# THROUGH PEMBERLEY WOODS

## A PRIDE AND PREJUDICE VARIATION

### EMILY RUSSELL

# CHAPTER 1

*E*lizabeth Bennet leaned against the carriage window and watched the surrounding countryside grow wilder and more rugged as they entered Derbyshire. Rolling hills gave way to scrubby brown peaks and cliffs. Dark forests replaced cultivated woodlands. The landscape was wild and romantic, more so than she expected from examining the pictures in her father's books. Elizabeth had never traveled so far north, and she smiled as she anticipated the weeks to come. She was impatient to explore the Peak District and meet the friends her Aunt Gardiner had spoken of so many times.

She gave her aunt an affectionate look. It had been a long journey from Hertfordshire to Derbyshire, and on the final portion of their travel, Aunt Gardiner had slept for several hours. She was wide awake now as if she'd sensed their approach to her beloved home county. She gazed out the window with the same eagerness as her niece while the carriage brought them closer to the town where she grew up and spent so many happy years.

"I am sorry Uncle Gardiner could not join us," said Elizabeth. "But I am sure we shall have a wonderful time in Lambton. I have always longed to see Derbyshire after all those years of listening to your stories. I intend to memorize every wood and stream and every mountain and hill. We shall not be like other travelers, jumbling them all together until we cannot tell one from the other."

Aunt Gardiner laughed. "It is a shame Edward could not come," she agreed. "If his clerk had not mislaid paperwork from the imports, he would not have needed to remain behind, and we would be on our way to the Lake District now. But I own I am looking forward to spending time at the place where I grew up. You will love it, Lizzy. There are so many scenic walks where one can ramble for miles without meeting another person. I doubt I will see much of you at all once you find your bearings! There is also a magnificent estate not five miles from Lambton, surrounded by woods and hills. The owner has given nature as free a reign as he could. I think you will explore every inch before we leave."

"An estate surrounded by woods and hills," said Elizabeth. She laid her head back against the carriage seat as she pictured it. She could already see herself rambling for hours, losing herself among the trees only to return home as the sun went down, tired but happy. "That is how it should be. What is the name of the estate? Who is the owner? Is he likely to be home?"

"I should not imagine so. It is still early in the summer, and many estate owners will linger in London for some weeks more. The estate is called Pemberley, and its owner is a young man called Mr. Darcy. I was not well acquainted with the Darcys when I lived here. They moved in far different circles to my own. But I remember old Mr. Darcy and Lady Anne as fine people, for all they were so grand."

She smiled. "I recall young Mr. Darcy when he was a small boy. His nurse would bring him out for air in a little phaeton his father had bought for that purpose. I think about that tiny boy from time to time, all dressed up with a little white bonnet on his head. I wonder how he has turned out."

"What is his age?"

Aunt Gardiner pursed her lips as she considered. "He must now be in his late twenties. Somewhere between seven and twenty or thirty."

"He is young to be master of an estate."

Aunt Gardiner nodded. "He is. It is a shame his father died so early. I remember reading of his death in the paper and thinking it was a pity the young Mr. Darcy was forced into such a responsibility at so young an age. But perhaps it has given him a strong sense of duty he might not otherwise have had. Edward considers it is the ruin of first sons that they cannot pursue other occupations while they wait to inherit. Most of them are bored and idle. They have nothing to do in the intervening years between finishing school and inheriting their estates but spend their fathers' money in disreputable activities. In my opinion, it can only have improved Mr. Darcy's character that he has not had the opportunity to do the same."

"Is he married?"

Aunt and niece looked at one another and burst into laughter. "It is a harmless question," Elizabeth said with feigned innocence. "I know his age and some information about his family. I even know the color of his childhood bonnet! It stands to reason I would then follow up with asking about his marital status."

"No, I do not believe he is married." Aunt Gardiner still smiled. "I heard no rumors of him being attached to a young lady, and the newspapers are full of such gossip. But I have not looked for news on him in particular, so if it was there, I might not have noticed." She gave her niece a sly look. "It is a shame he is probably still in London. What a fine thing it would be if I were to return you to Longbourn betrothed to the wealthiest landowner in Derbyshire. Your mother would never cease thanking me for my kindness."

"It is a shame," Elizabeth agreed with a sigh of mock regret. "If I knew I might encounter him, I would devise ways to throw myself in his path and adopt all the arts of captivation my mother has tried to teach us over the years - and at which I fear Kitty and Lydia have become far too adept. I would trap him with my charms and come home in triumph as Mrs. Darcy. Who cares a jot about the man's character if I am wealthy and secure? What does it matter if he has crooked eyes, an unseemly countenance, and a smell that makes birds fall from the trees as long as I have carriages, a house in Town, and a bank vault of jewels to call my own?"

The ladies laughed again. "I am sorry to say your mama would not realize you spoke in jest if you said as such to her."

"She would not. I once said something similar to tease her, and she only nodded and said she was surprised I could speak sense when I put my mind to it. "

Aunt Gardiner laughed again. "Poor Fanny. I cannot help but feel for her. With Longbourn entailed away from daughters, she has always been most concerned about your futures when your father dies. But it is not right she should attempt to throw you and your sisters into the paths of wealthy men with no regard for whether the men in question are worthy of you and whether you could respect and esteem your partners. I can understand her motives, but I cannot agree with her methods." She smiled at her niece. "Well then, it shall be a nice summer for you, my dear. For a few weeks at least, you need not fear anyone will try to throw you in the paths of wealthy, eligible men. You may enjoy yourself and give no thought to husband-hunting."

"And I shall never be able to thank you enough for inviting me. A few weeks without my mother trying to throw me into the arms of delightful suitors is welcome."

After a few more hours of travel, the carriage came to a stop outside a pretty manor house on the outskirts of Lambton. As the Gardiners' servant unloaded their trunks, Aunt Gardiner's old school friend, Mrs. Waters, flew down the steps to greet them, her face wreathed with smiles. Aunt Gardiner and Mrs. Waters embraced, their faces alive with delight at being reunited.

"I am so happy to see you, Marianne. You should not have left it so long to visit. It is very wrong of you."

"Well, Abigail, I am here now, am I not? But I am delighted to see you too, my dear friend."

They embraced again and spoke at high speed, their words tumbling over one another in their excitement.

When they finally drew back, Mrs. Waters turned to Elizabeth, who was attempting to tidy her hair after the long carriage journey.

"My dear, aren't you excessively pretty," she said after her aunt had introduced them. "Marianne often wrote of her charming nieces, but she did not do you justice. You are a beauty. Isn't she, Marianne? A beauty! Now —" She stood back, suddenly brisk. "I know you must feel exhausted after your journey, so I have had baths drawn up in your rooms. Come down as soon as you are ready, and we shall enjoy a nice dinner together. Just the family tonight, I am afraid. I thought you would not be desperate for company so soon after your long journey."

"You thought correctly," said Elizabeth with a smile. The thought of a bath and dinner heartened her, and the warmth of the older woman made her anticipate the coming weeks with even greater pleasure than she had already done.

# CHAPTER 2

*M*rs. Waters insisted on showing them to their bedchambers herself. She spoke at high speed all the way, not even pausing for breath.

"I chose this room for you, Marianne. It is near my own, and we can enjoy lovely chats by the fire. I want to hear everything about Edward and the children. How is London? What are the fashions this season? Is the room bright enough? I bought the counterpane especially — Now, Miss Bennet. You will come this way with me if you please. I chose this room for you. Your aunt told me you are a lover of nature and I hope this will answer your wishes. It looks out over the mountains. And look, see? There is Pemberley Woods. Beautiful, is it not? I did not arrange for the maid to light the fire. It is so warm today even if we are in Derbyshire, but if you wish it — no? Well, just as I expected. I understand you perfectly. Aren't you as pretty as a picture? Well, I shall leave you to prepare. If you need anything, just let me know, and it will be done."

She moved towards Elizabeth and, to her surprise, drew her into a warm embrace.

"Welcome to Trillings, my dear. I cannot tell you how delighted I am to meet you."

She released Elizabeth and left when Aunt Gardiner called for her. Elizabeth shook her head. The lady had not drawn breath from the time they entered the house.

Finally alone, Elizabeth looked around the room with appreciation. At home at Longbourn, she shared a bedchamber with her older sister, Jane. Beloved though Jane was, it always gave Elizabeth a thrill to have an entire space to herself.

She walked to the window and sat on the seat to admire the aspect for herself without the distraction of Mrs. Waters' breathless commentary. The house stood on a small hill, and in the distance, she could see the pretty market town of Lambton. Her eyes scanned over the chimney tops to the mountains in the distance and then across the lane outside Trillings, where endless acres of thick green woods spread before her. Elizabeth smiled. There was nothing she enjoyed more than a long tramp through the woods, and she knew all the forests and lanes around Meryton like the back of her hand. It was exhilarating to have somewhere so vast and new to explore. She was determined she would visit them first thing in the morning.

But for now, she had other obligations to attend. She turned with delight to the steaming bath.

The family was waiting for her in the drawing-room when she went down to join them. To Elizabeth's surprise, only her aunt and Mr. and Mrs. Waters were present. She understood from her aunt that the couple had two grown sons. It was the primary reason her mother had been so eager to allow Elizabeth to visit Derbyshire with

Mrs. Gardiner. She caught her aunt's eye, and they exchanged a grin. Mrs. Bennet would be beside herself if she realized she had sent Elizabeth away for nothing.

"My youngest son, Richard is away at school," Mrs. Waters explained. "And my oldest, Henry, is in the Navy. We are expecting him home in a few days, so you will have another young person around to keep you company when you are tired of us old folks." Mrs. Waters' eyes shone as she spoke of her son.

Elizabeth was uneasy at this news.

"I am sorry," she said, glancing at her aunt. Mrs. Gardiner looked just as uncomfortable as Elizabeth. "If we had known you were expecting your son home for a visit, we would not have imposed on your time with him."

"Abigail, why did you not tell us?" Aunt Gardiner chided. "It would have been no trouble for us to stay at the inn. We would not wish to intrude on your time with your son."

"Nonsense," said Mrs. Waters at once. "You will not be in the way, and you do us a great honor by coming to stay with us. Besides, you will not take any time we cannot spare. Henry is coming home to stay. He has earned his fortune, and he plans to settle down. This time we will not be obliged to part with him."

Elizabeth and Aunt Gardiner exchanged relieved looks.

"That must be agreeable," said Elizabeth. "For your son to come home to you, knowing he will not leave again. I can only imagine how painful it must feel to watch him depart for great lengths at a time. The Navy demands much from its recruits, but not enough consideration goes to what the families suffer in their loved one's absence."

The bell rang for dinner, and the family rose to move into the dining room.

"Thank you for your words, my dear," said Mrs. Waters as

they took their seats at the dining table. "You have remark-able feeling for one so young, does she not, John?"

Mr. Waters, who struck Elizabeth as a quiet man, had no time to respond before his talkative wife continued. "We do not see him for months and years at a time. And one hears such dreadful tales of shipwrecks and mutinies. I lost count-less nights of sleep wondering if I should see him again." She shuddered. "But we shall not need to worry about it ever again. It would be our fondest wish if he were to find a nice girl to marry. I know that is his plan."

Was it Elizabeth's imagination, or did Mrs. Waters' eyes flick towards her as she spoke? She schooled her face not to betray any response and pretended not to hear the hint if her hostess intended one.

"I am sure that will be a great comfort," she said. She cast around for a change of subject. "Mrs. Waters, I could not help but admire the extensive woodlands around the village. Walking is one of my chief delights, and I intend to explore as much of them as I can. Are there many pleasant walks here?"

Mrs. Waters tore her attention away from her son and any wedding plans she might have been making.

"Walks? Oh yes. Pemberley Woods is delightful at this time of year. I have not gone there myself in over twenty years, but I remember a few delightful walks, do you recall, Marianne?"

"I told Lizzy how we would sometimes see Lady Anne and old Mr. Darcy with the young Mr. Darcy in their carriage."

"Ah yes. The young Mr. Darcy is grown up now, of course."

"Are you acquainted with him?" asked Elizabeth.

"Oh, no. Mr. Darcy is far too grand for us. He mixes with

quite a different set. When he is here, he dines with other landowners and their families. I would never presume an acquaintance with him."

Elizabeth raised her eyebrows. "I can understand that is the normal way in Town, but in a small place like Lambton with less society, I would expect him to make a little more effort with his neighbors. If he does not wish to dine, that is one thing, but I am sure you must have dances and balls where he could mix with the neighborhood?"

"We do, but he never attends. I do not believe Mr. Darcy cares for dancing." Mrs. Waters pursed her lips as she considered. "I recall Mrs. White told me she had invited him to an assembly a year or two ago, but he sent back a brief decline. It was polite enough, but there was just that degree of coldness in it that discouraged the neighborhood from asking him again."

Elizabeth could not think well of this. As the leading landowner in the district, it would have been appropriate for this Mr. Darcy to attempt to mix with his neighbors even if he did not desire intimate friendships. There were many country villages where the elite might not attend private dinners with those below them, but they would still exert themselves to take part in social occasions where the classes mixed. She did not think much of a man who would withhold himself from those around him.

"You do not approve, my dear?" said Aunt Gardiner with a smile. "Perhaps you are right. Mr. Darcy should exert himself sometimes. But he is a young man, and he has a lot of responsibility on his shoulders. Perhaps he cannot find the time."

"I am sure he could find the time, Aunt. It is not as though he has a wife and children to demand his presence at home. Like all wealthy landowners, he will have stewards to assist him with his responsibilities. After all, they did not prevent him from spending a season in London." She shrugged and relented. "But then, we know so little of his life. Perhaps he has a good reason for not attending, as you say. Perhaps I should not be so quick to judge him."

Mrs. Waters laughed. "Mr. Darcy's friends would not be pleased if they knew you judged him and found him wanting. From my understanding, they think a great deal of him. You might be a revolutionary, Miss Bennet."

Elizabeth denied it. "Just one who has little patience for those who think too highly of themselves, Mrs. Waters."

As Mr. Waters had no other gentlemen to discuss topics with after dinner, the ladies remained at the table with him, and the conversation carried on for some time. It was late before Elizabeth finally climbed the stairs to her bedchamber.

# CHAPTER 3

*A*fter a long carriage journey and a late night, Elizabeth might have been forgiven if she had slept late, but her enthusiasm for being in a new place filtered through her sleep. When she woke, the sun was still low in the sky, with only the first few rays reaching into her room. She rolled over and looked out the window. The early summer sun rose over Pemberley Woods, lighting up the dark green trees invitingly.

Elizabeth threw off her covers and rummaged through her closet for a light frock. She didn't have the patience to pin her hair up, so she took the faster approach of tying her curls back with a ribbon. She did not expect to encounter many people so early in the morning, and she was sure she would be back in time to have the maid assist her with her hair to make her presentable before she joined the rest of the household for breakfast.

She gave herself one last check in the mirror and laughed. In her plain, loose frock with her curls held back in a ribbon, she looked positively rustic. It was as well no one was likely to see her apart from some curious birds and rabbits.

. . .

Elizabeth breathed in the sweet morning air as she walked down the lane towards Pemberley Woods. Dew clung to the grass along the edges of the path, dampening her boots and the hem of her frock. She hopped over a small stile leading into the woods and paused to tuck her hair back as some of it escaped her ribbon. The ground was dry and firm. At least she would not return to the house with a muddy skirt and shoes.

The trees were alive with birdsong as the upper branches swayed in the morning breeze. Multiple paths crisscrossed before her, leading in directions she could not see through the dense foliage. Elizabeth promised herself she would explore them all before she left Derbyshire.

As she was sure there was no danger of crossing paths with another soul, she ran as fast as she could through the trees, broken twigs scrunching and snapping under her half-boots.

She came to a wide stream. Several flat rocks rose from the water, offering her passage across to a sunny glade. Without slowing her steps, Elizabeth gathered her skirt and leaped onto the first one, pausing for a moment to steady herself before hopping from rock to rock. With one final leap, she landed on the other side, out of breath and laughing with delight at the exercise. Her hair tumbled about her shoulders, and she put a hand up to feel the loose curls. Her final leap had shaken her ribbon free. She spotted it on the ground behind her, and as she stooped to pick it up, she heard an angry voice call out.

"Hey. You there!"

Elizabeth started and looked around in alarm. A man strode into the little glade, a gun over his shoulder. She

14

guessed him to be a gamekeeper. He was in shirt sleeves and wore no jacket or cravat. His trousers were tucked into tall hessian boots. His sleeves were rolled up, and his face looked as if it had not seen a razor that morning.

The man's good looks struck Elizabeth. She guessed him to be a few years older than her. His dark hair was tousled and slightly damp as if he had washed and come straight out into the woods as she had done. He scowled at her, his eyes dark with irritation.

As she stared at him, a small spaniel came snuffling out of the woods. Without pausing, he ran right up to Elizabeth and sniffed around her skirts, his short tail thumping with delight. Elizabeth looked at the man defiantly, then knelt and caressed the dog.

"What are you doing here?" the man demanded.

Something about his arrogant tone riled Elizabeth up. She shot him a cool look.

"Poaching," she said with sarcasm.

The man tensed, and he took a step towards her with such a grim expression on his face that Elizabeth was alarmed. She scrambled to her feet, determined not to put herself at a disadvantage by having to stare up at him.

It did no good. Even standing, he was still much taller than her. She was forced to tilt her head back if she wanted to return his glare with one of her own.

"Do not be an idiot," she said. Her tone was sharp, but she felt apprehension as she eyed the gun on his shoulder. "I spoke in jest. Of course I am not a poacher. Do I look like a poacher to you?"

"I take it you are then familiar with how poachers should look, Miss..."

"Miss Elizabeth Bennet." She deliberately made her tone arrogant to match his own. "I am visiting from Hertford-

15

shire, and I wished to explore these woods. I assume it is not a crime for me to do so?"

"You are aware, are you not, that these are private lands? Perhaps not if you are not from here."

Elizabeth raised her chin. "I am aware that these lands are private. But is it not a common practice with landowners to allow others to pass through their woods? Perhaps things are different in Derbyshire. Perhaps Mr. Darcy does not wish his lands to be polluted by those he considers beneath him."

The man tensed and looked at her with curiosity. "Perhaps Mr. Darcy has good reason not to wish foolish young ladies scamper around his lands unaccompanied. Perhaps he has a sense of propriety, one that a young lady who runs around woods in a state of undress with her hair unbound might not understand."

Elizabeth gasped. Her face flushed with a mixture of fury and embarrassment. She had forgotten about her state of dress until the man called attention to it, and she was suddenly acutely aware of how she must appear. Her mother would be horrified. Elizabeth had not expected to meet anyone, much less this arrogant gamekeeper who behaved as if these woods were his personal property.

But it should not surprise her that someone as proud as Mr. Darcy might employ people who were almost grander than those found at an Almack's assembly. He might think it reflected well on him to have staff who looked down on others as much as he did.

"You have said enough, sir. If I am not doing wrong by being here, I ask that you continue on your way and leave me to mine. You have insulted me enough for one day."

She dropped a short curtsey and turned to leave. She had not gone many yards when the man called her again.

"Miss Bennet, wait."

Elizabeth reluctantly stopped and waited for him to come to her. She half-expected him to apologize for his rude behavior, but she knew it was unlikely considering how uncouth he was. He strode towards her, his long legs taking a shortcut through the undergrowth as if it did not hinder him.

"My dog," he said shortly.

Elizabeth stared at him in confusion, and he sighed with impatience.

"You are stealing my dog, Miss Bennet. Earl, come here."

Elizabeth looked down to see the little spaniel sitting at her feet. She'd been in such a pet over the man's rudeness she had almost forgotten about him. She had not realized he had followed her. The dog gazed up at her, his tongue lolling out.

"I do not believe I was stealing him so much as he realized he had the opportunity to switch his situation for a more pleasant one," she said pertly.

The man ignored her. He called the dog again. The dog looked at Elizabeth, then rose and trotted to his master's side, his tail still wagging. The man took a moment to scratch the dog's silky ears before straightening to meet her eyes.

"It is not safe for you in these woods," he said. Elizabeth scoffed, but he interrupted her. "Miss Bennet, I know what I am talking about. There are plenty of other places around Lambton you can explore, but these woods are not to be among them. I will escort you back to the town."

"I do not need you to escort me," Elizabeth protested at once. "I came this far by myself, did I not? And why are these woods not safe?" She raised her eyebrows in disbelief. "I suppose you will tell me there are desperate villains here about who will abduct me and carry me away?"

The man made a noise. "I would not think any villain would be desperate enough to carry you away, which is unfortunate as it would be a fitting punishment for his crimes. But yes, there are unsavory characters in these woods, and I have enough of a sense of responsibility not to wish anything to happen to you. I insist on escorting you, Miss Bennet."

Elizabeth glared back at him, but she could see he would not be moved. He had a stubbornness that even surpassed her own. She had no choice but to relent.

"I was about to return for my breakfast anyway," she said. She turned back the way she had come. The man followed at a short distance. "When people speak of unsavory characters, is it possible they are referring to the unpleasant gamekeeper?"

For a moment, there was silence, and only the sounds of sticks cracking beneath his heavy boots told her he was still there. Then she heard laughter.

"The gamekeeper?" He laughed again. "Miss Bennet, it is just as well I found you. You do not know what you are about."

Elizabeth declined to respond. The sooner she was out of these woods, the sooner she would no longer have to endure him.

# CHAPTER 4

The return journey seemed never-ending. Elizabeth did not remember it taking so long the first time she passed through this way until she recalled she had been running. She suppressed a sigh. There was no chance for her to run this time. She would not give the man the satisfaction of laughing at her again. His unpleasant company might also explain why the journey felt like it took forever.

She realized she still did not know his name although he knew hers. She turned to ask him but stopped herself.

No, why should she care? Let him think he did not matter enough for her to ask about it.

"Miss Bennet," the man said in a loud whisper. Elizabeth ignored him and continued walking until he grasped her arm. She spun around with a cry of outrage, but he put a finger to his lip. He looked into the woods, his body tense and prepared for — something.

Elizabeth peered in the same direction. There was nothing to cause alarm, as far as she could see. Leaves rustled, and an unseen creature moved through undergrowth somewhere nearby, but that was not unusual in woods that must teem with wildlife. The sun shone down through the trees as it rose higher, but Elizabeth still could not find what had captured the man's attention. However, something about his manner infected her with caution of her own.

"What is it?" she whispered.

The man shook his head. "Probably nothing. But..." He released her arm, and Elizabeth's unease increased when he drew the gun over his shoulder. "Stay there, Miss Bennet. It is just a precaution, but..."

The undergrowth beside them rustled, and Elizabeth froze. She turned towards the sound, ready to defend herself against whoever it might be. She heard the click of the gun and braced herself for the fire.

It never came. The man laughed and lowered his gun. He shook his head and moved forward as a second, much older man came through the trees.

"Keiths, you old fool. Do you realize I had a gun trained on you the entire time? I might have shot you. What were you about, sneaking up like that?"

The man took his cap from his head and glanced at Elizabeth. "I did not mean to sneak up on you," he said in an apologetic tone. "I took care to make noise. Sir, the Waltons had some of their poultry stolen during the night. And they live in that little community of cottages near the lake. They seem to grow bolder."

The man swore under his breath. "All right, Keiths. Thank you for telling me. Tell the Waltons I will come to them later and bring the magistrate. Whoever did this will not get away again. But right now, I must accompany this young lady to the town."

"May I walk with you, sir? I need to pick up supplies myself."

"Of course."

The man slung his gun back over his shoulder and strode ahead, leaving Keiths and Elizabeth to follow him.

"I am sorry for your misfortune," said Elizabeth. "We had a similar problem on my father's farm several years ago. The culprit was caught, but it was a distressing situation."

"It is," said Keiths morosely. "They took my wife's last week and the Smiths' some days before that. It makes us uneasy. My wife usually walks through the woods to the market, but I would not allow her this morning. I will not have her walking through the woods alone until we catch whoever is doing this. So far, he has not interfered with those on farms. It is us living in the woods who suffer from his actions."

Elizabeth fell silent. So that was the reason the game-keeper had been so forceful about her leaving. He might have told her that instead of snapping at her and ordering her to leave. She would not forgive him that part.

She watched him walk ahead, his back strong and erect. He had remarkable posture for a servant. Her conversation with Keiths made her realize how well the gamekeeper spoke. He was obviously an educated man. Perhaps his father before him had been the gamekeeper. Perhaps the son had been a favorite of the family, and they had offered to educate him as thanks for his father's service. It would explain his arrogance and high opinion of himself. What a shame a man as handsome and educated as he should be so unpleasant.

As the path took a turn, the gamekeeper stopped again. Keiths froze at once, and Elizabeth slowed down, her eyes darting around to find what had caught their attention. She was not too alarmed. It was more than likely yet another poor tenant who would emerge from the trees to see a gun pointed at them. She was about to say so when the game-keeper swore and plunged into the woods.

"Stay with Miss Bennet, Keiths," he snapped. "Do not allow her to wander off." He disappeared among the trees, Earl running beside him in a brown blur. Elizabeth moved to keep him in sight as far as possible, then turned to Keiths.

"What is he doing?" she demanded, her excitement making her voice high. "Has he seen him? Has he seen the thief?"

"I think so, Miss," said Keiths. His old face was white. "He should not run after him like that. Whoever this person is, they're dangerous."

"Well, should you not go after him and help him?"

Keiths stared at her incredulous. "Of course not. He ordered me to stay here with you."

"But if he is in danger..." She rose on her toes, trying to spot him. "I'm going after him. He might need help."

Keiths reached out to catch her, his face alarmed, but Elizabeth eluded his grasp and ran into the woods. If Keiths chose to stay behind, that was his affair, but she would not stand by and allow a man, no matter how unpleasant, to face criminals all alone.

Surely there was something she could do to help? A large stick caught her eye, and she stooped to pull it from the undergrowth. Thieves would not expect a woman to be a threat, so they would not be cautious. She would use the stick to defend herself and the gamekeeper if it came to it.

Her bold plan fell apart a moment later when the gamekeeper cut through the undergrowth towards her. His face was dark with annoyance, and it grew even darker at the sight of Elizabeth.

"Miss Bennet, what on earth are you doing?" He caught sight of the stick in her hand. He pinched the bridge of his nose and closed his eyes as if asking for patience from a divine source. "Where is Keiths? Why did he allow you to tear off like this?"

"I am sorry, sir," said Keiths. He came crashing through the undergrowth behind Elizabeth. He had chased her, and now he doubled over, his hands on his thighs to catch his breath. "She dashed off before I could stop her. I did not expect her to run after you."

Elizabeth raised her chin, her irritation building. "Forgive me, sir," she said with heavy sarcasm, "But I am not the sort to stand by and allow a man to face danger alone, even if he is such a man as you. I am sure you would have thanked me if a thief had attacked you and I arrived on time to help."

"Or I would have managed just fine until you came along, and then you putting yourself in danger would have obligated me to distract myself enough to save you, putting us both at peril," snapped the gamekeeper. "I told you to remain where you were for a reason, Miss Bennet. Fortunately for you but unfortunately for us, whoever it was got away. Come. The sooner I have you out of these woods, the safer we shall all be."

He strode past her, still scowling. Elizabeth stared after him, speechless with rage. She hurried after him.

"I wonder Mr. Darcy can endure having such a man in his service. Is this why he remains in London? So he does not have to deal with your dark moods and abrupt manner?"

The man looked down at her, and she saw a flicker of amusement on his otherwise scowling face. Before he said anything, Keiths spoke up.

"In London? What on earth does she mean, Mr. Darcy? Has the lady mistaken you for someone else?"

Elizabeth stared at Keiths. She heard and understood the words he said, but they did not register with her at first, and she merely stared at him in confusion. Why did he speak of

Mr. Darcy? Mr. Darcy was many miles away, no doubt sampling the delights of London. Finally, his meaning dawned on her. She stared at the man in shock.

"You are Mr. Darcy?" she said almost accusingly. The man she had thought to be the gamekeeper bowed.

"That is correct, madam."

"I thought you were the gamekeeper."

"Yes, I am aware you made that assumption."

Elizabeth was too stunned to say more. Finally, she blurted out, "You look like a gamekeeper."

It was true. His clothes were informal, but as she looked closer, she saw them in a new light. While before, she only saw shirt sleeves, now she saw a fine, expensive shirt that just wanted a waistcoat for him to fit into any salon in Mayfair. His trousers were of similar excellent quality, and his hessian boots gleamed with polish, despite the mud around the soles. All he required was a jacket and a cravat, and this man would not be out of place at the most elegant dining tables in the kingdom. Perhaps he would need a comb and a shave first, but it would take only minutes to transform him into a gentleman.

"I am not accustomed to dressing in a cravat and jacket to search for thieves in my woods, Miss Bennet," said Mr. Darcy dryly. "I am sure you can understand that. Surely you would not appear without a spencer or fichu or hairpins unless you believed you would be alone in your surroundings?"

Elizabeth looked down at her loose frock and flushed. He was not wrong. She turned without responding and walked on through the woods. She could not account for the extreme embarrassment she felt. It was a mistake she usually laughed herself out of, and no doubt she would later, but for now, she wished to be away from this man before she did something else to make herself appear foolish.

As she reached the path, Mr. Darcy walked by her side.

"I thought you were in London," she said.

"Yes, I was. I received letters from my steward about my tenants' distressing situation, so I returned early. I only arrived the day before yesterday. But may I ask how you know me and are informed of my whereabouts? I believe I know nothing of you."

Elizabeth flushed. "I was admiring your woods," she said. "I am staying with my aunt's friend, Mrs. Waters, and she informed me they belonged to you and that you were still in London. She did not seem aware you have forbidden the woods to visitors."

"They are not usually forbidden," said Mr. Darcy. He looked at her sternly. "But they are for now. I stress this again, Miss Bennet, because you have shown yourself to be stubborn and have an abominable amount of independence. I will not take on the worry for your safety as well as the concerns I already have for my tenants. For the time being, consider any venture into my woods as trespassing."

Elizabeth felt that same flash of irritation at his heavy-handed rudeness. There was no need for him to speak in that tone. She was not an imbecile who could not understand him unless he spoke with force. She decided she would not humor him with any more conversation or give him the undeserved flattery she knew anything of him. They walked to the edge of the woods in silence.

# CHAPTER 5

To Elizabeth's dismay, Mr. Darcy did not leave her once he had helped her over the stile. She had a missish desire to refuse the offer of his hand, but the jump was higher on this side than it was on the way in. It would be too embarrassing if she proudly spurned him, only to fall at his feet. She grudgingly accepted his help and jumped down beside him. He put his other hand on her arm to steady her as she stumbled against him. A shock of sensation jolted through her body, and, with a sharp inhale, she moved out of his reach, pulling her hand free from his.

"I can manage from here," she said. She hoped her face did not look as warm as it felt.

Darcy shook his head.

"I have walked you this far. It would be remiss of me not to escort you to your lodgings."

"Mr. Keiths can walk with me. You are going in the same direction, are you not, Mr. Keiths?"

Darcy hesitated. "No, Keiths will leave you on the next path. He is going towards the town. I will accompany you, Miss Bennet."

Elizabeth knew there was little point arguing. It would only prolong her time in his company. If he chose to walk beside her, she could not prevent him. She shrugged and walked on, consoling herself with the knowledge that in a few more minutes, she would no longer have to endure him.

The lanes were still quiet at the early hour of the morning. Elizabeth hoped she could return to the house without the family discovering her absence. She wished no one to see her with Mr. Darcy. It would only lead to awkward questions about why she walked in the woods in a state of near undress.

A little further down the lane, Keiths said his goodbyes and turned towards the town. Elizabeth was sorry to see him go. He was a welcome buffer between her and the proud, silent man by her side.

As they approached Trillings, Elizabeth's heart sank. Both her aunt and Mrs. Waters were in the garden. Mrs. Waters was tending to her rose bushes, and Aunt Gardiner sat beside her, a dish of tea in her hands. Elizabeth turned to Darcy.

"Thank you, sir, but I am home now. I am no longer in need of your assistance, and —"

"Lizzy! Is that you? I thought you were still in bed."

Elizabeth suppressed a groan. The older ladies turned in her direction, shielding their eyes against the early morning sun. Their smiles faded as they saw the tall man at Elizabeth's side. Mrs. Waters put down her shears, Aunt Gardiner her teacup, and they hurried down the path towards them.

Elizabeth bit back an unladylike curse she had once heard from her father. Why did Mr. Darcy not leave? He stood beside her as silent and immovable as a statue. Was this some strange punishment? That because she had inconvenienced him with her presence in the woods, he would now inconvenience her with his?

27

Mrs. Waters gasped and dropped a curtsey. "Mr. Darcy! What a pleasant surprise. I hope you and Miss Darcy are well? I thought you were in London, sir."

Darcy inclined his head. Although he had been nothing but rude since Elizabeth met him, he'd had an informality about his manner, moving through the woods like a man at ease with himself, a master of his domain. While he still had the same proud bearing, his manner was now stiff and formal. She had rarely seen someone look so ill at ease.

"I returned this week, madam. I met your niece in my woods this morning and considered it best to escort her home."

Aunt Gardiner looked concerned. "Was it a problem for Lizzy to explore your woods, sir? I am sorry if that is the case. We had no reason to believe walkers were not welcome there, and Lizzy is a great lover of nature."

"I have reason to prefer my woods be devoid of visitors at the moment. As I already told Miss Bennet, there are many places for her to explore that do not involve my property. She will not be deprived if Pemberley Woods is closed to her."

He gave the ladies a short bow and walked away. Mrs. Waters and Aunt Gardiner stared after him, their faces etched with astonishment. Elizabeth knew what a sight Mr. Darcy must make with his gun slung over his shoulder, Earl still scampering by his side.

While they stared after him, she hastily pulled her hair back into its ribbon. She hoped they were too distracted by Mr. Darcy's presence to notice her dishevelment. She would not have them ask questions about her being with him in such a state.

They turned back to her as she finished.

"Well, what a surprise. Mr. Darcy to accompany you back

to Trillings! It was good of him to exert himself so much. I have never known him to do so."

"Do not be surprised, Mrs. Waters. It is only in keeping with what you've told me of his usual character. He escorted me the entire way home because he wanted to make sure I left his precious woods. One of his tenants walked with us before leaving for the market, and his company would have done just as well."

"Mr. Darcy has turned out very well," said Aunt Gardiner. "He showed great promise as a boy, and he has fulfilled it. He is handsome, is he not, Lizzy?"

"It is a shame his character does not match his looks," said Elizabeth in an abrupt tone. "I found him to be a rude, unpleasant man. Lambton does not suffer by his absence, Mrs. Waters. It is best if he keeps himself and his high-handed manners to Pemberley. Now, I have been walking all morning, and I am eager for breakfast. May we go inside?"

Mrs. Waters and Aunt Gardiner looked as if they would like to ask more questions, but they agreed and followed Elizabeth into the house.

As Elizabeth returned to the table with a plate of rolls and cold meat and a cup of coffee, the older ladies waited for her, their faces animated with barely concealed curiosity.

"How did you come to meet him, Lizzy? He must have engaged you in conversation?"

Elizabeth shrugged as she buttered a roll. "Not as such. He was only interested in impressing on me that I must leave his woods. He made it clear he found my presence an inconvenience."

"But he must have spoken with you," said Mrs. Waters.

Her eyes were bright with anticipation of gossip. "Did he say why he returned early? Why does he not want anyone to visit his woods? Did he mention anything of the London season?"

Elizabeth found herself reluctant to speak of Darcy. "We walked mostly in silence, and I spent much of it speaking with his tenant, who had far more manners than his master. Mr. Darcy has little to recommend him."

At that, Mrs. Waters burst into peals of laughter. "Ah, Miss Bennet. If the other young ladies of Derbyshire and London could hear you, they would think you out of your senses. I do not believe there is one of them who would not leap at the chance to be Mrs. Darcy. He is the wealthiest landowner in Derbyshire, you know, and as you have seen yourself, he is so young and handsome and already the master of his estate. Not that he is more handsome than my Henry. Henry is his equal in all things apart from wealth and station. But when he is home, you may judge for yourself."

To Elizabeth's mingled relief and annoyance, the conversation once again turned to Henry. She was obliged to listen to Mrs. Waters' many hints about what an excellent husband he would make and how fortunate would be the lady he chose as his wife. Part of Elizabeth's purpose in coming here had been to escape the pressure of being thrown into the paths of eligible suitors, and she would not allow Mrs. Waters to push her son on her even if she considered him to be the finest young man in the kingdom.

But at least the conversation meant she no longer had to speak of Mr. Darcy. The sooner she could forget her unpleasant encounter with him, the better.

# CHAPTER 6

*D*arcy was lost in thought as he walked down the lane towards Lambton. He turned to look back at Trillings. There was no sign of Elizabeth. He partly hoped she might have lingered at the gate, eager for a last glimpse of him. He rarely left a house without a young lady dawdling on a doorstep or at a window but never before had he been disappointed when the lady did not materialize. He paused for a moment until Earl sniffed around his feet, recalling him to the present. He stooped to stroke the dog's silky head.

"You liked her, did you not, my little traitor?" Darcy had never seen Earl react to a stranger as he had to Miss Bennet. Ever since his uncle, the Earl of Matlock, had gifted him to Darcy as a puppy, he preferred Darcy's company to everyone else. Darcy scratched Earl's ear then stood up. He sighed. "Come. We have other matters to attend to right now."

He turned his back on the house and strode down the lane to Mr. Cole's house.

The magistrate rose from his desk with some surprise when Darcy was shown into the room.

"Mr. Darcy. I did not know you had returned so soon. How are you, sir?"

"I am well, Mr. Cole. But my tenants are not."

Mr. Cole gestured for him to take the seat opposite him. Darcy quickly outlined the new thefts that had taken place, including the one that had occurred at the Waltons the night before.

"Keiths is correct. If he is attacking people who live in a community together, he is growing bolder," he said. "And my biggest fear is that another incident like the one of last week will occur. I cannot allow that to happen again."

"No, of course not," said Mr. Cole. He fiddled with his pen, his eyes lost in thought. He rose from the chair. "Allow me to prepare myself, and I will return with you. Someone might recall seeing or hearing something during the night. I will not take long."

Cole hurried from the room. Darcy sank back into his chair as he waited for him, his mind busy with thoughts on how best to assist his tenants. A movement near the door caught his attention. Mrs. Cole peeked into the room. Darcy rose to his feet and bowed to her, but his heart sank at the sight. He had hoped he was too early to meet with her.

Mrs. Cole, for her part, looked as thrilled to see him as Darcy feared she would. She bustled into the room to greet him.

"I did not know you were home, sir. If Robert had told me, I would have insisted he invite you to dinner. How good it is to see you! Won't you join us for breakfast? I am sure you must be famished. All you young, unattached men dash about without a thought for yourselves. I fear you will not be properly cared for until Pemberley has a mistress..."

"I am quite well, thank you, Mrs. Cole. I wish only for Mr. Cole's assistance, and I shall be on my way."

He paced to the window, hoping to discourage her from further conversation.

It didn't work. It rarely did.

"And how is London?" she asked. "We are kept away from all that is exciting up here. You must have lots of news from Town?"

"None that will interest you, Mrs. Cole," Darcy said. He glanced back at her and tried to smile to soften the effect of his sharp words.

It did no good. It seemed no matter little interest he showed in conversing, Mrs. Cole was not to be dissuaded.

"Our Lucy is in Town. Perhaps you have seen her?"

Darcy winced as he recalled the Coles' daughter, an empty-headed flirtatious girl who made no secret of the fact that she desired a wealthy husband, no matter who the gentleman was. It was one of the reasons he declined invitations to mingle with the social life of Lambton. He had experienced enough tiresome evenings of being seated by her side while her mother looked on in breathless anticipation. And if it were not Lucy Cole, another lady would take her place. All gazing at him as if he were prime steak and they had been starved for a month. He grimaced at the thought.

"I did not have that pleasure, no."

"That is a shame. She will be surprised you have returned so early, but I am sure you know best. The Town is especially unhealthy in summer. All that heat and filth from the river. I wonder everyone does not fall ill, especially one as delicate and ladylike as my Lucy. Not that she is sickly, of course! She is one of the healthiest girls I know and will bear..." She broke off and spluttered with a cough to hide her gaffe as Darcy turned to stare at her incredulously. When she recovered, she continued, "Perhaps I should write and tell her to come home to Derbyshire..."

Darcy looked up in relief as the door opened and Mr. Cole returned.

"I will be home within a few hours, Julia."

"Oh. You are leaving already? But Mr. Darcy has just arrived. I hope nothing is amiss?"

"Just some estate business," said Darcy firmly. "And it cannot be delayed."

Mrs. Cole followed them to the door.

"And will you not invite Mr. Darcy to return for breakfast? I am sure he will find more comfort here than in a house that has been shut up for months."

"My house is always ready to receive me, Mrs. Cole. I am afraid I must decline your generous offer. I have much to do after my long absence."

Darcy bowed to her and strode down the path, Mr. Cole rushing to follow him. Once out on the lane, he took a deep breath of fresh air, feeling like a prisoner released from Newgate. He would never be free of such behavior until he married. But in order to get married, he would need to endure such behavior. It was a tiresome business. If a suitable bride should fall into his path without him having to weather such nonsense, he would be most gratified. But such things never happened.

As they walked down the lane past Trillings, Darcy glanced into the garden. His eyes swept over the lawn and among the trees and shrubs, searching for a sign of loose curls and bright eyes. The garden was empty. He felt a brief stab of disappointment that he immediately pushed away and turned to Cole to discuss the recent thefts. Speculation of who the thief might be kept his mind firmly from Elizabeth Bennet where it had no business wandering.

But as the house disappeared from view, he could not resist one last glance behind him.

· · ·

Mrs. Walton was visibly shaken by the theft, but she was doing her best not to allow it to unnerve her. She was washing clothes in a tub when the two gentlemen came along, and she rose at once and wiped her soapy hands on her apron when she saw them.

"Mr. Darcy." She dropped into an unpracticed curtsey. "You are very good to come yourself, sir. I am sure you did not need to put yourself out."

"It is no trouble," said Darcy. "Can you take us to your poultry house?"

There was little to see. The catches had been broken open, and nothing remained of any poultry except one lonely hen who clucked at them in a mournful tone.

"He might have heard a noise and ran before taking this one," said Cole. "Mrs. Walton, did any of you hear anything during the night?"

"My little boy, Jack did. He woke up during the night and heard the hens fussing. He was about to go out, but the noise stopped, and he fell back asleep." Mrs. Walton shuddered. "Thank goodness he did not go outside."

"Thank goodness indeed," said Darcy grimly.

Darcy and Cole spoke to the little boy, a fine fellow with bright eyes and ruddy cheeks. He did not have anything further to add than what his mother had already told them. Darcy sighed in frustration. He hated to see his tenants in distress, but they were still no closer to catching the fellow. Perhaps he might have caught him that morning if he had been fast enough.

The thought brought his mind back to Elizabeth Bennet once again. How she had chased him through the woods,

35

determined to help him...

He shoved the memory to one side. What on earth was wrong with him? He was not usually so easily distracted. He turned to Mrs. Walton.

"We will have your hen houses fixed, and I will assist you in replacing your poultry."

At Mrs. Walton's protests, he gently dismissed them.

"You have lived on this land for many years, and your family has been of great assistance to me on the estate. It is about time I showed some small appreciation towards it. We shall say no more about it."

Mrs. Walton swallowed and nodded. Darcy had to look away from the emotion in her eyes in case he betrayed his own. The keeping of poultry meant so much to the women on his land. It allowed them a measure of independence and a chance to earn money of their own that society would not otherwise permit them. It disgusted him to think of someone choosing to deprive them of it. He gave her a brief nod, then slipped a coin to Jack. He stepped outside, bending his head to avoid hitting it off the low lintel.

Darcy accompanied Cole back through the woods to the lane. On impulse, he offered to walk part of the way towards his house with him. If Cole thought anything odd about his offer, he said nothing, a fact for which Darcy was grateful. They strolled along the lane and talked quietly about Mrs. Walton. As they reached Trillings, Darcy once again glanced towards the garden. A glimpse of a pale dress caught his eye, and his heart pounded so hard he could not hear Cole's words. He stared eagerly, willing the girl to turn around.

She did.

It was not Miss Bennet. It was a servant girl who had nothing at all of Miss Bennet's height and build and not even her hair color. He had been so keen to catch sight of her he thought he saw her where she was not. He quickly scanned the windows, but no young lady sat at them. It was just as well. He could have no reason to wish to see her.

As they approached the Coles' house, Darcy slowed his steps. If Mrs. Cole caught sight of them from the window, she would believe he had returned for breakfast. And she would write a letter to Lucy Cole, who would take the first coach out of London to flirt her way into becoming Mrs. Darcy.

"I will return to Pemberley. Thank you for coming with me, Cole. I will keep you informed of anything else."

The two men shook hands, and Darcy walked back the way he came. This time, he kept his eyes resolutely turned from Trillings.

A fter his chase that morning, Darcy did not expect to encounter the thief again, so he was at liberty to relax and take pleasure in the walk. If he could catch the cursed fellow, he could truly enjoy being home.

How he missed Pemberley when he was in London. The Town had nothing to compare to the beauty of his home. Tiresome balls and tedious conversation with the *ton* paled compared to the satisfaction of being here where he could work and make a difference. Nonetheless, he was obligated to endure society if he ever wished to find a mistress for Pemberley and a mother for his heir. He had a responsibility, and Darcy was nothing if not dutiful.

He came to the stream where he first met Elizabeth and paused, unaware of the smile on his face as he recalled their meeting. He had been startled when she had come leaping across the stream, landing right in his path. Of all the characters he expected to encounter in the woods that morning, a pretty girl with her curls tumbling about her shoulders was not one of them. He had been shocked by her presence and anxious to remove her from any possible harm. All he could think about was getting her away and impressing her with the vital importance of not returning.

He had been horrified to think this young woman had walked through his woods quite alone when who knew what sort of brigands were around. If he had not come across her when he had, she might easily have walked further into the woods, and anything might have happened to her.

Darcy moved down to the water's edge. He picked up some pebbles and whistled to Earl. The spaniel bounded to his side and shuffled backward, his tail flying when he spotted the stones in his master's hands. Darcy threw them across the water and smiled as the little animal flew after them, bounding into the chilly water. He buried his face in the stream, then returned to Darcy's side and shook himself. Darcy bent to pat him, then walked on.

He glanced back at the stream, remembering how Elizabeth looked with her hair loose and her eyes sparkling. He smiled to himself when he recalled how she mistook him for a gamekeeper. When he realized her error, he had been about to correct her, but something stopped him. He found her pert manner rather refreshing. It was a welcome change from the practiced flirtations and attempts at allurement he had endured in London all season. He feared the moment Miss Bennet realized who he was, her manner to him would change, and she would treat him with the same artificial attentions so many ladies were prone to do. A rare spirit of mischief had come over him, and he had been tempted to allow her to continue in her error. If he could have prevented Keiths from revealing his identity without alerting the lady or arousing his tenant's suspicions, he might have done so.

So Darcy had been pleasantly surprised when revealing his identity did not change her behavior towards him. She had been surprised, yes, but she did not suddenly try to engage him or make herself pleasing to him. If anything, she had seemed even more irritated by him than before. Darcy had found her fascinating, and it had been a spur of the moment decision to accompany her back to Trillings that he might spend as much time with her as possible before he was obligated to part with her.

To see her after this incident was out of the question. He could tell by the manner of her dress, and her stay at Trillings that her condition in life was decidedly below his own. There would be no reason for their paths to cross again. She would not come to his woods, and he would not see her in Lambton.

Yet every time he thought of her leaping across the stream, her eyes sparkling with the exhilaration of exercise, her dark curls flying tumbling about her shoulders, he smiled once again. It was a sight he would not be averse to seeing more often. It was yet another reason, a more selfish one, to regret the thief raiding the poultry houses on his lands. If he had not been required to forbid his woods to her, he suspected she would have rambled there often, and perhaps he might have found excuses to converse with her and even to walk with her some of the way. He would have taken great pleasure in showing her his favorite beauty spots and seeing her bright eyes glow with appreciation.

He sighed with frustrated disappointment. It was for the best that he ensured she did not come through there again. It was for the best.

The trees were heavy and full with the promise of summer. The day was already warm, but a pleasant breeze cooled his face as he breathed in the fresh air. His mind turned to other matters. He had been so close to catching the culprit that morning. He was sure the person he had chased through the woods was the thief. If only he had been fast enough to catch him.

It was impossible for him to recall the incident without also recalling Elizabeth. His irritation melted, and he smiled at the memory of her coming after him, so slight yet prepared to take on criminals to help him, a stick clutched in her hand for a weapon. She had a fierceness and spirit about her he felt irresistibly drawn towards. He decided it was an excellent thing he had banned her from his lands. If he had not, and he was obliged to spend more time in her company, he should find himself in great danger. He might be compelled to forget everything he owed his family and make an offer for a woman who was utterly unsuited to be Mrs. Darcy.

He once again forced her from his mind. Georgiana would arrive tomorrow. He could not wait to see his younger sister again before she left for Ramsgate. He had been surprised and not a little disappointed when she told him she would cut her summer at Pemberley short to visit the seaside at Ramsgate, but if it were her desire, he would not prevent her. He would have to do his best to make the most of his time with her.

And he would not allow anyone to take some of that precious time. Not even pert ladies with bright eyes and a sparkling spirit.

There! He was doing it again. Thinking of her when he knew he should not.

"Come on, Earl," he called over his shoulder. The spaniel

bounded to his side and then raced ahead of him, his nose twitching with excitement.

# CHAPTER 7

*E*lizabeth spent the next few days accompanying her aunt to Lambton. After visiting the shops, they spent hours with many of Aunt Gardiner's old friends, who were thrilled by her return. Elizabeth found them to be pleasant company, but no one was close to her age.

Another problem occurred to her to dampen her earlier excitement. Because their original plan had been to travel to the Lake District and had only changed at the last minute, aunt and niece had not had time to make firm arrangements about how they would pass their time in Derbyshire. Although her aunt promised to explore the peaks with her, Mrs. Gardiner was not a great walker, and she tired easily. Any excursions they took could only involve short distances, not the long rambles Elizabeth loved. And her aunt also desired to spend a lot of time in the town itself where she could enjoy the company of her old friends. Elizabeth did not begrudge her the house calls and evening dinners which must make up much of their time there, but she was at a loss for how she could explore the county as much as she desired. A letter from Jane had followed not long after their arrival in

Derbyshire. Jane was the dearest to Elizabeth of all her sisters and her closest friend. She wished Jane could be here. Reading her words made her realize how much she longed for the company of someone her own age.

E lizabeth had been in Derbyshire for a week when she walked into Lambton to visit the market. She promised Mrs. Waters she would look out for some house pieces she desired as an excuse to stay out for a few hours.

Lambton was crowded with people for market day. Farmers had traveled from all the surrounding areas to show their produce, and many of the stores set up small stands to display their wares without obliging people to step inside the shops.

Elizabeth's attention was caught by a stall selling antique books. She loved old volumes. The smell of cracked, yellowed pages thrilled her, and she always purchased far too many.

She was leafing through an old novel when she was aware she was not alone. She looked up to see a young lady, some years her junior, standing opposite her. Like Elizabeth, she was leafing through a book, a small smile on her lips. She was engrossed in the volume but looked up when she sensed Elizabeth's eyes on her. Elizabeth was pleased to see a young lady not too far from her own age. She was just considering whether to speak with her when the young lady replaced the book she held, only to cause the others around it to topple to the ground. She gasped, and her cheeks flamed as she dropped to her knees to recover them before the ill-tempered looking book-seller could notice.

Elizabeth ran around to help her. They arranged the

43

books as they had been on the table and glanced across at the book-seller. He was too busy bickering with someone at a neighboring stall to notice the lady's accident. The girls looked at one another and giggled.

"Thank you for helping me," whispered the young lady.

"It is my pleasure. I did something similar once in London and was heartily scolded for it," said Elizabeth. She gestured back to the display. "But I am always so happy to come across stalls like this." She held up a particularly old book. "One never knows what treasures they will find. I always discover an old volume someone else no longer wants. I never leave these places without being weighed down with new purchases."

The young lady blushed, and she smiled shyly and picked up a new book.

For a moment, Elizabeth thought their brief conversation was at an end. The young lady wore a dress of expensive muslin, and Elizabeth guessed her to be of a higher circle than her own. She wondered if the lady took offense at her for conversing with her so freely. She was about to wish her a good morning and move away when the lady spoke.

"I agree," she said. "There is something about exploring these stalls. There are many bookstores in London, some of them enormous, but I always know what I will find there. When I come to a place like this, I am always surprised."

"There is another bookstall on the opposite side of the market. I saw a volume of Shakespeare with an inscription from the original owner. I believe the date was 1650."

The young lady's face lit up with interest, and Elizabeth laughed. "Come, I will show you."

They strolled across the square to the stall. It took a moment for Elizabeth to locate the book. She opened it, and they bent their heads to examine it, speculating as to the original owner. The lady was so absorbed in their conversation some of her shyness had faded.

"Are you a reader of books or a collector?" Elizabeth asked.

"Both. Or perhaps I am the great reader, and my brother is the great collector, although he loves to read too. He is always happy when I return with some new volume for our library."

Elizabeth laughed. "My father is just the same. He insists one can never have enough books, and while our library at home is rather small, it is overflowing. He has crammed every shelf from top to bottom. Books spill out into piles on the floor, and my mama complained of tripping over them until my father forbid her access to it. He says the library is his refuge."

"His refuge from what?" The young lady put the book down without realizing it, engrossed in Elizabeth's story.

"His refuge from us, I'd imagine. He is the only man in a house of women. He is surrounded at all times by myself, my four sisters, and my mother." Elizabeth grinned. "He does not mind my older sister and me so much. But my younger sisters are rather loud, and my mother is similar. The library is his escape from the endless chatter he has to endure."

The lady smiled and blushed and looked as if she did not know how to respond.

"Forgive me for chattering on so," said Elizabeth. "My mother often scolds me for the wild way I run on. It is my way, I suppose."

The lady looked up quickly. "Oh, I do not mind it," she protested. "I was thinking how nice it must be to be so at ease with one's self. I should like that."

"There is nothing wrong with being quiet in nature," said Elizabeth. "In fact, I often envy those ladies who are. They strike me as so much more mysterious and elegant." She smiled. "Perhaps we can influence one another for the better. Do you live near here?"

"Yes, Derbyshire is my home, although I only spend a little time here. But I can tell from your voice you are not from Derbyshire. In fact, I know you are not, or I would recognize you."

"No, I am from Hertfordshire. My aunt grew up here, and she invited me when she wished to pay a visit to some old friends. I have heard much of the peaks, so I was eager to accept."

"Have you seen much of the district yet?"

Elizabeth's smile faltered. "I am afraid not. My aunt is rather tired, and I do not wish her to feel guilty by speaking of how much I long to explore. But it is further than I could travel alone in a carriage."

The young lady looked as if she were pondering something. She turned back to the book and hesitated. She started to speak, then stopped. Her face reddened with the effort it took to get the words out.

"I should - if you would like - please say no if you would not like it, I will not be offended. But if you should - I would be happy to accompany you to the peaks. My brother would accompany us or even send a servant along if he cannot spare the time to come with us." She spoke in a rush as if eager to get the pain of speaking over with all at once. "It is just an idea. I have not seen the peaks in some time, and I should like to see them again. And I have only my companion, though it is not the same as having a friend, and..." She broke off, her face a picture of agony at having spilled so much of her thoughts.

Elizabeth's heart leaped at the offer. "I should be delighted to accept," she said eagerly. "You do not know how much I hoped to make a friend here and that we might explore together. My aunt will be relieved to be released from the obligation to come with me. The journey here has left her exhausted, and that was a week ago."

The lady's eyes lit up with such excitement Elizabeth was touched. It had taken the girl a lot of courage to make such a bold offer, and her evident delight Elizabeth had accepted it was endearing. She was such a sweet, shy girl Elizabeth felt a great desire to be good to her and encourage her to come out of her shell. Such a pretty, sweet girl should not hide away. If Elizabeth could impart some of her self-assurance, she would be happy to do so.

"I am so glad you like the idea," said the lady, her voice light with relief. A smile lit up her face as she spoke, although her cheeks were still pink with the exertion of speaking as she had done. "My brother will be astonished I have done so. He desires me to make friends, and worries I find it difficult. He will be pleased." She paused, and a worried little frown crossed her face. "Would it be too bold of me to invite you and your aunt to dinner? My brother will wish to meet you if we are to spend time together."

"Not at all," said Elizabeth. "I can answer for my aunt that we would be delighted to accept. I would have made the same suggestion. My aunt will also wish to meet you." She tilted her head to consider. "We are engaged tomorrow as our host's son is to come home, and I am required to be there to meet him. But any evening after that, I should be most glad to attend."

"You may bring your hosts too, of course," said the lady quickly. Elizabeth smiled and shook her head.

"I do not imagine they will wish to share their son's company so soon after he is home. They protest otherwise, but they will be happy if myself and my aunt are out for the evening and allow them time alone with him."

The lady nodded. "I will tell my brother we shall expect you, Miss..." She paused, then ducked her head with a shy laugh. "I cannot believe we have spoken so and still not exchanged names."

Elizabeth started with surprise and laughed too. "How foolish. Can you imagine me returning to my aunt and you returning to your brother to announce we shall spend time together and we have forgotten to discover the other's name? My name is Elizabeth Bennet."

The lady smiled and held out her hand for Elizabeth to shake.

"My name is Georgiana Darcy. I know my brother will be as delighted as I am to welcome you to Pemberley."

"Miss Darcy..." said Elizabeth faintly. Her stomach flipped. What were the chances she should make a new friend, and it would be none other than Mr. Darcy's sister? Now she was obliged to spend an evening with him and possibly travel around the countryside with him. How unfortunate.

But she would not change her mind now. She liked Miss Darcy. She would not wound her by withdrawing from their fledgling friendship for the sake of an arrogant man was beneath her consideration.

"Is something wrong, Miss Bennet?" asked Miss Darcy. Her face was anxious.

Elizabeth smiled and shook her head. "Nothing is wrong. Your name startled me. I am already acquainted with your brother."

Miss Darcy gasped. "Are you? When did you meet him? He said nothing about a new acquaintance."

"I think perhaps acquaintance is too strong a word." She

hesitated. She was reluctant to hurt her new friend by offering her candid opinion on Mr. Darcy's conduct. "We met briefly."

"Well, that is wonderful," said Georgiana. "He will be more at ease than ever when I tell him he already knows you."

She paused and looked behind Elizabeth. Elizabeth turned to see what had caught her attention. A tall woman walked towards them through the crowds. Her lips were pressed together in a look of displeasure. Elizabeth wondered if it was her usual expression or if she had reason to seem unhappy at the sight of their conversation. The woman joined them.

"This is my companion, Mrs. Younge," said Georgiana. "Mrs. Younge, this is Miss Elizabeth Bennet, from Hertford-shire. We have just been..."

"Charmed, Miss Bennet," said Mrs. Younge. Even her smile was tight-lipped. "Miss Darcy, we must take you home to your brother. He will desire your company."

"I must return too," said Elizabeth. "I have a few things to buy for my hostess, and I have been most delightfully detained. It was lovely to meet you, Miss Darcy."

Georgiana pressed her hand. "I will send you a note," she promised.

Elizabeth watched as Mrs. Younge led her charge away. She seemed to be speaking to her in a low voice, and Elizabeth would have been very curious to hear their conversation. She smiled and walked away to find Mrs. Waters' house pieces.

# CHAPTER 8

"Miss Darcy, I confess I am surprised at you," said Mrs. Younge. The carriage rumbled over the dusty road on the journey back to Pemberley. "It is not like you to converse with strangers, especially someone new to the area. We know nothing of who she is."

"I spoke with her long enough to see she is pleasant company," said Georgiana. Her voice was faint as it always was when she contradicted another person. "And it is nice to have someone near my age. Not that I don't enjoy your company," she added with an anxious look at her companion.

Mrs. Younge sniffed and looked out the window. Her demeanor suggested one who was grievously hurt but doing their best to hide it.

"Of course you must prefer the company of younger people," she said. "I cannot imagine the friendship of one who is old, tired, and sad after losing a beloved husband can be enjoyable. I understand."

Georgiana felt a rush of desire to comfort the older woman, but she could not feel she was in the wrong this time. It was to Mrs. Younge's benefit she had younger ladies to befriend. It lessened her duties and gave her time to attend to her interests. She could not imagine why Mrs. Younge was acting so ill-used. Her brother had only engaged her a couple of months before, and it was not as if the two were bosom friends already.

"It is not that your company is less valuable," she said. "But you must allow, my company can be trying for you. Having to please a young girl cannot be easy. Now you will have time for other matters."

Mrs. Younge continued to stare out the window. Georgiana could not tell if the idea consoled her.

"How long does Miss Bennet intend to stay in Derbyshire?" she asked after some silence.

Georgiana looked up in surprise. "She did not tell me the exact number of weeks, but she gave me the idea she would be here some time. She told me her aunt grew up here, and she would like to spend time with her old acquaintances."

"Some weeks," said Mrs. Younge. "Well, I daresay it will be nice for you to have a young person's company for a few weeks before we go to Ramsgate. I trust you will not allow Miss Bennet to disrupt your plans?"

Before Georgiana replied, Mrs. Younge laughed. She turned to her and patted her arm. "I speak in jest, Miss Darcy. You are not so weak and irresolute that you would change your plans for someone you have only just met, be she ever so delightful. I know you will not change your mind and ask that we stay here instead." She turned back to the window, still chuckling softly as if the idea was ludicrous.

Georgiana fell silent. It had been Mrs. Younge's idea that they visit Ramsgate. Her companion had raved about the health benefits of sea bathing and the salty air and how it would put roses back in Georgiana's cheeks, which she insisted had developed an unhealthy pallor. She mentioned a pleasant little guest house where they would be most cozy. She spoke of walks along the promenade and the surrounding countryside.

Mrs. Younge had been so excited at the idea Georgiana found she had agreed to it without realizing it. She promised she would consider the proposal, but when Mrs. Younge returned a few days later, beaming and holding up a letter in triumph telling her she had booked their rooms, Georgiana came to understand that agreeing to consider a plan was as good as accepting it in the minds of others. And if Georgiana's words or actions raised someone's expectations, it was only right that she met those expectations. Mrs. Younge had been most insistent on that fact. Georgiana was sorry to leave her home and brother earlier than she might otherwise have done, but she tried to console herself with the idea that the sea air might do her good. Besides, it would not do to let Mrs. Younge down when she was so enthusiastic about it. Georgiana turned her head to the window, her heart sinking.

Georgiana found Fitzwilliam in the drawing-room. He was reading an agricultural magazine, and he looked up with a smile when she entered the room.

"There you are, Georgie. I hope you had a pleasant trip to Lambton?"

"It was pleasant. There are many new stalls, and I believe everyone within fifty miles traveled to be there today."

While she told him about the stalls and the crowds, Darcy rose and rang the bell for tea. Georgiana waited until the footman laid the tray down and left the room before telling him her other news.

"I made a new friend today," she ventured.

"Oh yes?" Darcy looked surprised. "I am pleased, Georgiana. Who is this friend? Is her family known to us?"

Georgiana hesitated. "Not exactly. But you do know her as we discovered by accident."

Darcy looked up sharply from pouring the tea. Usually, the lady of the house attended to such matters, but when it was just the two of them, it pleased him to take care of his sister.

"I already know her," he repeated. His mind flew at once to a lady with sparkling eyes leaping over a stream to land in his path. His mind revisited that memory more than he would have liked over the past few days. "What is her name?"

It must be her.

"Miss Elizabeth Bennet."

Darcy returned to his task to hide the reaction he knew must be visible on his face. "How did you come to meet?"

Georgiana told him about how they had spoken over their shared love of books. When she reached the part where she offered to take Miss Bennet touring around the peaks and how she planned to invite her to dinner, Darcy stopped what he was doing and looked up. He pushed the dish of muffin towards her and sat back to look at her.

"How did Miss Bennet take that offer?"

"She was delighted." Georgiana delicately picked at her food. "She said she despaired of meeting friends closer to her age. Her aunt tires easily, and Miss Bennet did not like to ask her to come traveling too far. We were both very pleased the other wished to further our acquaintance."

Darcy nodded. "And when she accepted your offer, was it before or after you told her you were my sister?"

"Before. We had been chatting so much we forgot to introduce ourselves." Georgiana chewed thoughtfully, staring into the fire. "There was a moment when I thought my name troubled her. As if she would not have been so quick to talk if she'd realized who I was." She shrugged with a smile. "But perhaps I am not used to making friends and am not so wise at reading people. She rallied and said she would be happy to come to dinner if I extended an invitation."

Darcy pressed his steepled fingers to his lips. For a moment, he feared Miss Bennet pursued a friendship with his sister to get closer to him.

She would not be the first lady to have tried it. His friend Bingley's sister would fall on Georgiana's neck when she saw her and declare it an age since they last met. But from his observations when Miss Bingley did not realize he was present, she scarcely acknowledged Georgiana's existence apart from that. It was gratifying to know Miss Bennet was not such a lady.

But why should Miss Bennet seem uncomfortable? Had he made such a terrible impression on her? He had been abrupt, but that was his manner. His friends in London forgave him for it. Miss Bennet did not resent him, did she? Did she dislike him?

And why should it bother him? Miss Bennet was nothing to him. He would value her as a good friend to his sister if such proved to be the case. But for himself, she could be nothing.

"I hope you will not delay in inviting Miss Bennet for dinner," he said. Georgiana looked at him, her eyes bright.

"I will write and ask her at once. And her aunt. She is so pleasant and easy, Fitzwilliam. She spoke as if it did not trouble her at all to converse with a stranger, and she made me laugh. I should be glad to become friends."

"And if it pleases you, I will do all I can to encourage it," Darcy promised. "Here, take more strawberry jam. Hudson will be devastated if we send it back. He told me several times he made it, especially because it's your favorite."

# CHAPTER 9

$\mathcal{M}$rs. Waters was sorting through letters when Elizabeth came downstairs. She looked at her guest and smiled.

"Well, Miss Bennet. It seems you are popular already. A card has come for you."

Elizabeth's heart pounded as she took it. If it were what she suspected, it would mean she would soon spend an evening in the company of Mr. Darcy. Once again, she reminded herself of how much she enjoyed his sister's company. Mr. Darcy's society would be a small price to pay.

"Who is it from, dear?" asked Mrs. Waters as Elizabeth moved away. Elizabeth suppressed an irritated sigh. Mrs. Waters was kind and an excellent hostess, but she was incurably intrusive and desired to know all about her. The housekeeper came down the hall and spared her the need to respond.

"Madam, Cook wishes to speak with you in the kitchen. The partridges for dinner arrived, but she would like your direction in how you wish them prepared."

"Oh, roasted. Henry loves roasted partridges above all things. I will tell her."

She hurried down the hall, and Elizabeth sighed with relief. Today was the day Captain Henry Waters returned home, and Mrs. Waters was beside herself with excitement. Only a meal fit for a king would do for her precious boy. Elizabeth was curious to meet this paragon of manhood, but she was even more curious to read the contents of her note.

Elizabeth slipped into the library in case Mrs. Waters should return. She read the note with a smile. She could almost hear Miss Darcy's shy, hesitant voice as she begged her and her aunt to be good enough to join them for dinner the following evening. Elizabeth was already looking forward to seeing her again and continuing the acquaintance. She knew her aunt would be fond of the girl and should be glad to meet her.

What had Mr. Darcy said when Miss Darcy returned home and informed him they had met? Had he been annoyed? Did he even remember Elizabeth, or did he see her as nothing more than a temporary nuisance he had forgotten once she was out of his sight?

Or worse; would he be suspicious? Would he find it too much of a coincidence that after discovering who he was, she might have deliberately sought his sister and befriended her to get closer to him? He was an eligible, wealthy bachelor, after all.

She shook her head and laughed at her thoughts. What did she care what he thought of her? Even if he suspected her motives, one evening in her company would cure him of any notions she had designs on him. He would not mistake her indifference once she made it plain she was there for Miss Darcy's sake alone.

Besides, she had more important concerns than the

thoughts of one man who was nothing to her. What on earth would she wear to a dinner at a house as grand as Pemberley? She was sure her gowns, which had pleased her when she chose them for her visit to Derbyshire, would seem shabby compared to the grandeur of such an estate.

She would ask her aunt's advice. Aunt Gardiner would know which she should choose.

Elizabeth and Aunt Gardiner stood just inside the hallway as the clock struck four. Mr. and Mrs. Waters stood on the steps. Mrs. Waters was almost sobbing in her eagerness to hold her son again, and though Mr. Waters appeared calm, his frequent pacing to the lane spoke of his anxiety.

Elizabeth, for her part, was bored by the wait and a little apprehensive about the meeting. She and Aunt Gardiner had suggested they leave the house for a few hours so the Waters' might welcome their son in private, but the couple refused. Mrs. Waters had not let up on her hints she hoped Elizabeth would make a match with her son, and Elizabeth knew from her own mother how uncomfortable it was to have a mama trying to force a match between her child and another prospect.

She hoped Mrs. Waters would recognize Elizabeth's lack of enthusiasm and cease her attempts. There would be plenty of women in Derbyshire for Henry Waters to make a match. Elizabeth was not about to be forced into an alliance with a young man who needed his mama to sing his praises. She doubted very much if he would live up to them.

It was more than half an hour after four when a carriage turned into the gate and drove up to the front of the house.

Mrs. Waters shrieked and ran down the steps while her more sedate but visibly happy husband followed her.

Elizabeth could not see the young man when he emerged from the carriage. As soon as he stepped down, Mrs. Waters launched herself at him, burying him in a flurry of kisses and hugs and scolding him for his lateness. When she finally released him, Mr. Waters' tall form stood before him and blocked their view as he embraced him.

"I am glad the Darcys invited us to dinner tomorrow, Lizzy," said Aunt Gardiner in a whisper. "My friend will protest, but I am not comfortable being here while they welcome their son. It is an intrusion."

"I quite agree, Aunt." Elizabeth sighed with resignation. "But Mrs. Waters is determined to keep us as guests."

"I wonder why?" Aunt Gardiner gave her a sly smile. Elizabeth laughed.

"It seems until I wear a ring on my finger, I am doomed to have no peace from matchmaking mamas. But I am certain I will not find Captain Waters anything close to as agreeable as his mother paints him. She is a partial mama, and we must..."

She broke off as Mr. Waters moved out of the way, and at last, they saw him.

Captain Henry Waters was a tall man. His years in the Navy gave him a proud carriage, and months at sea gave his face a light tan which made his blue eyes shine. He smiled at them, and Elizabeth saw the whiteness of his teeth. His sideburns were neatly trimmed, highlighting his strong jawline. Elizabeth realized she had forgotten to breathe as she admired him. Perhaps his mama was not so partial after all?

Once the Waters' had introduced their son to their guests, they repaired to the drawing-room. Mrs. Waters hung on her son's arm, dabbing at her eyes with a handkerchief as she beamed up at him.

"You're home," she kept repeating. "You're home. Why were you late? I was dreadfully afraid something had happened."

Captain Waters laughed with a little embarrassment at his mother's caresses. He caught Elizabeth's eye and gave her a conspiratorial grin. Elizabeth felt a flutter in her stomach at his attention, and a warm sensation rose up her neck.

"I am not that late, Mama. Portions of the road were in poor condition, and I was not about to risk the horses."

"Which way did you come?" asked Mr. Waters. "I expected you to come around the Derby Road, but you came by way of Lambton."

His quiet voice was drowned out by Mrs. Waters. "Oh, those terrible roads. Well, no matter. You are here now." She wrapped her arms around him once again. Captain Waters patted her hand and turned to Elizabeth.

"I was pleased when Mama told me we would have guests on my homecoming," he said. "Home is always pleasant, of course, but a home filled with pleasant society and intelligent conversation is essential."

"I hope when you marry, you will live close by, and your own home will be filled with all the society you desire," said his mother. "I told you my son came home to settle, did I not?" she asked, turning to their guests. Her eyes were wide and innocent as she looked at Elizabeth.

Captain Waters blushed. Elizabeth wondered if Mrs. Waters had dropped as many hints to him as she had to her. She thought he gave her an apologetic smile before he patted his mother's hand.

"That is my reason," he said. "But there is no rush. I should like to take my time getting acquainted with a young lady and forming a deep friendship as a solid foundation for marriage. I do not wish to marry for the sake of it."

This was just how Elizabeth felt, an attitude that caused Mrs. Bennet great distress. She looked at the new arrival with renewed interest, noticing yet again how well his uniform became him. Every girl in Derbyshire would be in a flutter when news spread of his homecoming. For the first time, Elizabeth was relieved there were so few young women in Lambton, and she blushed at the thought. She was not the sort of silly girl who lost her heart to any handsome face. But she was also willing to allow that Mrs. Waters might not be entirely wrong in wishing a match between them.

As if reading her thoughts, Mrs. Waters spoke up. "It is a shame there are so few young ladies in Lambton. I would like you to find someone close by, dear. Someone connected to the family and at liberty to move here."

Elizabeth felt as if her fichu was strangling her. "Shall I play music?" She rose suddenly and crossed the room to the pianoforte.

"Oh - yes." Mrs. Waters twisted around in the chair, surprised at her sudden manner. "Yes, of course. Henry loves music, do you not, dear? And Miss Bennet plays so beautifully. It will delight you."

Elizabeth pretended she had not heard her. Her own mother lacked propriety and was devoid of subtlety in arranging her daughters' marriages. But Mrs. Bennet had a kindred spirit in Mrs. Waters. It was somewhat surprising she was such close friends with the sensible Aunt Gardiner rather than the gossipy, intrusive Mrs. Bennet.

Elizabeth played a lively tune she had learned before leaving Hertfordshire. Mary, her middle sister, despaired when she played it, declaring it had no taste and no genius. But Elizabeth did not pretend to have Mary's affectations for music. She played whatever delighted her, and lively Irish tunes were a favorite. If Captain Waters wished for something more refined, he could find someone else to play or learn the instrument himself.

Elizabeth was so absorbed in the music that Captain Waters was before her before she realized it. She missed a note in her surprise, and he hastily apologized. She played on, pretending to focus on her performance. If she looked up, she knew she would see Mrs. Waters gazing across at them with ill-disguised delight.

"You play beautifully, Miss Bennet," said the captain. "It is just the music I like. I wish I could say I preferred high-brow tones, but something about this music is irresistible for rousing the spirits."

Elizabeth looked up and flashed him a smile to show she appreciated his words.

"Will it not be strange for you to settle after so many years of travel?" she asked after a pause. Captain Waters leaned on the pianoforte and gazed thoughtfully out the window at the rose garden as he considered her question. His eyes were the most astonishing blue. His return would cause a sensation in Derbyshire. Far more than a certain unpleasant landowner for all his wealth and breeding.

"It will," he admitted. "Even though there is always a chance I shall be called back into service. I shall not know what to do with myself. I wish to purchase a farm nearby where I can make myself useful. I could not bear sitting around and being a gentleman of leisure. Not when I have known so many years of activity. But it is good to be home. I have longed to stay in one place and not wonder where the Navy might send me next. I wonder at the men who can do it year after year. Some are married and do not see their wives and children from six months to the next. I do not under-stand how they can bear it."

"Perhaps they have not had your good fortune." Elizabeth gave him a playful smile. "Your mother has told us again and again how quickly you have risen through the ranks to take command. Few have such talent. And it enables you to retire early and live just as you choose. I consider you blessed."

Captain Waters gave a short laugh to hide his discomfort. "My mother is fond of me, but you must not mind all she says. I have been fortunate, but she will make me out to be finer than I am. I am sure your mama is just the same with you." He grinned. "I am sure if I visited Hertfordshire, I would hear nothing but boasts of her Elizabeth's beauty, of her wit, of her skill at playing the pianoforte."

Elizabeth laughed out loud, only stopping when she saw Mrs. Waters' gleeful look in their direction. She tried to compose herself, but she could not suppress her amusement.

"I am afraid we have rather different mothers. Mine is not liable to boast of me. My father is a different matter. He does me too great an honor in his opinion of me."

"I am sure that is not the case."

Elizabeth only smiled and returned to her playing. She was aware of Captain Waters' eyes on her and wondered if he found her as attractive as she thought him. She could not suppress a surge of glee that such a handsome man looked on her with admiration.

*If I am not careful, I shall be a fair way to falling in love,* she thought. *How fortunate that Lydia and Kitty are not here. They would be head over ears for him and make fools of us all.*

"Mama tells me you have been forbidden to visit Pemberley Woods," he said.

Elizabeth looked up in surprise and shrugged. "It is no matter. There are other places to explore."

Captain Waters laughed. "So you had an interesting first meeting with Mr. Darcy then?"

"That is one way to describe it. Are you acquainted with him?"

"Not well. His family is not of the sort to mix with the town. It is a shame as Mr. Darcy, and I are of an age, but I cannot imagine we would have much in common even if we were friends."

"He would hardly object to making your acquaintance now, not having served in the Navy," Elizabeth reminded him.

"That is true. But still, the fact remains I do not think we would have much in common. He will speak of the London Season, and I will speak of navigating around the West Indies."

"Your temperaments are so different," Elizabeth agreed. "There is nothing easy and friendly about him, and you converse so delightfully. You are affable, and he is reserved. I can't imagine him laughing and speaking easily, even with friends."

Captain Waters laughed and thanked her for the compliment. "And yet he has invited you and your aunt for dinner tomorrow night. He cannot be all that proud and reserved."

"I am afraid that is nothing to do with him and all his sister's doing. We met yesterday, and as both of us are eager to continue the acquaintance, she invited us for dinner. I cannot imagine Mr. Darcy was pleased, but perhaps he indulges his sister."

"Well, I shall be sorry to lose your company for an evening, but it is a small price to pay if you carry home news of what it was like to dine in the home of the great Mr. Darcy. I shall be eager for your report."

Elizabeth laughed and agreed.

The rest of the evening passed pleasantly, and no one was happier than Mrs. Waters. Not only did she have her precious son by her side, but the young people conversed with as much spirit as she would have wished. Elizabeth wondered why she should be so eager to promote a match between them. The Waters' were from trade, and as a gentleman's daughter, she was above them, but she would bring little fortune on her marriage.

But she supposed Mrs. Waters was keen to forge a closer alliance between her dearest friend, and if she could do so by marrying her son into gentility, she would not miss such an opportunity.

# CHAPTER 10

"*I*t never rains, but it pours," announced Mrs. Waters. She had just returned from Lambton, where she had taken her son to show him off to their neighbors. Captain Waters took the seat beside Elizabeth as soon as he came in and leaned towards her to admire her needlework. Elizabeth half listened as Mrs. Waters spoke. "We were just lamenting the dearth of young people in this neighborhood when who should I see walking down the street but the two Miss Carters."

At Elizabeth's inquisitive look, she was happy to continue.

"They are cousins of Mrs. Jones, and they have not been to stay with them at the parsonage for some time. They are pleasant girls, of course. Miss Helen Carter has not much to recommend her. I am sure she is a good-hearted girl, but she is plain - very plain. But her sister, Miss Rebecca Carter, is quite handsome. Such a true English beauty. It seems a shame a girl with her looks can have such low prospects."

"What do you mean?" asked Elizabeth, putting down her needlework.

"Mama," said Captain Waters with an exasperated sigh. "Please do not gossip so. The Miss Carters cannot help their circumstances."

Elizabeth's curiosity was stirred even higher, and she would not be satisfied until she had an explanation. Even Aunt Gardiner had put her book to one side and was listening.

Mrs. Waters threw her son an apologetic look. "I am sorry, my dear, but of course they will wish to know of them. It is only natural, and besides, they may run into them."

"And be polluted by the experience, I am sure," said Captain Waters, rolling his eyes. "Well, tell them then. Now you have awakened their curiosity, they will find out anyway."

Mrs. Waters hesitated for a moment as if to show reluctance, then moved closer, although there was no one else in the room.

"I am afraid the Carters are the natural daughters of nobody knows whom," she whispered in a scandalized tone.

Captain Waters shook his head at his mother's manner.

"Well, someone must know who their parents are if they are staying with their cousin," Elizabeth pointed out. Captain Waters looked up and gave her a grin.

"They are not exactly their cousins," began his mother.

"They are not their cousins in any sense, Mama. There is little point in making a show of delicacy towards them if you will then follow it up with scandalous tales of their origins." He looked at Elizabeth. "They were left with a good family in Portsmouth. No one knows why the family took them in. My guess is one of the family was friends with one of their parents. Mrs. Jones is a cousin of that family. They are very good to them, I understand."

"Well, that is fortunate," said Aunt Gardiner. "Poor girls.

They had no say in the manner of their births, and it is a shame they should go through life with it hanging over their heads. I am glad they fell in with a family who seems to cherish them. Where is their usual residence?"

"It is a school at Portsmouth," said Mrs. Waters. "They spend their holidays with their foster family and then return to school where they are parlor boarders. Most of the other girls go away for the summer, so they take the time to visit their different adoptive relatives.

"How old are the ladies?" asked Elizabeth.

"Helen is about nineteen, and Rebecca is twenty. It is a shame they don't have connections. They are charming girls, and Miss Rebecca is a beauty. She could have made a fine match if she had a family. Now, it is impossible to guess what will become of her and her sister. No respectable family will wish to form an alliance with them."

"Well, it seems they are dear to their foster family. I am sure they will always have a home with them," said Aunt Gardiner. "And we cannot say they will never marry. Women with unknown origins have made matches in the past. Perhaps they will meet respectable, kind-hearted farmers who will be happy to love them and marry them?"

"Oh, I hope so with all my heart," said Mrs. Waters. "There might be someone who could make them respectable. I would like to see them settled among their people."

"Their people? Do you mean farmers, Mama?" asked the captain. He looked as if he did not know whether to be amused or annoyed at his mother. His mother responded with an indulgent smile.

"Among those who are not genteel, of course."

Elizabeth exchanged a glance with her aunt and grinned. Having a son in the Navy appeared to have gone to Mrs. Waters' head. It caused her to forget that her beloved Marianne Gardiner, who enjoyed a happy marriage to a tradesman, was among those not considered genteel.

Aunt Gardiner rose from the table. "I will walk into Lambton. One of my gloves has become loose around the wrist, and I wish to buy a new pair before tonight. Will you join me, Lizzy?"

Elizabeth agreed.

As the ladies walked down the lane towards the town, they heard Captain Waters call Elizabeth's name. They paused and waited for him to catch up with them.

"I must apologize for my mother," he said. His handsome face looked embarrassed. "She speaks without thought sometimes. I hope she has not offended you?"

Aunt Gardiner laughed. "My dear boy, I am far too old to be offended by such a trifling thing. I am aware it was simple thoughtlessness."

He sighed in relief. "I spoke to her often as to the importance of considering what she says. Her attitude can be — but perhaps I am too harsh. I have seen much of the world, and the privilege has caused me to think differently about attitudes my mother holds dear. I am relieved you are not offended."

"Not in the slightest." Aunt Gardiner's expression was too cheerful for him to disbelieve her. He smiled.

"Which glove makers will you visit?"

"I am not sure. It has been too long since I lived here, and I am unfamiliar with the newer establishments. I am sure there is someone you can recommend?"

"White's is a popular place. It is where most of us buy our gloves, and we visit there almost every day of our lives. You will find it to the west of the main square. Anyone may direct you there."

"And will you join us?" asked Elizabeth. "You will be eager to see your old friends, I am sure."

Captain Waters hesitated, and for a moment, Elizabeth's spirits were in a flutter to think he might accompany them to spend time with her. But he shook his head with a smile of apology.

"I have a few matters I must attend. And besides, my mother has arranged for all the neighbors to visit and welcome me home. I should think I'll meet the entire town by dinner." He affected a pained expression to make the ladies laugh.

"The conquering hero returns," said Elizabeth with a teasing smile. "We should go, Aunt. The day is already half done, and if White's does not offer us what we need, we will have to search elsewhere."

"I can guarantee you will not. White's will provide all you need."

"Do you perhaps work for White's, sir?"

He laughed. "Well, perhaps I might consider it. But no, I thought you would find what you need there and be able to hurry home to prepare for the grand dinner tonight." His eyes narrowed with a playful threat. "It would not do to keep Mr. Darcy of Pemberley waiting."

The ladies laughed again.

"He is a pleasant fellow," said Aunt Gardiner with a fond smile as they walked arm in arm to the town. She glanced at Elizabeth out of the corner of her eye. "I suspect you find him rather more interesting than you expected?"

"Well - perhaps a little more," said Elizabeth. She smiled at her aunt. "Now, don't you start too. Come, we must hurry. He is right, you know. If we keep Mr. Darcy waiting, he might forbid us his house as well as his woods."

# CHAPTER 11

*E*lizabeth gazed out the window as the carriage approached Pemberley. The magnificent limestone mansion was lit up by lamps, and the evening light swept across rolling lawns.

"It is beautiful, is it not?" said Aunt Gardiner. "I have seen many such homes in my time, but I still believe none are as fine as Pemberley."

"It is splendid," agreed Elizabeth.

She gazed in admiration at the many windows and the impressive sweep of parkland. If she had not experienced Mr. Darcy's unpleasant manner for herself, she would have been surprised such a place did not have a mistress. Surely every lady Mr. Darcy encountered was eager for the role of mistress of Pemberley?

"Perhaps its beauty renders its owner a little more agreeable?" said Mrs. Gardiner, interrupting her niece's thoughts with a teasing smile.

"Well — perhaps," said Elizabeth with a show of reluctance. She looked at her aunt and laughed. "Perhaps a very little."

Mr. Darcy and his sister appeared at the top of the steps to greet them. To Elizabeth's surprise, Mr. Darcy himself came forward to hand them out of the carriage before the footman approached. She thanked him and tried to appear unconcerned by his presence.

To her annoyance, she realized she had forgotten how handsome he was. Perhaps even more so than Captain Waters. Her hand tingled where he held it. To hide the effect it had on her, she looked past him to where Georgiana waited, looking beautiful in a white gown, her golden curls arranged about her face. She smiled shyly and pulled at her shawl and seemed so out of her depth in the role of hostess, Elizabeth's heart ached for her. She moved towards her at once.

"I so looked forward to seeing you again," she said after she had shaken the younger girl's hand.

"And I, you, Miss Bennet. I worried — "

Elizabeth looked at her quizzically.

"I worried you might change your mind," she admitted.

"Not at all. I told my aunt all about you, and she has been eager to meet you." Elizabeth turned and introduced her aunt to the Darcys.

Mr. Darcy himself stood apart from the group.

"We should go in," he said.

They were brought into an elegant drawing-room. Elizabeth looked around in admiration at the old portraits on the walls showing long-gone Darcys. The furnishings were old but well-maintained and spoke of the owner's taste. A great fire roared in the hearth despite the evening's warmth. In a room that size, a fire would not go amiss.

Another woman rose as they came in. She was tall and had thick hair bound up in curls. Her face had a pinched expression, and she pursed her thin lips before rearranging them into a smile that did not meet her eyes. Her gown was of rich material and well-made.

Elizabeth remembered she was the lady who had pulled Georgiana away when they first met. Their first encounter had been so brief it had taken her a moment to recognize her. That she had not welcomed them outside as Mr and Miss Darcy had done suggested the woman was not a member of the family, for all her fine clothes.

It was also plain this lady was not pleased to meet Elizabeth and her aunt, though why that should be, Elizabeth was not sure.

The woman dropped a curtsey and gave a bigger smile when she saw Darcy, her demeanor at once becoming warm and friendly.

"Mrs. Gardiner and Miss Bennet, may I introduce my companion, Mrs. Younge." Georgiana glanced towards the lady from under her eyelashes, and Elizabeth had the impression she seemed apprehensive about Mrs. Younge's reaction.

But why should Miss Darcy be apprehensive about her companion? Perhaps Mrs. Younge considered Elizabeth's friendship with Miss Darcy a threat to her position, but that was silly. Elizabeth would only be in Derbyshire for a few weeks. Still, some people were jealous and did not care to share those in their lives with others. Perhaps Mrs. Younge was one of them.

The ladies greeted one another.

"It is a pleasure to meet you, Miss Bennet," said Mrs. Younge. "I am sorry we had to leave so suddenly the other day when Miss Darcy met you. I hope you did not think me rude?"

"No apology necessary, Mrs. Younge," said Elizabeth. From the corner of her eye, she saw Darcy watching the exchange. His eyes were alert, and she knew he did not miss a word. Elizabeth ignored them both and turned back to Georgiana.

"Miss Darcy, my aunt and I are grateful for your invitation. I looked forward to seeing you again."

Mrs. Gardiner smiled. "I am so happy Lizzy found a young person. I worried she might be lonely without people of a similar age. I am happy to explore with her, but I cannot keep up with Lizzy's energy. She will not be satisfied until she has explored every hill, field, and wood in Derbyshire."

At the mention of woods, Elizabeth could not resist a little peek at Darcy. He appeared similarly struck and turned to stare at her. She smiled.

"On my first morning, I explored some of Pemberley Woods," she said. "They are delightful. Everything a woodland ought to be without too much interference from man beyond well laid out paths. The gamekeeper was most accommodating about showing me the best spots. He even escorted me home, which was generous of him."

"The gamekeeper?" Georgiana tilted her head in confusion. "Fitzwilliam, did you appoint a new gamekeeper? I did not realize you had found one so soon after Thompson retired."

"Miss Bennet speaks in jest, Georgiana," said Darcy. He stared at Elizabeth, and she could not work out if he was angry at her levity or amused and trying to suppress it. "It seems she has a rather peculiar sense of humor. The gamekeeper she refers to is me. That is whom she mistook me for when I encountered her exploring my lands."

Mrs. Younge gave an audible gasp she made a great show of trying to suppress. Her hand went to her mouth, and she shook her head in a chiding gesture as if she did not wish to offend Mr. Darcy's guests but could not hide her disapproval of such an error.

"It was an easy mistake to make," said Elizabeth lightly. "You dressed in casual clothing, walking through the woods with a gun over your shoulder and a dog by your side. The perfect image of a gamekeeper." She gave Mrs. Younge a pointed look. "And it is not an insult. There is no shame in being a gamekeeper and so no shame in being mistaken for one."

"None at all," said Darcy. He stared at her again as if examining her. Elizabeth returned his stare frankly, refusing to be intimidated into looking away first. The rest of their party was slightly perplexed by the atmosphere between them.

"I suppose you cannot be offended by my taking you for a gamekeeper when you took me for a poacher," she added with a mischievous smile.

To her surprise, Darcy's expression relaxed, and he gave her a small smile.

"I did not take you for a poacher in all seriousness, Miss Bennet. I spoke to be contrary, and I think you know that. If you were a poacher, you would have made a poor one in your frock with your hair unbound. Unless you intended to charm my game into following you from the woods."

"You discovered through my plan, sir," said Elizabeth with mock horror. "I am the Pied Piper of animals. Why even Earl was charmed and would have happily exchanged one master for another if you hadn't prevented us."

Georgiana laughed, although there was a nervous note in it. She glanced at her brother to see how he took Elizabeth's teasing tone. To her surprise, he was much more relaxed than she expected and even seemed to be enjoying it.

"What does Miss Bennet mean, Fitzwilliam? Earl will not go to anyone else if you are there, even when offered a treat. I should know, for I tried many times."

"Miss Bennet thought she could abduct Earl without my knowledge, Georgiana," he replied. His eyes were still fixed on Elizabeth's face. "She is so skilled at charming him, I did not notice he had left with her until they had gone some distance away. Another person might have missed her trick until it was too late. I am sure if I had not intervened when I had, I would have found Earl under a new name, having forgotten who I am."

"It seems I will have to poach elsewhere from now on, sir," said Elizabeth. "You see through me. I see my tricks will not work here."

Darcy gave a short laugh. He bowed to her.

"Excuse me. There is still time before dinner, and you will wish to renew your acquaintance with Georgiana. I shall leave you for now."

He left the room. Elizabeth stared after him, more perplexed by him than ever. He was such an odd man, she did not know what to make of him. Her eyes met Georgiana's. She looked just as bewildered as she did.

"Won't you sit down, Miss Bennet?" she said when she had recovered her voice.

Most of the conversation comprised Elizabeth and Mrs. Gardiner speaking of their journey to Derbyshire. Georgiana ventured to contribute to the discussion, but she was shy and often glanced at Mrs. Younge for her approval.

That lady said little and seemed most put out that the evening should happen at all. Elizabeth suspected her way of talking to Mr. Darcy had forever set her up as an impudent upstart in that lady's mind.

Elizabeth did not care for her opinion, but she felt a slight concern about how it might affect her friendship with Georgiana. The young girl apparently needed her companion's approval. There was an anxiety about her that was more than simple shyness. Elizabeth was concerned that if Mrs. Younge put it in her mind that Elizabeth was not a suitable friend, the girl might feel obligated to agree. She hoped it would not be the case, and she hoped if Georgiana enjoyed her company, the grumbles of her companion would not dissuade her. But she was so young, Elizabeth would not think poorly of her if she was deterred.

"Do you think you would like to accompany me to the peaks this week, Miss Darcy?" Elizabeth asked. "The weather has been perfect for exploring parties, and the views will be at their best."

"Miss Darcy will need to speak with her brother before deciding," said Mrs. Younge before Georgiana replied. "She would not wish to show him disrespect by accepting an offer before he has granted his permission."

Georgiana looked mortified by her companion's presumption, but though her cheeks burned, she did not protest. Elizabeth shot Mrs. Younge a cool glance.

"You are kind to speak on Miss Darcy's behalf, I am sure," she said smoothly. "But Miss Darcy has a mind of her own. I am sure she can tell me so herself in her own good time."

A flash of anger crossed Mrs. Younge's face, but she quickly smothered it with a smile.

"Of course she can. I am simply reminding her of what she owes her brother."

"I do not forget what I owe my brother," said Georgiana. Her voice was small, and her cheeks were still red, but Elizabeth rejoiced to see this small beginning in speaking up for herself. "I will speak to him at dinner, Miss Bennet. I am sure he will agree."

Mrs. Younge sat stiffly and took on a wounded expression. She sniffed and looked to the window with the air of one who had been terribly injured but was bearing up bravely.

Georgiana looked at her anxiously, but Elizabeth caught her eye and grinned at her. She shyly returned it, and the conversation turned to the beauty spots they could explore once they had Mr. Darcy's permission.

# CHAPTER 12

*M*r. Darcy returned just as the bell rang for dinner and escorted them to the dining room. As they sat down to dinner, Elizabeth watched him interact with his sister. He wanted her to take the role of hostess, but he was gentle about it and encouraged her with a supportive smile. It pleased Elizabeth to see it. From her brief encounter with Darcy, she would not have realized he possessed a softer side. She caught her train of thought and paused to reflect why she should care so much about making out his character, but she told herself it was because her friendship with Georgiana depended upon it.

She watched as Darcy leaned forward and whispered something to his sister. Georgiana nodded, and he gave her an encouraging smile. As he straightened up, he caught Elizabeth's eyes upon him. Elizabeth dropped her eyes to her plate, embarrassed he should catch her staring at him. A wave of annoyance came over her. What did it matter what he thought? She looked up at him again and met his gaze with an unwavering one of her own.

"What are you thinking, Miss Bennet? You regard me as gravely as I might study one of my account sheets."

"I am merely trying to make you out," said Elizabeth with a show of unconcern. "You are a riddle, Mr. Darcy, and I enjoy riddles."

Darcy's eyebrows raised at her bold response. Out of the corner of her eye, she caught Mrs. Younge shaking her head in sorrow.

"And what do you make of me?" he asked. "I do not consider myself complicated. I am a straightforward man and speak as I find. Nothing to justify being the topic of such an important study, I am sure."

"Ah, well, that is for me to decide, sir," said Elizabeth with a smile. "I find human nature fascinating. I am sure your modesty does you credit, but if I find your character interesting, it is not for you to decide otherwise."

For a moment, Darcy did not respond. He exchanged a glance with his sister, who looked on anxiously.

"Well, when you put it like that, I suppose you are right, but I still say there is nothing so complicated about me. What are your findings so far?"

Elizabeth shrugged and turned back to her plate.

"I do not get on at all," she said. "You are a riddle, like I say. You appear to possess many contradicting qualities. For example, right now, you are all gentleness to your sister. And while I am the first to agree she deserves nothing but the kindest treatment, it is in stark contrast to your behavior towards me when you marched me from your woods. When I met you then, I would never have realized you had it in you to be so soft-hearted." She gave him an arch smile. Darcy looked as if he was not sure how to respond.

"I am sure you have great confidence in your abilities to make people out, Miss Bennet, but I should remind you, this is only our second meeting, and our first was under very different circumstances. We can not have spent over two hours in one another's company. You do not know me so well yet."

There was just that edge in his voice that suggested he was offended. Elizabeth did not care if he was insulted, but she did not wish him to prevent Georgiana from seeing her, which he might do if he considered her an unsuitable companion. She let the matter drop for now.

"I must thank you again for inviting us to dinner, Miss Darcy," she said. "I am delighted to spend time with you. Without realizing it, you provided us with a perfect escape this evening."

"Lizzy." Aunt Gardiner shook her head. "Do not run on so. The Darcys will not realize you are joking."

"I speak in jest," said Elizabeth. "Our hosts are charming people. I refer only to the fact that their son has returned him from the Navy to stay. There is much excitement in the house, and we are happy to allow them some time alone with their son. They missed him so much, and his mama especially is thrilled to have him back."

"From the Navy," said Darcy. "That would be Captain Waters?"

"It would. Do you know him?"

"Only by reputation. I have heard of his achievements."

"What sort of man is he?" asked Georgiana.

"I consider him a fine man. He is pleasant and charming and is happy to converse at length about all topics. He has told me many stories of the countries he has visited. As one who would love to travel, it was exciting for me. I would love to visit Italy and Malta and Madeira."

"You would not be afraid to travel?" asked Darcy. "Few manage it now."

"Oh, my mother would never allow it, and I could not manage her reaction if I were to do so," said Elizabeth. "I am in no danger of taking on an army to view a painting in Florence, not that I would not be tempted. But things will eventually settle down. I hope I may travel one day."

Whatever Darcy thought of young ladies traveling, he refrained from saying. Instead, he said, "What age is Captain Waters?"

Elizabeth and Mrs. Gardiner looked at one another.

"I am not too sure," said Mrs. Gardiner. "I suspect he is of an age with you, sir. His mother wishes for him to settle down, and he says it is his intention."

"And is he..." Georgiana paused, her color rising. "Is he a well-looking man?"

"He is well looking. He is too young to have that weather-beaten appearance so many of our men develop from years at sea. I would say few ladies would not find him pleasant to look at."

"Are you betrothed, Miss Bennet?" This question came from Mrs. Younge.

"I am not," said Elizabeth.

"And you are staying in the home of an eligible, handsome young man?"

"That is enough, Mrs. Younge," said Darcy. His voice was firm.

The woman quickly apologized and turned back to her plate. A silence followed. Darcy glowered and seemed in low humor. Elizabeth was taken aback by such a sudden turn of mood. She could not believe it was displeasure at his employee's rudeness. She suspected he was often so; the sort of man who could be agreeable one moment but grow quiet and ill-humored in the next.

How tiresome it would be to have such a companion. His

wealth and personal attractions would not make amends for having to live with a man whose temper changed from one moment to the next.

Captain Waters would never behave so. He was amiable, and the few times Elizabeth had seen him out of humor was when his mother earned it. But his temper never lasted long, and he readily laughed himself into a good temper. It was a trait Elizabeth shared and valued in others. For a moment, she wished she had stayed home, but she reminded herself she came here for Georgiana, not her brooding older brother.

Determined that Mr. Darcy's black humor should not ruin the evening for the rest, she looked at Georgiana.

"I hope you will play for us before we leave, Miss Darcy? I should love to hear you."

Georgiana looked nervously at her brother and companion and agreed shyly. She offered her opinion on some new pieces of music from the continent. Mrs. Gardiner joined in, and the three ladies soon had a pleasant conversation and almost forgot about their two silent companions. Elizabeth noticed Darcy watching Georgiana. As his sister pushed herself to converse more, Elizabeth saw a distinct softening in his features. He seemed to shrug off whatever had affected him and joined the conversation.

# CHAPTER 13

*D*arcy joined them when they retired to the drawing-room. Elizabeth begged Georgiana to perform on the elegant pianoforte set before the window.

"Come, I will play afterward if it suits you. Or if you like, I will play before you," she said when Georgiana demurred. "Perhaps that would be best. Once you hear my terrible playing, you will understand yours can only be an improvement."

Georgiana giggled.

"I shall play, but please do not make me sing."

"Of course, if you would rather not."

Georgiana seated herself before the pianoforte and played a tune. Elizabeth took a seat near her and watched her while humming along to the song and tapping her foot. She was so intent on listening to her new friend she did not notice Mr. Darcy approach her until he was at her side. She looked up at him expectedly. His manner of approaching suggested he wished to speak with her, but no words were forthcoming. At first, Elizabeth was tempted to allow the silence to grow in awkwardness, but she was too provoked by his presence to let it pass.

"Your sister plays very well," she said.

"She does." He looked at his sister and smiled. "I might be prejudiced in her favor, but I do not know there is a finer performer in London."

"My sister, Mary would take umbrage at that remark, sir," she replied with a smile.

"Your sister is a superior performer?"

"My sister considers herself a superior performer. But she does not have your sister's talent. That is the difference between yours and mine. Mine has all the confidence and none of the talent. Yours has the talent without the confidence."

To her annoyance, Darcy took the chair beside her. He listened in silence to Georgiana's playing for some moments before speaking again.

"Do you have other siblings?"

"I am the second of five sisters."

"No brothers?"

"None."

"You must miss your family while you are away."

Elizabeth gave a short laugh. "Well, my younger sisters and my mother can be a little high spirited, although I miss my father and my oldest sister, Jane. Jane writes to me all the time, but it is not the same as being with her. My happiness would be complete if she were here." She smiled. "But my favorite aunt is here, and now I hope I will have a new friend in your sister. And Derbyshire is full of beauties. I have much to be cheerful for."

"Ah yes, Derbyshire's beauties." Darcy paused. "As an older sibling of younger sisters yourself, I am sure you can appreciate how protective I am towards my sister, Miss Bennet. And I am happy for her to explore the peaks with you. But I am still not altogether easy. I have matters to attend to here, and with the thief still around, I sometimes need to visit my tenants. I cannot always go with you."

"I understand that," said Elizabeth in surprise. "I did not think of asking you to escort us."

"I take it you planned to ask Captain Waters?"

"I have not asked him yet, but yes. He is pleasant and good-humored and from a respectable family. Your sister will be in safe hands with him."

"And you as well."

"Presumably." Elizabeth gave him a puzzled look. "I would hope he would not just attend your sister and ignore me."

"I have not met him."

"That is easily remedied."

Darcy was silent. Elizabeth could not make him out. It seemed as if he wished for her and Georgiana to be friends but was being unnecessarily difficult about it.

"I am sure I can spend some days exploring with you," he said. "It is not as though you will travel for weeks at a time. I can spare a few hours from the estate. And I will be easier if I am not leaving my sister in the care of an unknown man."

Elizabeth laughed. "You need not be uneasy about Captain Waters, sir. You know his family, though not personally, and they are highly regarded in the town. But if it makes your mind easier, I am happy to join parties and for us to all go together."

"Join parties?"

"I am sure you would not object to my aunt or Captain Waters joining us on occasion, even if you are with us? My aunt cannot do all the walking I would like, but that does not mean she cannot make the occasional excursion if the destination is not too far. And it would be remiss of me to spend time with new friends and neglect one of my hosts. Captain Waters has a carriage of his own, so it would be no burden.

He also has a little phaeton that would take two easily enough."

"I am sure my carriage is large enough to transport anyone, even those with as impressive a reputation as Captain Waters," said Darcy shortly.

"I never said otherwise."

Elizabeth's irritation grew. Why should Darcy approach her and push his foul humor on her? If she were not a guest in his home, she should have told him to take his temper elsewhere and not spoil her evening. But she could not say so here, so she fell silent instead, determined not to humor him.

"Forgive me, Miss Bennet," said Darcy after some silence. "I have been out of sorts this evening. I have a lot on my mind, but it is no excuse."

Elizabeth was startled by the unexpected apology. She did not know what to say, so she inclined her head. Darcy shifted in his chair towards her.

"And Miss Bennet, I must tell you I appreciate your friendship with Georgiana. She is a shy girl and finds it difficult to meet others. We have that in common," he added with a wry smile. "But I am most sincerely glad she has a friend."

"And Mrs. Younge does not answer your idea of friendship?"

They both looked across the room. Mrs. Younge had been speaking with Mrs. Gardiner, but they had parted when Mrs. Gardiner rose to turn Georgiana's pages at the pianoforte. Mrs. Younge sat alone by the fire. Her mouth twisted as if she had tasted a lemon.

Darcy paused. "Not exactly. A companion one pays is no substitute for a friend of one's age, chosen for the pleasure of being together."

"Even though Mrs. Younge seems so joyful and full of

laughter," said Elizabeth dryly. Darcy looked as if he was trying not to smile.

"I cannot be severe on her there. I am hardly so myself," he replied.

The music changed as Georgiana played a lively tune. Elizabeth's foot tapped to the music.

"I danced to this one at the Meryton assembly rooms just before coming here," she exclaimed. "It was a favorite with everyone, and we requested they repeat it. It is impossible to sit still when I hear it."

Darcy paused. "Then would you like to steal the opportunity to dance a reel with me, Miss Bennet?"

Elizabeth looked at him in alarm and laughingly demurred. "I think not. Please do not suppose I spoke to hint you would ask me to dance, sir. I had no such notions in mind."

"No, I do not believe you would. Such arts are not in your nature. But I would be honored if you would dance with me."

Elizabeth declined again and turned back to Georgiana to end the conversation.

She would have enjoyed a dance, but she did not believe Darcy wished for it. He regretted his ill-temper and wanted to rectify it by offering her a reel.

Well, he had no need. He was not of such importance to her that she needed him to make amends to her. She would spare him the necessity of dancing.


Darcy stood at the top of the steps as the carriage rolled down the drive taking Miss Bennet and Mrs. Gardiner back to Lambton. Georgiana stood at his side, waving until the carriage turned a corner. Her eyes were bright.

"Oh, Fitzwilliam, that was a splendid evening, was it not? Do you think they enjoyed it? I hope they enjoyed it."

Darcy draped his arm around her shoulders.

"I know they did, Georgiana. Miss Bennet is looking forward to seeing you again. I would say the evening was a success, and you were an excellent hostess."

Georgiana's cheeks flushed with pleasure at his praise. When she had finished playing the pianoforte, Darcy had told her of his and Elizabeth's idea for all of them to explore together. Georgiana had been thrilled, and she and Elizabeth discussed the peaks at length, with Darcy offering recommendations for local beauty spots.

Seeing how happy Georgiana was made Darcy's heart clench. It brought before him more than ever how very lonely she was. Mrs. Younge was all very well in her way, but Georgiana needed more. She needed a lively, caring friend, and Miss Bennet fitted the bill perfectly.

After the siblings said goodnight and retired to their rooms, Darcy walked to the window to look out over the darkening countryside. In the distance, he saw the faint outline of lamps in the direction of Lambton.

He was not pleased with his conduct that evening. Georgiana relied on him to promote her new friendship, and he was afraid he had been more unpleasant than necessary. Miss Bennet had accepted his apology, and he was relieved it did not seem to discourage her from pursuing an intimacy with Georgiana. His guilt if he had cost her a friend would have been enormous.

But something about the mention of Captain Waters unsettled him. He was familiar with the man's reputation as a naval hero. There had been much excitement in the county when word got around that he was coming home to stay. Every young girl in Derbyshire would not fail to lose her heart to a handsome hero with tales of adventure to tell. Darcy would not lose sleep over those other ladies.

It was another lady who troubled him. Elizabeth lived under the same roof as this man. She would see him every day. Such close quarters could not help but promote intimacy. Surely a lively young woman like Elizabeth would lose her heart to a man like Captain Waters? The idea made a bitterness burn in Darcy's chest.

Elizabeth could be nothing to him. He repeatedly reminded himself of the fact. She was far too unsuitable to be mistress of Pemberley. So why should the idea of her falling in love with another man cause such a burning feeling in his chest? It was beneath him. For all his honors, Captain Waters was nothing to a Darcy of Pemberley. He and Elizabeth would probably make an excellent match. But the thought of having to invite him and seeing the two together troubled Darcy more than it should. He could not master the irritation he felt at the idea.

Perhaps it was that he felt obliged to invite a man he was not acquainted with. That must be it. How could it be otherwise when he hardly knew Elizabeth and when she would be nothing to him anyway apart from his sister's friend?

And, of course, he had a young sister to worry about. Georgiana was young and shy, and with thirty thousand pounds to her name, she was the perfect prize for an ambitious man. He would have to keep an eye on Captain Waters and not allow him the opportunity to woo her.

Yes, that was why the idea of him troubled him so much. What a relief to have that clear.

But as he drifted off to sleep that night, he wondered why Elizabeth's smile was before him.

Or why it was the first thing in his mind on waking up the next morning.

# CHAPTER 14

hen Elizabeth returned from her walk the following morning, the sound of unfamiliar voices coming from the parlor caught her attention. She paused with her bonnet in her hand, uncertain whether she should intrude.

The matter was settled for her by the door opening. Captain Waters came out. He did not notice Elizabeth at first, and he glanced behind him into the room, laughing at some remark. He turned and started when he saw Elizabeth. As always, Elizabeth's face grew warm at the sight of him. He would cause a sensation in Meryton if he were to visit. She felt a pleasant flutter when his face lit up.

"Ah, Miss Bennet. Just the person I missed. Mama said you had gone for a walk."

"I left very early. I wished to explore the path by the river." She held up a handful of damp flowers and smiled. "I will bring Aunt there during the week. It is too beautiful to miss."

As she spoke, she glanced behind his shoulder to look

into the room. A pair of grey eyes met hers before their owner quickly withdrew their stare.

"If I had known you were going, I should have tried to go with you," he said with a grin.

"That would hardly be proper, sir," she replied with mock offense.

"Ah, but if we were to meet by chance, there could be no criticism. Two people having the same destination in mind on a beautiful summer's morning is hardly unusual."

"Who are you speaking to, Henry? Invite them in for heaven's sake and do not keep them at the door."

The door opened out, and Mrs. Waters emerged. "I am afraid the Navy has caused you to forget your manners — why, Miss Bennet. I am so glad you are here. Come and meet our friends."

Before Elizabeth could protest the state of her gown, Mrs. Waters had gripped her firmly by the hand and pulled her into the room. Four pairs of eyes turned to gaze at her, and she dropped an awkward curtsey, more aware than ever of her damp gown and muddy hems.

"Miss Elizabeth Bennet, this is Mr. and Mrs. Jones, who you already met at church, and Mrs. Jones's cousins, the Miss Carters. This young lady is Miss Rebecca Carter, the eldest, and this is Miss Helen Carter."

The visitors smiled at her.

"Out rambling, I see," said Helen. "I should love a walk. I miss the countryside around here when we are away."

"Miss Bennet is a great walker. I do not doubt, but she knows the entire county of Derbyshire by now," said Captain Waters with a grin.

"Not quite, Captain Waters, but I am getting there," said Elizabeth.

"How far do you walk, Miss Bennet?" asked Mrs. Jones.

Elizabeth told her, and she responded with some favorite walks of her own. Helen joined in, and as they spoke, Elizabeth sensed the eyes of Miss Carter on her.

It was not in Elizabeth's nature to be intimidated, but something about the woman's calm scrutiny made her squirm with discomfort. Miss Carter was the sort of lady who would intimidate even the most self-assured woman.

She was possibly the most beautiful woman Elizabeth had ever seen. Her grey eyes were bright and intelligent. Her glossy chestnut hair was bound in elegant curls, unlike Elizabeth's unruly tendrils, which had come loose during her ramble. She was tall and her figure slim. Despite her unfortunate origins, she held herself with all the grace and dignity of a queen. Elizabeth felt at once that being a natural daughter would be no hindrance to such a woman. No man would blush to introduce her in London society, and no one would wonder at his choice.

"Do you like to walk, Miss Carter?" Elizabeth told herself she asked only to include her in the conversation. But a rebellious voice whispered she merely wanted to prove she was not intimidated by this goddess as she sat there in a muddy dress with her hair loose around her shoulders as it fell from its pins.

"I am not a great walker, I am afraid," said Miss Carter. "I love to enjoy the view, but I prefer to do so from a carriage. It is remiss of me, I know."

"I am sure with so many beauties around you, you must desire to experience more than a carriage can show you," said Elizabeth. "Carriages are all well, but they do not allow you to explore the hidden places only accessible by foot."

Miss Carter only inclined her head but did not respond. After an awkward silence, Mrs. Waters spoke.

"The Darcys invited Mrs. Gardiner and Miss Bennet to dine at Pemberley last night."

The visitors turned to stare at them with deeper interest.

"Dine at Pemberley!" said Mrs. Jones. "That is grand. I have never been to the house although I keep telling Mr. Jones we must pay a visit. How are the family?"

"I am surprised Mr. Darcy extended an invitation. I thought he held himself apart from most people," said Miss Carter.

Elizabeth felt a brief stab of irritation at her words, but she was unsure why that should be.

"Do you know Mr. Darcy then?"

"Only by reputation," the lady replied.

"Our cousin speaks of the family, and we spent several summers here," added Helen. "We have never known him to interact with the neighborhood. May I ask how he came to invite you?"

Elizabeth told them of meeting with Miss Darcy at the market. She declined to mention her first encounter with Darcy in the woods. They did not need to know that. Besides, unlike herself, they did not strike her as the sort of ladies in danger of trespassing on his land.

"Friends with Miss Darcy," said Helen. "Well, that is lucky. And what sort of man is Mr. Darcy? I hear he is rather proud."

"Nonsense, Helen," said Miss Carter. "I am sure he is amiable. He should not have to run on like other young men to be agreeable."

"He is rather proud," said Elizabeth. "And I would not describe him as friendly, but he was perfectly cordial to us last night, was he not, Aunt? He is eager that my acquaintance with his sister should continue."

"I would not object to meeting Mr. Darcy, but I can not imagine he would grant me the privilege just yet," Captain Waters added. "Perhaps that might change at a later date. I have a mind to buy land next to his, and I am sure we shall have matters to discuss as new neighbors."

"Oh my love, have you settled where your new home should be?" his mother asked. Her eyes glowed with delight as she looked at her son.

"Just some ideas. Nothing settled as yet. In fact, with Miss Bennet's love for rambling, I thought she might like to accompany me and offer her opinion?"

"I would be glad to," said Elizabeth with enthusiasm.

Mrs. Waters smiled at them.

"Miss Bennet and my son are firm friends already," she told their guests. "I have never seen two people more alike and whose tastes are in such alignment."

"Mama," said Captain Waters in a reproving tone. Their guests looked between the two with renewed interest. Elizabeth could have cursed Mrs. Waters for her indiscreet remarks. Now, the entire town would watch them constantly, on the lookout for signs of attachment or the impending announcement of an engagement. Mrs. Waters could not be worse than her own mama for intruding on her children's affairs and playing matchmaker.

"It must be pleasant for Captain Waters to come home and find such an agreeable companion to spend his time with," said Miss Carter.

"Most agreeable. With Richard away, it is nice for Henry to have a friend. Especially one as lively and active as Miss Bennet," said Mrs. Waters.

Miss Carter nodded. She turned to her cousin.

"The time, Agnes."

"Oh gracious me, yes. Look at the time. I am afraid we must run away. We have far overstayed our welcome," said Mrs. Jones. She scrambled to her feet, searching for her parasol. "Thank you for the tea, Mrs. Waters. It has been too long since we visited with you."

"I hope we shall see more of you now. We plan to have a welcome home dinner for Henry in the next week or two. I shall be sure you all receive an invitation."

With much goodbyes, the visitors finally departed. Captain Waters sighed.

"What a to-do. It is always nice to meet old friends, but it is hard to enjoy one's home when it is crowded with people passing in and out."

"Henry! They are excited to see you. And there will be plenty more where they came from. The Miss Stands are coming this afternoon to pay their respects. They will be most happy to — "

"Miss Bennet," said Captain Waters, turning decisively towards Elizabeth. "May I prevail on you to come with me to view the site I think to purchase? If you are not too tired from your walk, that is."

"Too tired?" Elizabeth arched an eyebrow and grinned. "Never. It would take more than that to tire me out. If you allow me to change, I will be ready in a matter of minutes."

"Henry! The Miss Stands. You shall miss them, and..."

"I am sorry, Mama. You can see I am otherwise engaged with Miss Bennet. Please make my apologies to the ladies. Or better yet, send them a note and ask them to call later. That way, you and Father and Mrs. Gardiner can follow after us in the carriage."

Mrs. Waters sighed and relented.

"Very well." Her smile was sly. "I am sure one cannot

object to you wishing to spend the morning in such pleasant company."

Elizabeth expected Captain Waters to object, but instead, he replied with a firm "No indeed." She left to change her clothes before she could hear anything further.

# CHAPTER 15

*E*lizabeth ran outside, tying her bonnet under her chin as she looked around for Captain Waters. She stopped with a laugh when she saw him sitting on a phaeton. His grey mare tossed her head, eager for the outing.

"What is this?" she asked as she approached. "Too tired for a walk? I am surprised at you, Captain Waters."

Captain Waters laughed as he jumped down to assist her.

"Not at all. This is for your benefit, Miss Bennet. I do not care what you say. I can see the exhaustion in your eyes."

"Exhaustion?"

"Extreme exhaustion. I believe you are in danger of fainting at any moment. I cannot risk it. Your health is too delicate."

"How considerate of you," she said as he climbed up beside her. "To think of me when you are huffing and hardly able to breathe just from the exertion of climbing into your seat. How noble of you to worry about my health when you seem about to expire at any moment. It is a shame I have no medical training. I am sure I shall need it before the day is out."

Captain Waters grinned at her and clicked his horse forwards. "Aside from my undying devotion to your health, I do have another reason for taking the phaeton." He nodded as they turned a corner and pointed with his crop. "Look over there."

Elizabeth turned and gasped. The added height of the phaeton meant she could see more than ever the surrounding peaks stretching before them for miles.

"It is beautiful," she exclaimed. "I am sure I would be happy to stay in Derbyshire forever."

Captain Waters cleared his throat, and Elizabeth realized what she had just said. She winced. Surely he would believe her willing to go along with his mother's plan for their marriage?

"But then, I said the same thing about almost every county I visited," she added firmly. "My uncle once took us for a picnic to Box Hill, and once I experienced the view from there, I declared I would be happy never to leave Surrey. I am a fickle creature, am I not?"

"I would not say that. You speak as you find, and it is refreshing. It is a change from those who are cold and careful and never say the wrong thing but also can never be known and loved."

"You speak as if you know many such people."

Captain Waters grinned. "Not too many, thank goodness. But I met such a one today, and it put it in my mind. What is your opinion of the Miss Carters?"

"Miss Helen seems a pleasant, friendly girl. I should not object to getting to know her better."

"And Miss Carter?"

Elizabeth paused as she considered how to answer. "I cannot say with confidence when I met her so briefly," she said. "But she strikes me as just such a one you mentioned.

Very quiet and difficult to know. But then, it is not fair for me to say so when I spend so little time with her. Perhaps she is only so with people who are not well known to her?"

"I wish I could say so, but it is not the case. From my understanding, she is just the same even with people she has known for a long time."

"She is lovely," said Elizabeth. She was not comfortable speaking ill of the lady. Her sense of fairness struggled with the instinctive dislike she took to her and wished to say something to ease it. "I have rarely seen her like. My sister, Jane, is lauded for her beauty everywhere she goes, but even I, impartial as I am, can say she is not quite Miss Carter's equal. Miss Carter has a way of carrying herself that adds to her beauty."

"She is famed for it in Portsmouth. I met her there; we were introduced due to having connections to the same place. But I knew of her by reputation long before I met her, and all I heard was of her incredible beauty. It is a shame she does not have the warmth to match it. Nothing makes a woman more appealing than the openness of character." He smiled and changed the subject. "How did you find Mr. Darcy? You did not say much in the company of everyone, and I cannot blame you for that."

"Mr. Darcy is — " Elizabeth paused. "In some respects, he is rather like Miss Carter. He can be reserved. At first, I found him rather odd and severe, but I detected a slight softening last night. I do not think he is as cold as he comes across at first. Merely uncomfortable with strangers. But if you are curious about him, I might have the means of satisfying it," she added in a playful tone.

She told him of their proposed outings they discussed the night before.

"I would like it if you joined us," she said. "My aunt will

not come with us all the time. I am fond of Miss Darcy, but she is rather quiet and will take time to draw out. Mr. Darcy is - well, he is Mr. Darcy. I expect many long hours of silence if I am with him. I should like to have someone by my side who enjoys conversation as much as I do."

"I should be delighted," said Captain Waters. His tone was surprised. "It is good of Mr. Darcy to invite me when we are unacquainted."

"Well, I rather insisted," said Elizabeth with a laugh. "He has heard of you, and I think he should be as curious to meet you as you are to meet him."

"Well, I shall not object to anything that provides me with your company for whole days at a time," said Captain Waters. "You may thank Mr. Darcy for my part of the invitation and tell him I gladly accept."

Elizabeth was flushed and pleased by his response. She had worried that a day exploring with the Darcy party would mean a day spent much in silence. She was sure Georgiana would make a pleasant friend once drawn from her shell, but until then, it was good to know she would have someone to converse with. Especially if Mr. Darcy should continue alternating between silence and haughty remarks.

Captain Waters pulled the carriage to a stop and swept his arm out.

"This is it," he declared. "Tell me what you think, Miss Bennet. I want your honest opinion, now. None of that cold and careful attitude from you if you please."

Elizabeth looked around and shook her head in admiration. The land was at a height with a pleasant slope towards woods. It was vibrant and green, in contrast to so much of the stark Derbyshire countryside. A sparkling natural stream flowed through a thick bed of wild summer flowers. Birds swooped in among them.

"It is perfect," she said in awe. "It is just what it ought to be."

Captain Waters jumped down from his chair and helped Elizabeth down. She walked over the soft, fragrant grass and took a deep breath. The air was sweet and filled with the warm scent of vanilla from the gorse bushes nearby. Butterflies fluttered through the wildflowers.

"This is beautiful," she said. "I congratulate you, Captain. You could not choose a more perfect place to make your home."

"I am glad you approve," he said. He smiled as she tilted her head to the sun and sighed with pleasure. "As soon as I came here, I knew I had to have it."

"Where will you build your home?"

He pointed to a gentle hollow where a house would nestle into the countryside as if part of it. Elizabeth imagined how an evening sun would light up windows to gold. It would make a bewitching sight.

"It will not be as large as Pemberley, of course," he added with a smile. "Nothing so grand as that. But it will be a large, comfortable, modern home. Perfect for raising a family."

"And within easy reach of your parents," added Elizabeth. "Your mother will be thrilled to have you and your children at such an easy distance."

Captain Waters laughed. "I do not mind. I am ready for all that now. I had great adventures, but I am tired of wandering. I want a home and a family I love."

The warmth in his voice captured Elizabeth's attention, and she hesitated. She continued to look at the hollow as if she imagined the future house, but her mind raced.

What did he mean by talking so? Was he hinting at

making her an offer? He had remarked on his mother's desire to match them when he first arrived, but that did not mean the idea had not grown on him. She felt flustered and moved away from him.

"And you have spoken to the lawyer about buying the land?" she asked. She was determined to put the conversation back on a more business-like setting, and fortunately, it worked. Captain Waters was instantly diverted.

"He has drawn up the papers. I am setting up the transaction with my bankers in London, and once I sign it, it is mine."

He turned to point in the opposite direction to where the house would face. "It is part of the reason I should like to meet Mr. Darcy. Once I own this land, he and I will be close neighbors. Look. You can see Pemberley from here."

He was right. Through a gap in the woods, Elizabeth could see the grand limestone house.

"You will be able to invite him hunting by firing shots in the air," she said lightly. "And he will respond in kind."

"One shot for yes, two for no," said Captain Waters. "We shall create a whole new language if we form a friendship. We shall not waste time messing about with carriages and horses if we wish to speak to one another. It is a splendid arrangement."

"You have it all worked out," said Elizabeth. She looked about her once again. "Well, you wished for my opinion, and I gave it. You have made an excellent choice, and I wish you well with it. I think it would be impossible for someone not to be happy here."

"Thank you, and I quite agree." He looked around in satisfaction. "Well, it is a beautiful day, and I have the phaeton out already. Shall we explore some more? Assuming you are not overcome, of course, and require a sofa and smelling salts."

"Your mother informed me you had taken my last batch," said Elizabeth. "And yes, I would like to explore more. Assuming I will not end with having to carry you to a physician."

Captain Waters gave a low laugh as he followed her towards the phaeton. Elizabeth grinned to herself. She could not remember enjoying a man's company so much. Could she learn to like him in a more particular way?

Just as Captain Waters took her hand to help her into the seat, he paused and stared at something behind her. Elizabeth followed his stare and started when she spotted Mr. Darcy. He was walking towards them, and he had not noticed them yet. He waved his stick at the grass and called to Earl, who snuffled around in delight. He looked up and did a double-take when he noticed them. Elizabeth raised a hand to wave. He raised his own then started towards them.

"Well, you had a curiosity to meet Mr. Darcy," she murmured to Captain Waters. "It looks as though fate has arranged for you to have it sooner than expected."

She dropped a curtsey when Darcy reached them. He responded with a bow.

"Mr. Darcy, may I introduce Captain Waters."

The two men bowed to one another.

"I am pleased to meet you, Mr. Darcy," said Captain Waters. "Miss Bennet has told me all about you, and of course, I am aware of you by reputation."

"Likewise, Captain Waters."

The two men stood in awkward silence as Elizabeth bent down to scratch Earl's ears and crooned soft words to him.

"Captain Waters wishes to buy this land," she said when she straightened up. There was an odd tension between the men, and she could not account for it. She looked between them. Captain Waters still looked cheerful as always, but

Darcy stood even stiffer than usual, and his demeanor was cold. Captain Waters picked up on it as well and looked a little nonplussed.

"What is your opinion of his choice, sir?" asked Elizabeth. "Is it not a fair prospect? I think it is utterly delightful."

"I do not know," he said. "It is exposed in the winter, and the ground will flood. I would not build a home here myself. I am sure Captain Waters can find a better place."

"Flood? What do you mean, sir?" Captain Waters looked slightly alarmed. The two men walked away. Darcy pointed about with his cane. Captain Waters nodded as he listened to him, and his face was troubled. They spoke together more before Darcy broke away from him to approach Elizabeth.

"Miss Bennet, my sister wishes to send you a note, but now I see you, I can spare her the trouble. With your permission, she would like to call on you and your aunt at your convenience."

Elizabeth had been expecting a return visit, but she was surprised that Mr. Darcy should put himself out to arrange it for her.

"Yes, my aunt and I would like that very much. Is tomorrow morning suitable?"

Darcy bowed. As he turned to leave, Elizabeth could not resist asking him,

"What has become of your poultry thief? Has he returned?"

"Poultry thief?" Captain Waters came to her side and laughed. "Turkey houses being plundered, are they? I had better tell Mama. She is proud of her hens. But surely Mr. Darcy is not trying to catch a thief himself? No, Miss Bennet. I am sure you are wrong."

"I am here on my land, and there is mischief afoot. I am not sure why you presume I would prefer to cosset myself at the house and allow someone else to manage what I am not prepared to do myself," said Darcy abruptly. He bowed. "I shall allow you to continue with your day."

He whistled to Earl, who came tearing out of the undergrowth in a little blur of brown and white. He rolled over at Elizabeth's feet, begging her to rub his belly, then tore off after his master.

Elizabeth watched him walk away. Much as she disliked him, she had to admit he made an impressive sight, striding across the fields in his shirt sleeves, his hair tousled. He would make a romantic figure if he were not so cold. She turned back to Captain Waters.

"Well. And what do you think of Mr. Darcy now you have met him? Does he answer all your expectations?"

"He is an odd man, is he not? Quite severe. But I must admit I am indebted to him. I was not aware there is an underground spring here which would cause me endless problems with the foundation of the house. I am still determined on this land, but I shall have to look for a more suitable area to build."

"I am sure he does not wish you to build a house that might rival his," teased Elizabeth. "He wants to be the only one with a fine dwelling in the area."

"And he still will be. I do not pretend to build anything as fine as Pemberley. But no, he did not wish to discourage me, although he does not seem pleased with the prospect of having me as a neighbor. His advice was sincere." Captain Waters sighed and looked about him at the soft hills. "Well, I shall consider some more. Now, Miss Bennet. What do you say we take the scenic route home so you might see some peaks?"

"Should we wait for your parents?" Elizabeth asked. She

looked back towards Lambton, but there was no sign of them."

"Mama is always late leaving the house. She will have recalled a million things to do while Father waits patiently for her. But she knows the route I am most likely to take to show you some of the sights. They will have little difficulty following us. Come. I want to show you a hill that will allow you to see all the way to Derby if you wish to visit it."

Elizabeth only had one answer to that. They climbed back into the phaeton, and as Captain Waters called to the ponies, Elizabeth grabbed her bonnet and laughed with delight at the speed of the carriage. She was so occupied with laughing and exclaiming over the views she did not see Mr. Darcy watching her as they raced by, his eyes lost in thought.

# CHAPTER 16

*E*lizabeth prepared her aunt and Mrs. Waters for a
visit from Miss Darcy. Mrs. Waters was in a fluster
to prepare the house for such a prestigious guest until Elizabeth laughingly reminded her Miss Darcy was not to
spend the day with them. Elizabeth could not imagine she
would stay any longer than the usual fifteen minutes. While
the girl was gentle and friendly, she was excessively shy and
would feel uncomfortable in a house with so many
strangers.

And Miss Darcy would, of course, be accompanied by
that haughty companion of hers, that sour-faced Mrs.
Younge. She would be sure to exert her influence to prevent
Miss Darcy from staying longer, whatever Miss Darcy's
inclinations.

Elizabeth had calculated they would arrive around noon.
So she was astonished when she came downstairs half an
hour after ten to hear voices in the parlor. She paused to
listen and was startled to hear a particular voice, deeper than
all the rest. She walked into the room, and her suspicions
were confirmed when Mr. Darcy rose from his chair and

bowed to her. Elizabeth dropped a somewhat confused curtsey then greeted his sister with more warmth.

"I did not expect to see you here, sir," she ventured when she had taken a seat beside Georgiana. "I thought Mrs. Younge would accompany Miss Darcy."

"She usually does, but I preferred to accompany my sister this morning," said Darcy. His face softened when he looked at Georgiana. "I do not see her as often as I like, so I enjoy spending most of my time with her when I can."

"An ideal older brother then," said Elizabeth with a smile as she looked at Georgiana's blushing face.

"Lizzy, Mr. Darcy and Miss Darcy were speaking of an excursion to the peaks. He is insistent on taking all of us, but if you do not mind, I would prefer to stay with my friend and enjoy our time together. I am not uneasy now I know you have agreeable company to join you," said Aunt Gardiner.

"There is plenty of room for Captain Waters if he wishes to join us," said Darcy.

"Room is no concern," said Captain Waters. "I can drive myself and Miss Bennet. We shall not be crowded."

"Captain Waters, if it is all the same to you, I would prefer to ride with Miss Darcy. She and I first arranged this excursion so that we could explore together. It will rather defeat that purpose if we were to travel separately."

"Of course. How inconsiderate of me. Well, I am content to ride. There will be no need for a carriage for most of the journey. Where did you hope to visit? There are fine houses in Derbyshire that I am sure you would love to see, Miss Bennet. It is not all mountains though I understand your enthusiasm for them."

"I should like to experience as much as I can. All the mountains, woods, and fine houses in the area. I understand Hardwick Hall is a fine example of Tudor architecture."

"You are a student of history, Miss Bennet?"

"I find it interesting, but I am more interested in old architecture."

"Well, I hope you will advise Henry when he builds his own house," said Mrs. Waters, beaming at them. "My son is here to stay, Mr. Darcy, and hopes to build a home. He and Miss Bennet have become firm friends even though it has only been a few days since they met."

"Mr. Darcy knows of my plans, Mama. We met him yesterday, and he offered me sound advice, for which I am very grateful. But yes, I would appreciate Miss Bennet's suggestions. I am sure a mind as lively and creative as hers will have some interesting contributions to make." His eyes were warm as he smiled at Elizabeth.

Elizabeth laughed and demurred, her face flushed with embarrassment. She turned her attention back to Georgiana.

"Well, what do you think, Miss Darcy? Would you like to visit Hardwick Hall?"

"I am sure I would. I am told it has a grand music room."

"Well, when shall you all go? You should do it sooner while you have this fine weather. It can be unpredictable even at this time of year," said Aunt Gardiner.

Captain Waters hesitated. "I must ask that you wait a few days before we go. I have business in Manchester tomorrow and plan to stay there for a few days. But once I am home, I am at your disposal."

"Oh, Henry," said his mother in disappointment. "Only home and away already? What business is this that it must take you away from us so soon?"

Captain Waters burst out laughing and affectionately patted his mother's hand. "Do not stare at me like that. I am not taking a ship to the West Indies. I shall be home again within a few days."

"But what business can be so important?"

Captain Waters still smiled, but Elizabeth thought he looked irritated by his mother's persistent questioning.

"An old friend from the Navy, Mama. I have not seen him or his wife for some years."

"Oh, yes, of course you will want to visit your old friends. Why you should bring them here. I would love to meet them."

"I am afraid they cannot stay long enough. Mrs. Croft's brother is getting married, so they must return to Somerset-shire for the ceremony. I would like the opportunity to see them before they leave again. But I will be home within a few days. I say, Mr. Darcy. You must tell my mother about this dreadful business you've been having with poultry thieves. She will want to keep a closer watch on her own birds."

Mrs. Waters was instantly diverted. "Oh yes, Mr. Darcy, you must tell me. Have you found the fellow?"

Mr. Darcy's face darkened. His fingers tapping on the arm of his chair spoke of his irritation.

"Not yet. But there have not been more in a few days. I hope it is at an end."

"And dare I hope your woods will be open to exploration again soon?" Elizabeth asked with an arch look. "Or do you plan to close them permanently to the public for fear of another thief?"

Captain Waters laughed. "Close his woods? Because of a few chickens? Surely not, sir. Some hungry poor fellow rummaging for his dinner is not a danger to anyone."

"I pray you to pay me the compliment of knowing what I am about," said Darcy. His voice was cold. "I do not close my woods because I am overly anxious." All eyes in the room were fixed on him, and he sighed, visibly irritated. "I would not do so unless I had a good reason. But I have received no word of robberies in the town or on the farms. It is those living in the woods who are affected. Mrs. Waters has nothing to fear. Her turkeys are safe."

An awkward silence fell over the room. Georgiana looked so uncomfortable Elizabeth stepped in.

"I am sure Mr. Darcy has his reasons. He knows the situation better than any of us, so he is the best judge for what actions to take. I hope you will forgive my teasing, sir."

Darcy gave her a searching look and nodded. The tension left his shoulders, and he smiled briefly.

"Thank you, Miss Bennet."

Elizabeth nodded. She still felt he was severe in his approach, but she would not expose him to criticism in front of his sister.

"It is highly inconvenient, though," added Captain Waters. "Pemberley Woods is a shortcut from Lambton to Derby. Having to travel around it adds a lot to the journey."

"If anyone wishes to travel through my woods by carriage, I will not stop them. My concern is for young ladies who wander through the woods alone at unsociable hours." He gave Elizabeth a pointed look, but she thought she detected a certain softening in his manner.

"Well, you might have explained that to Miss Bennet," said Captain Waters. "I am sure you can see why she thought you overreacted to her presence."

"I am not accustomed to explaining my reasons."

Elizabeth was about to roll her eyes at his arrogance, but she remembered his sister sat by her side and was sure to see it.

"Well, back to the topic at hand. Shall we say we shall visit the peaks within a day or two of Captain Waters' returning home? What say you, Miss Darcy?"

Georgiana agreed as eagerly as her shy nature would

allow, and as Mr. Darcy and Captain Waters had no objections, they settled on the second day after Captain Waters' return. Mr and Miss Darcy took their leave shortly afterward, and Miss Darcy and Elizabeth had the pleasure of knowing their acquaintance would continue in a few days.

# CHAPTER 17

*A*s soon as they returned to Pemberley, Darcy kissed Georgiana on the forehead and told her he would be in his study. He had been subdued ever since their visit to Miss Bennet and had been even quieter than usual on their return journey. Georgiana was anxious about the cause.

"Fitzwilliam," she said as he turned to leave. He paused and raised his eyebrows, waiting for her question. "You like Miss Bennet, do you not? You have no objection to our friendship?"

Darcy looked surprised by her question, and she bit her lip while she waited anxiously for his response. To her relief, he smiled.

"No, Georgiana. I have no objection to Miss Bennet."

"Forgive me for asking, but it sounded as though you disapproved of her when you spoke of young ladies walking alone in woods."

Darcy shook his head. "You must not mind me. I worry about her walking alone in the woods when we do not know who is about. I did not mean to speak as harshly as I did. I am preoccupied, but it is not something with which you need concern yourself."

A worried frown still crossed her face, so he walked over to her and placed his hands gently on her shoulders.

"To put your mind at ease, I can tell you I think highly of Miss Bennet, and I believe she will make you a fine friend. She is just the person I would like you to have in your life."

Georgiana's face lit with a smile. Darcy returned it then left the room.

She spent the rest of the morning practicing her music. Darcy had bought her a harp in London, and though she did not play it so well as the pianoforte, she was eager to master it. She sat in the sunshine, strumming the strings and singing to herself.

Aside from her worry that Darcy disapproved of her new friend, she had been pleased with the events of the morning. She did not think her brother would put an end to the friendship if it gave her pleasure, but she found it difficult to do anything that might make him unhappy. The idea her actions might bring distress to another was one she could never bear, especially if it was to the brother she adored.

Why then should he grow so quiet afterward? He had surprised her by accompanying her that morning and had seemed almost nervous for the visit. He had exerted himself to talk more to help her with her stilted conversation. But somewhere along the way, he had fallen into silence and had spoken little on the journey home. She hoped whatever troubled him would soon be resolved. She did not like to see him so unsettled.

As Georgiana plucked at the strings, she heard the door open. She continued to play, assuming it to be a maid. She jumped in alarm when a shadow fell across her.

"Mrs. Younge!" she exclaimed. "I did not know it was you.

You gave me a dreadful fright." She gave a little laugh to ease the sudden knot in her stomach.

Mrs. Younge did not return her laugh. She took a seat beside Georgiana and gestured for her to continue playing. Georgiana obeyed, but she felt on edge as she often did when her companion was close by. Something about Mrs. Younge's presence gave her the sensation of being smothered under a thick blanket, and she could not place why that should be. By anyone's standards, Mrs. Younge did her duty as a companion and was polite and pleasant. She was more than happy to accompany Georgiana wherever she went and did not even like to be out of her presence to have time to herself as other companions might wish for. Since her husband had died, it was as if she made Georgiana her entire world, and Georgiana was ashamed of being uncomfortable with the idea. She tried to put Mrs. Younge out of her mind and played on.

"You play well, Miss Darcy. I am gratified to see how much you have improved. I told you, did I not, that you must practice more? I am sure you are glad you listened now you are profiting from my advice."

Georgiana tried to recall a time when Mrs. Younge had needed to advise her to practice. It was something she seldom needed to hear, so diligent was she about her music. If Mrs. Younge offered her this advice, Georgiana had no memory of it. She must have forgotten.

"It is always gratifying to feel my progress," she replied softly. "There is a deep satisfaction in comparing where I am now with where I was when I started."

"Yes, well, we must not grow too proud, must we?" said Mrs. Younge with a laugh. "We must always be humble and remember that no matter how far we come, there is always room for improvement, and there are always those who are better than us."

Georgiana felt deflated at the rebuke. Her face flushed with shame, and she ducked her head to recover from her embarrassment before she played on. Mrs. Younge was right. Her playing was far from perfect, and there was much room for improvement. But surely there was no harm in being proud of her accomplishments?

"Did you enjoy your visit to Miss Bennet this morning?"

"I did."

"I confess, I was surprised and a little hurt that your brother did not wish me to attend you. I wonder what he meant by it? Perhaps he is not happy with my work. Or perhaps he decided you do not need a companion now you have Miss Bennet to replace me?"

Even with her back to her, Georgiana noted the catch in Mrs. Younge's voice. She stopped playing at once and turned to her.

"Oh, Mrs. Younge, do not say such things. Of course, you are not to be replaced. My brother merely wished to spend time with me and took the opportunity the journey provided. Please do not be upset."

Mrs. Younge stared out the window and shrugged, but her face was still long.

"If you say so," she said in a tremulous voice. Georgiana was at a loss for what to do. She watched her companion's face anxiously for some sign her mood was improving while her mind raced for something else to say that would ease her distress.

"What is Mr. Darcy's opinion of Miss Bennet?" Mrs. Younge asked.

Georgiana was a little taken aback by her suddenly brisk tone. "Fitzwilliam assures me he likes her very much. He said he —" She paused, afraid of wounding her companion yet again. "He is happy for us to be friends."

"Well, I am sure your brother knows what he is about, but between the two of us, I urge you to be careful, Miss Darcy. Not everyone is as trustworthy as you or I."

"I do not see any sign that Miss Bennet is untrustworthy," said Georgiana with a little more heat. Mrs. Younge sighed and placed a placating hand over hers.

"Oh, I am sure there is none. But a friendship with you is a valuable connection for someone to have, especially one with so little. Just be careful. That is all I ask. Do not be tempted to confide in her. Enjoy her company for the few weeks she is here, and then you can part and continue writing to one another if you wish." She paused at the sight of Georgiana's crestfallen face. "Please don't think I mean to take from your happiness in your new friendship," she said in a gentle voice. "I merely seek to put you on your guard. You are young and have not seen as much of the world as I have. I only urge your caution. That is not too much to ask, surely? Allow your friendship to grow slowly, and it will stand the test of time."

"No, there is nothing wrong with your advice," said Georgiana, though her tone was uncertain. "I had not thought of it the way you say. But I am sure Miss Bennet is trustworthy."

"Then she will be just as trustworthy even if you allow your friendship to develop slowly," said Mrs. Younge. "Now," She removed her hand from Georgiana's and sat back with an abruptness that startled the younger girl. "Tell me; what did you talk of? What plans have you made? Are you and Miss Bennet to explore together? I will discuss the arrangements with your brother so we shall all fit in the carriage."

Georgiana's heart sank. So, Mrs. Younge planned to come with them. She had hoped to persuade the older woman to take the day to herself to allow Georgiana to spend time with Miss Bennet. She knew if she were to suggest such a thing now, Mrs. Younge would be deeply hurt.

But surely she should not mind her companion coming with them? After all, who had been at her side these last months, if not Mrs. Younge? Her companion was right in what she sometimes needed to say to her - she must guard herself against her tendency towards selfishness.

She told Mrs. Younge of their plans, and she nodded.

"Yes, that is right. You shall see much of the peaks by that route and many of the county's beauties. I was afraid your new enthusiasm for this Miss Bennet would mean endless excursions day after day, but you have chosen sensibly and put much into one day. At least you will not feel as though you are missing out when we leave for Ramsgate."

She rose from her chair. "I will see what arrangements can be made. You need not worry, my dear. Leave it all to me."

Georgiana watched her leave and waited until Mrs. Younge closed the door before sinking her head into her arm. She had always wanted a friend more than anything. And now she had found one, it was more complicated than she expected.

# CHAPTER 18

"We have received an invitation, my dears."

Mrs. Waters came out to the garden where Elizabeth and her aunt strolled beneath the trees. She held up a card, beaming with excitement as she hurried across the lawn. She stopped to catch her breath. "It must be in compliment to Henry and you because the Altons have not given a dinner in some time. You will like them. They are charming people. They know Henry is home, and I am sure they mean to honor him." She looked down at the card again and made a face. "They will be disappointed when I tell them he is in Manchester, but I am sure they shall be happy to hold another dinner when he returns."

"When is this dinner?" asked Elizabeth with interest. They had dined out little since they had arrived, and she looked forward to mixing more with the neighborhood.

"On Thursday evening. Mrs. Alton said there would be a few people from the neighborhood." She lowered her voice. "They are not what you would call nice, the Altons." She pursed her lips and nodded. "Though they come from an old family, they are not genteel, and I do not know who will be there. They became quite wealthy in trade, but they do not like to think of their origins too much. I sometimes suspect they seek to rise though I should never express such a suspicion to others. But they are pleasant, good-natured sorts and I am sure we shall have a nice evening. Well, shall I accept?"

Elizabeth and Aunt Gardiner agreed and then smiled as Mrs. Waters hurried across the lawn to return the note.

"My friend has a good heart," said Aunt Gardiner. "She can be a little attentive to rank, but she means no harm."

"She sees the value in you as a friend and has been a kind hostess to us. I am not disposed to think badly of her," said Elizabeth. "But I shall be glad to attend the evening. I hope the Altons are agreeable people."

"I daresay they are. Mrs. Waters thinks so, even with her reservations about their ambitions."

Elizabeth laughed. "Yes, but Mrs. Waters' idea of agreeable and mine might not match. I suspect Mrs. Waters will consider them agreeable if they dress well and smile a great deal. My idea of agreeable is intelligent conversation and enquiring minds. I wonder whose ideas they will answer?"

"Well, we shall find out soon enough." Aunt Gardiner took Elizabeth's arm and linked her own through it. "But if nothing else, they and their party will provide you with interesting character studies. You have enough of your father in you to find them agreeable if they should prove themselves ridiculous just as much as if they should prove themselves intelligent and spirited."

Elizabeth looked at her aunt with feigned joy. "Why, that is true, Aunt! This evening might provide us with all we could wish."

Aunt Gardiner gave her a reproachful look while trying to hide a smile. "Nonsensical girl," she scolded gently.

Elizabeth's smile was genuine, and she leaned into her

aunt with affection. "Well, if the Altons invite as many people as Mrs. Waters expects, I do not doubt of the evening being entertaining. It could not be otherwise with such a mix, and it will be a fine opportunity to meet others in the town. I, for one, am satisfied with this invitation."

F ive miles away, the same invitation was received with much less enthusiasm.

Mr. Darcy opened the card and read it with a raised eyebrow. A dinner in the town given by the Altons. Darcy had to think for a moment before he recalled who they were. A family of no great importance and not of high note, but Darcy remembered reading something in the London papers about Mr. Alton doing well in trade. Darcy was always happy to see a man do well for himself and his family, but for them to presume to invite the head of the principal family in the county hit a sour note. While they celebrated their newfound wealth with superior houses and chaise and fours, that was their affair, and he would not begrudge them. But when their wealth led them to extend invitations to the leading families of the area, he did not approve. To accept such an invitation was to set a bad example. The world worked best when people knew their correct place.

He was sorry to disappoint the Altons - and he had no doubt they would be disappointed; to be noticed by Mr. Darcy of Pemberley would be a tremendous honor for them - but he would not accept. He would not sit at their table and make conversation with them or whoever else they invited. The idea was absurd. It was better if he maintained his usual manner — polite and willing to help those less fortunate and always ready to offer an opportunity to anyone who desired to work hard and improve their lot in life. But no intimacy beyond that.

He folded the card and told himself he would answer it later.

In the meantime, he had promised his sister he would collect a new book of music sheets for her from the bookstore in Lambton. He went to Georgiana's parlor to invite her to join him but paused outside the door when he heard the sound of her playing the harp. He smiled. For the past few days, she had been diligent about practicing the harp, even more than she usually was when it came to her music. It would not do to disturb her while she was hard at work. He would see her at dinner.

Darcy arrived at his destination; a small bookshop off the main square. He had arranged for a small packet of books to be sent from London as a surprise for his sister along with the new music sheets, and although the shop would have sent it to Pemberley if he required it, he felt the need to be out of the house. The ride into town would offer him relief from the troubling thoughts of Miss Elizabeth Bennet and Captain Henry Waters and the very real possibility they might share a future together.

The smell of books hit him at once, and some of his tension eased. It was a scent he never grew tired of. He moved behind a shelf to examine some new books for his library.

As he leafed through one, he heard two female voices on the other side of the shelf. Half-listening to the conversation told him they were servants on errands for their employers. He turned his attention back to his book until some words reached his ears, causing him to pause at once. Darcy never liked listening in on other people's private conversations, but he could not resist this one.

"You will be in a fine state to prepare the house for the Altons' dinner. Have many responded to the invitations?"

"Not yet, but they were only sent out this morning, so we shall expect more back over the next few days. The Greens are coming, of course, and the Alcocks. I suppose the Winthrops will come. Oh, and the Waters and their two guests. A Mrs. Gardiner from London and her niece, a Miss Bennet from Hertfordshire. We received their note accepting the invitation just before I came out."

"And what of Captain Waters? Is he to join you?"

"No, sadly not. He is away from home for a few days. But we are all eager to see him. He is fiercely handsome, and..."

Darcy had stopped listening. Praise of Captain Waters held no charm for him. Besides, he had already learned the one piece of information that captured his attention.

Elizabeth Bennet was to attend the dinner. A rush of exhilaration coursed through him at the idea of seeing her again. He clumsily pushed the book back onto the shelf and walked away to a different one, taking care not to alert the two girls to his presence.

Elizabeth Bennet was to be at the Altons. She would entertain them all with her clever remarks and her lively wit. The whole town would speak of this pretty, charming girl from the south.

And what of it? She was nothing to him. He was not like his friend, Bingley, to have his head turned by a pretty face and dark, sparkling eyes. He was Fitzwilliam Darcy, a man who was not prone to losing his heart.

Besides, she was almost certainly intended for Captain Waters. If it had been a mistake to consider her before, it was more so now.

And yet...

What harm would it do to spend time in her company? A dinner would only last a few hours. There would be many other people in attendance, so it was not as if they would be alone together. If he wished to avoid conversing with her, it would be easy to do.

He felt a powerful curiosity to know more of her. He wondered how she would behave in company, dressed for society. Would she be so bewitching without her hair loose while roaming through woodlands? What would it be like to converse with her in the relative privacy of a public setting rather than in his own home surrounded by a more intimate and, therefore, less private party?

And more importantly, what would it be like to have an evening with her without Captain Waters or even Georgiana by her side? The temptation to converse with her and discover if she was sincerely attached to another man was a powerful inducement, and he could not deny the idea was attractive to him.

No, this would not do! He had no interest in Miss Bennet, and he already had reasons not to dine with the Altons.

Besides, he had too much to do. He had promised himself he would spend as much time as possible with Georgiana. She was not out yet, so she could not accompany him. It was an idle thought and nothing more.

He waited until the girls had moved away, then collected Georgiana's books, congratulating himself on his good sense.

# CHAPTER 19

*M*rs. Alton, a short woman with golden brown hair streaked with grey, bore down on Elizabeth and her companions as soon as they entered the room. After a warm introduction by Mrs. Waters, she turned to her in a state of high excitement.

"My dear, you will not believe who has accepted my invitation," she hissed. Her voice was a whisper and intended for Mrs. Waters' ears alone, but the lady had never mastered the art of lowering her voice sufficiently to avoid the notice of others. "I cannot believe it — bless me, I never for a moment thought he would — thank goodness I insisted Mr. Alton order new china, especially from London. I am beside myself. I did not believe he would come until he arrived, although he accepted my invitation, which was shocking enough."

"Whoever do you mean, my dear?" asked Mrs. Waters. "You sound as though you've received a visit from the Prince Regent himself."

"I hope she has ordered more food if she has," whispered Elizabeth out of the side of her mouth to her aunt. "Derbyshire will be drained of all its wine and meat if that gentleman should come to call."

Mrs. Gardiner gently nudged her with a smile.

"The Prince Regent? No, indeed. I would never presume to send an invitation to royalty," said Mrs. Alton with such earnestness it was all Elizabeth could do not to burst out laughing. "No, no. It is Mr. Darcy."

She paused as she waited for her words to land with the impact she hoped it would, and she was not disappointed. Mrs. Waters gasped and clutched Mrs. Alton's hand, and Elizabeth froze with astonishment.

Mr. Darcy, here? She had been sure he never accepted invitations to mingle with the town. Did Mrs. Alton refer to another Mr. Darcy? A distant cousin, perhaps, who shared the gentleman's handsome looks but not his high-handed manner.

"Mr. Darcy is here? That is shocking! I wonder what has affected this change. I did not know you had invited him."

"I almost did not, but then I thought why not? I assumed he would not accept, but at least no one could accuse me of being deficient in my manners. I was as shocked as anything when I received his acceptance and even more so when he arrived. I fully expected to receive a note with an apology for some unexpected situation that demanded his attention."

The two ladies spoke together, their words tripping over one another in their excitement.

"I am astonished Mr. Darcy has come here," whispered Aunt Gardiner. "It is most unlike him. Perhaps he wishes to mix with the neighborhood for his sister's sake? Whatever his reason, it is surprising."

"I cannot imagine his presence is worth all this specula-tion, Aunt," said Elizabeth with a wry smile. "By all accounts and by my experience of him, he is a proud man, and I am

EMILY RUSSELL

amazed he deigned to come here. I should like to believe he is improving in manners and deciding to be more courteous to his neighbors or even that he is attending for his sister's sake. But it is more likely he suspects one among the crowd tonight is the thief who has been rifling through his tenants' poultry houses. Perhaps he hopes to find a culprit with feathers in his pocket?"

She turned to her aunt with a laugh, but her laughter trailed away at once.

"Mr. Darcy."

The gentleman stood beside her, regarding her gravely. She cleared her throat. "I did not see you there, sir." Her face colored, but if the gentleman had overheard her remarks, he gave no sign.

"Miss Bennet. Mrs. Gardiner." He stood looking at Elizabeth in a manner that made her wish to put a hand to her hair to see if there was something amiss. Why did he stare at her like that? "I hope you are well?" he asked.

"Very well, thank you. And you?"

"Quite well. Thank you."

A movement at Elizabeth's side alerted her that Mrs. Waters had summoned her aunt, leaving her alone with Mr. Darcy. If she could have done it discreetly, she would have grasped her aunt's hand to keep her by her side. As it was, there was nothing she could do but turn back to Darcy and try to look as unconcerned as possible.

"How is Mr. Keiths?" she asked after some moments of awkward silence. "I did not have a chance to ask you previously."

"Keiths is in good health. I shall tell him you asked for him."

"Do that." She paused. "And have you had any success in finding your poultry thief?" As soon as she asked, her face

128

burned again. Had he heard her quip when she first came into the room?

"I have not. There have been no further thefts in recent days, so we might hope the culprit has left the area."

"No doubt he was terrified to learn the master of the estate was home," Elizabeth said with a smile. "I am sure he fled into the night when he discovered your presence at Pemberley."

"Perhaps he did. I am known for taking an interest in my estate and my people. He would know I would do all I can to find him," he said with a touch of arrogance.

"Well, any man who approaches a girl with a gun is intimidating indeed. I cannot blame them for running."

Darcy raised an eyebrow. "Come now, Miss Bennet. I hardly think you were intimidated, gun or not."

"Oh, quite terrified, I assure you. I used up all my aunt's smelling salts and have scarcely come out of a swoon since."

"Somehow, I doubt it." There was a faint flicker of a smile on his face.

They lapsed into another silence. As the only other people in the room she had been introduced to were occupied, she had no choice but to stand with Darcy. At first, she was determined she should not do all the work of maintaining the conversation, but on suspecting he would find it a greater punishment if she forced him to speak, she turned to him again.

"I am surprised to see you here, sir. I understood you did not attend social events in the town."

"You are as well informed of my habits as ever, Miss Bennet."

"Hardly. You are the main landowner in the county. It is not unusual that people should speak of you."

Darcy hesitated. Was it the effect of candlelight, or did

Elizabeth see a faint color on his face? She could not imagine why her question should embarrass him. It was not as though such an arrogant man would care about what anyone thought of him.

"I rarely attend social events, no. I do not enjoy them, and I do not feel the need to mix with my neighbors as I have seen others do."

"You do not value their friendship?"

"I value friendship, yes, but I am particular about who I bestow mine on."

"Oh, I am sure your friendship is a great honor," said Elizabeth with sarcasm. To her relief, her aunt turned and gestured to her to join her. She dropped a curtsey before Darcy could reply and walked away.

D arcy stared after her, feeling wrong-footed. What had he said? He wished to do her the honor of being honest about his true thoughts, and somehow she had taken offense to it and walked away. Surely she did not expect him to join in every barn dance in the county? She must know there were lines he needed to draw between himself and others.

This was precisely why he needed to remind himself that for all he was drawn to her and her perplexing spirit, she was unsuited for anything more than that. She would never understand or fit into his world. Perhaps he had been a fool to come here.

# CHAPTER 20

*D*arcy did not know if he was relieved or dismayed when his hosts placed him beside Elizabeth at dinner. If Elizabeth had overcome her pique with him, he could not tell.

He considered conversing with his companion on the other side but found himself at a loss for how to speak. He resisted dining out even in London unless he had intimate friends such as Bingley by his side. Bingley's cheerful, natural manner meant he made friends everywhere, while Darcy was always mystified about how to converse with people who were little known to him. He could not catch their tone or appear interested in their concerns as he observed others do in such a natural manner. As a result, he often stood apart, his tongue tied as he tried to think of a topic to discuss with those around him.

He glanced at Elizabeth. She conversed with the person on her other side, a young lawyer called Anthony Ainsworth, who practiced in Derby. Darcy knew him by reputation. He watched as Elizabeth laughed easily and spoke of the countryside with her companion. She mentioned her home and the town called Meryton, where she liked to walk with her sisters. He made a mental note of that information, and as soon as she was disengaged by Mr. Ainsworth speaking to someone else, he took his chance.

"I think you must have always been a great walker, Miss Bennet. How does Derbyshire compare to Meryton? Does it answer all the ideas you must have formed before coming here?"

"It does." Her voice was still a little cool, but there seemed no danger she would refuse to converse with him. "I am fond of exploring and am never satisfied until I experience everything a place has to offer."

"Then I hope you will be satisfied by our excursion. My sister is looking forward to it."

Elizabeth's face softened into a smile. He was gratified to see her enjoyment of his sister's company was sincere.

"I am also looking forward to it. Your sister is a sweet girl. I will be happy to spend more time with her."

"And will it be enough to satisfy your need to explore?"

She laughed, and he was relieved she had lost some of her coldness. "Oh, no. I shall not be satisfied until I see more of the world. Every time I imagine it, I add more places to my itinerary. I should like to visit Italy, France, and Spain. To experience great palaces and works of art and walk where legends once strode." She tilted her head. "In that light, I should like to add Greece and Egypt to my list."

"Your list has grown even in the few days since we last spoke on this." He smiled. "You shall have trouble seeing all of them but especially France. I do not know when it shall be safe to visit. Not for some time, perhaps."

Elizabeth shrugged. "I do not expect it to be an easy stroll. And I understand I shall have to avoid Paris for the time being. But you cannot deny it has its beauties, for all its recent tragedies."

"I am sure it does. And for what it's worth, I agree with you. I, too, would love to explore more of the world. Between the war and my excellent father dying, it was not possible. I hope I will do so one day when a more suitable opportunity arrives."

"You have had the running of your estate and responsibility for your sister from a young age." There was a note of sympathy in her voice, and it lifted his spirits.

"Yes. I should say responsibility for my sister is the more difficult challenge and the one I dread failing in most of all. She is at an age where she needs a woman's guidance. There is only so much I can do for her. I feel hopelessly deficient."

"You do not have aunts who might answer?"

"My uncle is widowed, and my other aunt is my mother's sister. Lady Catherine de Bourgh." Darcy laughed a little. "I would not subject my shy sister to her. I have seen Aunt Catherine's effect on my poor cousin, Anne."

He caught himself and started. Why on earth was he telling her such private family matters? His cousin, Colonel Fitzwilliam, was the only one who knew of his opinion of his aunt and only then because his cousin shared them, albeit much more vocally than he did.

He looked at Elizabeth. If she found anything remiss in his confidences, she did not show it. She listened to him attentively with none of the coquettish looks he endured in London. He felt oddly at ease with her and not like an aloof outsider, which was so often the case with him.

"In short, Miss Bennet, I am afraid I lack female relatives who can help my sister."

"And what of Mrs. Younge? She is older. Does she not provide a suitable alternative?"

EMILY RUSSELL

Darcy paused. "Mrs. Younge is a paid companion. She is there for her wages. I am sure she is fond of my sister, but I do not know if she answers the need for sincere affection." He cleared his throat and reached for his wine glass. "Miss Bennet, may I say again how happy I am that my sister has met you? I watch the growing closeness between you with pleasure. I want to thank you for your kind attention to her. I appreciate it."

Elizabeth looked up, startled at Mr. Darcy's words. He had expressed similar sentiments before, but there was a warmth in his voice that caught her attention. His words were far more heartfelt than anything he had ever said. There was a flush about his cravat as he spoke, and she felt an unexpected rush of affection and protectiveness at the sight of his nervousness. There was something endearing about such an aloof man expressing his deeper feelings. She smiled, her face flushed with pleasure.

"You are welcome, Mr. Darcy, and it is kind of you to say so. But I am also enjoying my friendship with Miss Darcy. I am attached to her. She is a sweet, artless girl and just the sort of person whose companionship I value. I am thankful to have met her."

Darcy looked at her with such warmth in his eyes that Elizabeth had to look away in a fluster of confusion.

"Thank you, Miss Bennet. I am more gratified than I can express you should feel so about my sister. And I will do all I can to encourage your friendship. You are always welcome at Pemberley."

The intimacy of the moment was almost too much for Elizabeth. How had the atmosphere between them shifted so suddenly? She eased the tension with a little laugh.

"Just not welcome in the woods," she said with an arch smile.

Mr. Darcy smiled back at her, but there was something about him that made her think he wished to say more. He paused, and she waited for him to continue, holding her breath.

"I do wish to apologize to you for my behavior the day we met. I was alarmed to see you and could only think what might have happened to you if I had not found you." He swallowed. The words did not come easily to him. "I feared for my tenants, and it made me sharper than I meant to be."

"Thank you for the apology. I admit, your attitude towards me unsettled me. But may I ask you something? Why were you so strongly against my being there? Poultry thieves are sadly common. My mother had a problem with them several years ago. Such people are a nuisance, but they are hardly dangerous. If one of these people has ever harmed someone while stealing from them, I never heard of it."

Darcy was silent. Around them, the rest of the diners talked and laughed. Knives chinked on plates, and glasses clinked as they were refilled from wine carafes, but Elizabeth was oblivious to all of it as she looked at the man by her side.

"This is just between the two of us, Miss Bennet. The magistrate knows, of course, and my tenants, but as the houses of Lambton have been left unmolested, I do not intend to cause fear and panic for nothing."

"It will not go past me."

"I know." He paused as a footman placed another dish before them, then spoke. "If it were merely a case of a few mischievous turkey thieves, I should not be so cautious, but I am afraid there is more to it than that. You see, one of my tenants intercepted a fellow as he was running away. He tackled him, and the man fell to the ground and cut his forehead on a rock. My tenant, an excellent fellow, called Graham, approached him believing him to be unconscious when the scoundrel rolled over and pulled a pistol from his pocket. He shot him."

Elizabeth had to stifle her shocked reaction to avoid drawing attention to their end of the table. She stared at Darcy in horror. He had turned back to his plate, but his jaw was set, and she could see the emotion he attempted to hide.

"I am so sorry, sir. Was your tenant — he was not — ?" She could not bring herself to say the words.

"He is not dead, no. Thank god for that. The scoundrel missed his heart and wounded him in the shoulder before he got away. He left Graham for dead. It was Keiths who found him before he bled out. He and his wife visit him and his family daily to attend to their needs. My gamekeeper had retired only a few weeks earlier, and I had not replaced him. No doubt the fellow knew of this and took advantage. My steward wrote to me in London, and I returned at once. I will not allow any more harm to come to anyone."

He turned to meet her eyes, and his own were dark and serious. She could see the resolution in them, and she nodded.

"I understand," she said softly. "I am relieved to hear your tenant will recover, and I am sorry for all your estate has been through. It must be terrifying for them." She gave him a wry smile. "I suppose I can understand why you reacted to my presence the way you did. I am sure I would have done the same."

"Thank you for that."

"Do you have any suspicion who it might be?"

"I would like to say yes, but I am afraid I don't. He had his face covered, and when Graham moved closer to him, he turned and shot him, so he did not get a good look at his features. The only comfort is the thefts ceased since I came home. He knows how close he came to being caught, and perhaps it unnerved him. I am hoping he will not return, but I will not be easy for some time to come."

"I am surprised you returned yourself," said Elizabeth. "I am sure most landowners would have appointed someone else to oversee matters."

"And you supposed I am such a one?" Darcy smiled. "I can see why you would think that. But no, Miss Bennet. It is my land and my tenants. I am responsible for them, and I will not pass the burden to anyone else." He made a face. "Besides, I would have gone mad if I had to attend another *ton* gathering. I was glad to escape even if the circumstances were dreadful."

Elizabeth smiled. She felt she understood him better. He was not quite the hardened, arrogant man he had appeared at first. His social skills were somewhat lacking, and he did seem above his company, but she considered that in essentials, he was not who she believed him to be at first.

"Well, in light of what you have told me, I suppose I can forgive your manner towards me when we first met," she teased. "I concede you had good reason to behave the way you did. I will make an allowance for you."

"You are all kindness, Miss Bennet." Darcy smiled at her. Elizabeth experienced a strange jolt in her stomach, but she pushed the feeling to one side.

However, for the rest of the meal, she was acutely aware of the man beside her and found it difficult to join in the general conversation.

# CHAPTER 21

*A*fter dinner, the less worthy women from the town joined the party. Elizabeth had the pleasure of once again speaking to Helen Carter. Helen excused Rebecca's absence.

"My sister is staying with friends in Derby," she said. She sighed with mock tragedy. "She is always in demand everywhere she goes. I must forever be in her shadow."

Elizabeth laughed. She could well imagine it. Miss Carter had the sort of beauty that would draw people to her even if she found her too cold for her tastes. She far preferred her less pretty but much warmer sister even if the world at large did not. They chatted together for some time, and Helen told her about Portsmouth.

As they spoke, Elizabeth looked up to see Darcy standing nearby. To her surprise, he was speaking with her Aunt Gardiner. From the snatches of conversation she heard, they discussed a favorite tree both enjoyed climbing in their respective youths. He looked up at Elizabeth as soon as she turned in his direction as if he had sensed her eyes on him. He smiled. Elizabeth returned it then turned back to her companion. She hoped her face did not appear as warm as it felt. Helen watched him with interest.

"I saw you speak with Mr. Darcy when we entered. He is handsome, is he not?"

Elizabeth could not help but agree.

"We have not seen him often," Helen continued. "Either he is away from Derbyshire, or we are, and besides, we move in very different circles," she added with a wry laugh. "But Rebecca and I agree he is the most handsome man either of us has ever seen. She will be most put out that I spent an evening in his company. No one expected him to be here, but if she had known, no friends, no matter how dear, would have kept her away."

"Oh?" Elizabeth tried to sound light-hearted but something coiled in her chest at the idea of the strikingly beautiful Rebecca setting her cap at Mr. Darcy. They moved in very different spheres, but Darcy would not be the first man who forgot himself in the face of such beauty. And while London society might sneer behind painted fans at his choice of bride, few would not blame him for losing his heart to a woman like that. "Shall you write and tell her? Make her green with envy?"

Helen laughed. "I might do that. Although she will probably never believe me." Her eyes lingered on Darcy, and she gave a lusty sigh, not even trying to hide her desire for him. "Speaking of handsome men," she added. "What is your opinion of Captain Waters? Every girl in Derbyshire will be wild you stay under his roof. He is well regarded everywhere he goes. I do not believe there is a woman who can speak with him without falling madly in love."

Elizabeth smiled. "I can assure you while I like Captain Waters very much, I am not in love. It will take much more than a few pleasant conversations before I give my heart. I am not so easily won over."

"His mother approves. She seems quite set on having you for a daughter-in-law."

Elizabeth groaned. "Do not say such things. I do not wish rumors to fly around the town. And with all due respect to Mrs. Waters, it is not about what she wants. The people whose wants matter are Captain Waters and me. I try to be as clear as I can without being indelicate, but she chooses not to hear it."

The two girls looked across the room to where Mrs. Waters stood to talk with the Altons. For all her reservations at their new money, she seemed to have no qualms about speaking to them at length, although about what, Elizabeth could not say. Elizabeth turned back to her new friend with a grin. "The only thing she wishes to hear from me is that I am in love with Captain Waters and will marry him. I suspect anything else will fall on deaf ears."

Helen burst into laughter. "Well, you have a problem most people would envy. A devoted mama wishes you to marry her handsome, wealthy, heroic son. I will trade places with you in a heartbeat, Miss Bennet, although I am sure you would not do so with me." She smiled, but it faltered, and there was a note of sadness in it. "I cannot imagine any mama, much less Mrs. Waters, being eager for her son to marry a woman of my background."

Elizabeth had few experiences with people of natural origins and even fewer experiences with someone who expressed her opinion of it so openly, so she was not sure how to respond.

"I am sure there are many people of similar background to meet with," she ventured. "The Prince Regent and his brothers have many natural children, and no one would see it as a shame to be with them." She smiled even as she knew it was a weak response. There was a difference between the natural daughter of royalty and the natural daughter of unknown parentage.

Helen laughed, her easy humor taking the remark in her stride. "That is just what I tell Rebecca. She feels the stain even more strongly than I. I remind her there are many people in the world with our background, but she sighs and reminds me we do not know who our papa is, never mind whether he is royalty. She is only one year older than me so she has no memory of him. But I tell her even if we do not know, that means we can imagine him to be whoever we wish him to be." She smiled. "Ah, Miss Bennet. Children born under the law do not realize how fortunate they are. Status might cause a barrier but nothing to the same extent." Her face was morose, and Elizabeth was at a loss for what else to say when Helen shrugged away her mood with a smile.

"Do not listen to me. It is a party. We are only just acquainted, and I am already speaking of such intimate matters. What must you think of me? We should talk about more pleasant things. Let us return to the subject of whether there is a possibility of a match between you and that divine Captain Waters?" Helen raised an eyebrow archly, and Elizabeth shook her head with a smile.

"You must not fixate on the subject so much. Mrs. Waters already does that enough."

Helen laughed. "Ah, but you are coy. I shall not push you any further. Though I will add, and I am sure you will admit, your home must be sadly the quieter with him away."

"It is quieter, but I have my aunt, and I have my explorations. I am not at a loss without him."

"Still, it will be nice when he returns."

"No doubt."

"Well, I have teased you long enough. Will you play a duet with me, Miss Bennet? This room needs music! It wants people moving about and dancing. I will open the pianoforte if you join me?"

Elizabeth was happy to agree, and the two played a lively duet. The rest of the party pushed back the furniture, and several couples stood up in the middle of the room, clapping hands and crossing over and back as they danced down the line. Helen was a superior player, and after a few songs, Elizabeth was happy to leave the music to her.

She moved about the room. Her aunt was sitting near the fire chatting with one of her old friends, and Elizabeth was about to join her when Darcy appeared by her side. His demeanor was awkward, and he cleared his throat.

"I would like to praise your performance, Miss Bennet. You play with great spirit."

"Well, I cannot take all credit for that. Miss Carter is a splendid player, and I am afraid she carried most of the tune." Her smile deepened. "I assure you, she covered a multitude of my sins. Without her, I would have been exposed."

"I have had the pleasure of your acquaintance for long enough now to know you are free from that affected habit of demurring and pretending you do not believe you deserve praise, so I can only assume you mean what you say. But I stand by what I said. Your playing gave me great pleasure."

Elizabeth thanked him again. She felt unaccountably shy, an emotion she was not used to experiencing. She excused herself and was about to continue on her way to her aunt when he spoke again.

"They are coming to the end of this dance." Darcy nodded to the dancers lining down the center of the room. "They will form again for another one. Will you do me the honor of dancing with me, Miss Bennet?"

"Oh — " Elizabeth was so astonished, she could not frame an answer. "I had not — I had not thought to dance this evening."

Darcy's smile faded, and a closed look came over his face. "Ah. I understand. You have a particular reason not to dance. Forgive me."

He bowed to her. Elizabeth dropped a curtsey and walked away, her heart racing.

# CHAPTER 22

*E*lizabeth drew out her fan to cool her suddenly warm cheeks and moved closer to the window where someone had thrown up a sash to allow in the night air. Shielded by the drapes, she heard Mrs. Waters walk close by. She was about to emerge to speak with her when she caught the sound of her name.

"Well, what did I tell you? Miss Bennet has refused Mr. Darcy. Mr. Darcy! A man I believe no woman ever refused. Does this not answer all my hopes? Why else would she not dance if she were not in love with my son?"

"Perhaps Miss Bennet is tired? She walks a great deal." Mrs. Jones' voice came to her.

"Oh, no." There was a flat refusal in Mrs. Waters's voice. "A lady would only reject an offer to dance with such a prestigious gentleman if her heart was otherwise engaged. She has mentioned how much she looks forward to Henry's return several times. It will be the answer to all my wishes when my dear Marianne and I are joined as a family. Poor Mr. Darcy. I do not believe he has ever been rejected before, but he is not to know he asked a lady whose heart belongs to another man."

Elizabeth tapped her fan against her lip and frowned. Mrs. Waters would persist in this delusion she and Captain Waters were to marry. Elizabeth was not averse to the idea, but she did not appreciate being pressured. If Mrs. Waters carried on this way, Elizabeth would find herself engaged in the eyes of Derbyshire at least. The voices moved a little further away, and Elizabeth made up her mind.

She strode across the room and walked directly up to Mr. Darcy. He stood near the door, speaking to a servant in a low voice. Elizabeth lightly touched his sleeve, and he turned with a frown that melted into a look of astonishment at the sight of Elizabeth looking up at him, her jaw set and determined. He raised a hand to the footman to indicate he should wait and turned back to her.

"What is it, Miss Bennet? I am preparing to leave."

"Mr. Darcy, I must apologize for my behavior just now." Elizabeth's voice was higher than usual, but she still looked determined.

Darcy recoiled slightly and immediately waved away her apology, but she stopped him.

"I did not expect you to ask me to dance, and I believe you misunderstood my hesitation. I do not have a particular reason not to dance apart from being slightly tired after a long walk today. But if your offer of a dance still stands, I would — I would like to accept it."

Her expression was so fierce Mr. Darcy looked startled. The footman started towards Darcy with his overcoat in his hands. At the sight of Elizabeth's face, he hesitated then swallowed and tiptoed out of the way.

"I — yes, Miss Bennet. My offer still stands."

Elizabeth nodded briskly. She placed her hand on the one Darcy offered and steered him to the line of dancers just as the previous song ended. As they stood opposite one another, she saw the frown on Darcy's face, and mortification overwhelmed her.

Oh god, what had she done? Thrown herself at a man and all but ordered him to dance with her. It was the sort of thing her sisters Lydia and Kitty would do and something that would earn them a scolding from Elizabeth herself. What must Mr. Darcy think of her? No wonder he looked at her with such disapproval.

As the dance began and the couples moved closer to one another, Darcy took her hand for them to cross in opposite directions.

"I am sorry, sir," Elizabeth said. All her earlier determination had fled, and now she simply felt embarrassed. "You must wonder at my actions. I rather do myself."

"You need not apologize."

Elizabeth nodded, and they continued dancing. There was still tension between them. Elizabeth glanced across the room and was gratified to see Mrs. Waters watching them. The lady frowned a little, and Elizabeth was relieved. Perhaps it would prevent her from making marriage plans before Elizabeth or Captain Waters knew what they were about.

She saw Darcy watching her and gave him a small smile.

"I daresay you have not had a lady ask you to dance before."

"I certainly have not." His tone was so clipped Elizabeth felt that same wave of embarrassment. His expression softened. "But I did not experience it tonight either. You did not ask me to dance. I asked you, and I walked away before you had a chance to respond to my request."

"Well, yes, you did," said Elizabeth. She smiled. "I do not believe you often invite ladies to dance even though you dance well. Am I right?"

"I will admit I dislike the occupation in particular. I usually find it a punishment to stand up with someone unless I have known them a long time."

"Do you consider me someone you have known for a long time?"

"Not at all. But I still wished to dance with you."

As Elizabeth smiled, he added, "My sister will ask me if there was any dancing tonight and if I partook in any. When I tell her I danced with you, she will be thrilled."

"Oh." Elizabeth forced herself to appear unconcerned, but her heart sank.

So he wished to dance with her for his sister's sake.

Well, of course he did. What other reason did he have? He had already told her he would do all he could to promote his sister's friendship with her. Asking her to dance was a natural extension of that.

Elizabeth told herself she was pleased he thought highly enough of her to forward her friendship with Georgiana, but she could not help feeling disappointed. For a moment, she had flattered herself he wanted to dance for herself alone.

But that was nonsense. She would not be the sort of foolish lady who fancied a man in love with her if he so much as paid her the slightest bit of attention. She would not allow her imagination to run away with her.

"Well, you must tell her we were the finest dancers in the room," she said. "Everyone was in awe of us. All the other dancers stopped and stood back to allow us the whole floor because they knew their dancing could not agree once we had exposed them to ours."

"I shall tell her one of the kitchen boys ran out into the street to inform every one of the marvels taking place in his house," added Darcy. His expression was grave, but there was a twinkle in his eye. "Neighbours rushed in to witness this sight. One man ran for his carriage and, deciding it would not carry him fast enough, commandeered another to take him to London that he might inform the papers."

Elizabeth struggled to stifle a laugh lest they draw too much attention and gossip on themselves, but it was difficult. She did not know Darcy had it in him to engage in playful conversation.

"People everywhere will despair when they hear of it. They will give up dancing for good. Even Almack's will be no more."

Darcy made a face as he took her hand and crossed over. "That would not be a bad thing."

"I am sure the patronesses would not be pleased to hear you say that. You will be denied your voucher for the next season."

"I do not know how I could bear such a punishment," said Darcy dryly. He looked down at Elizabeth, his eyes warm. "No, Almack's has nothing to this evening right here. I would not trade it for the world."

Elizabeth found it hard to meet his eyes when he looked at her like that. Her stomach fluttered, and she laughed a little to hide her confusion.

"How provincial of you, Mr. Darcy. But do not worry. Your secret is safe with me."

"Thank you, Miss Bennet." His eyes were warm when he smiled.

. . .

I t was with reluctance Darcy released her when the dance ended. At the end of the evening, he attended her to her carriage and watched it depart with a curious sensation in his chest. He remained where he was until even the sound of the horses faded to nothing. He sighed and returned to his carriage, his heart more confused than ever.

# CHAPTER 23

"It was a pleasant night, was it not?" Aunt Gardiner sighed as she leaned on her niece's arm. "The Altons are such pleasant people. It was wonderful to see faces I had not seen in years. The Becketts traveled from Derby, especially because they heard I was attending. I have not seen them in more than a decade, but it was as if no time had passed since we parted."

"That is always the way with true friends."

Aunt and niece strolled down a lane near the boundaries of Pemberley Park. They had spent little time together, just the two of them since their arrival, so when Elizabeth left for her usual walk, Aunt Gardiner offered to accompany her. Elizabeth had eagerly accepted her offer. The park boundary was close to Lambton and would not overtax her aunt.

"You seemed to enjoy yourself," her aunt added archly. "I was surprised to see you and Mr. Darcy converse with such ease. You seemed engrossed by one another. Should I write to Longbourn and request the banns be read?"

Elizabeth made an exasperated noise and turned to her aunt just in time to catch the twinkle in her eyes.

"Oh, you speak in jest." She shook her head and laughed at herself. "Well, that goodness for that." She dramatically placed a hand to her chest and her other hand to her forehead. "It seems everywhere I go, I meet with a matchmaker desperate to have me married off. What is a poor maiden to do?"

Aunt Gardiner smiled and patted her hand. "I am afraid this will continue until you marry, my dear, and even then, you will find yourself pestered relentlessly with demands to know when you will have children. Such is a woman's lot. But I am partly serious. You enjoyed Mr. Darcy's company last night, did you not?"

"I confess I did. He is far easier to talk to than I expected. Not nearly so proud and disdainful. I enjoyed our conversations. And I will own it was a welcome relief to talk to a man without people watching in breathless anticipation to discover if wedding bells are pending."

Aunt Gardiner sighed. "I am afraid my friend is overzealous. I have told her to leave you and Captain Waters alone, but she insists she is not interfering, only expressing her wishes. She thinks it would be a fine thing if we were family."

"I like Captain Waters, but I will not wed him to please anyone but myself. But it is not just Mrs. Waters who pushes it. Even Helen Carter last night asked me about it in a most particular manner. I fear it is a sign of rumors spreading."

"Well, we are only here for a few weeks. If you and the captain can form an attachment, you will have time to do so on your excursions. And if you do not, it is of little matter once you are home in Hertfordshire."

"Consider how enthusiastic Mrs. Waters is, I may need to flee under cover of night if I dare refuse a match with her son," said Elizabeth dryly. "Be prepared, Aunt. I may come to you when the house is in darkness and urge you to pack your things so we might flee at once. We shall have to take back roads to throw Mrs. Waters off our trail when she hunts me down, determined to kidnap me and carry me to the altar by force."

Mrs. Gardiner gave Elizabeth a chiding look even as she tried to suppress a smile. "Well, let us hope it will not come to that. I am sure my friend will be reasonable, and — " She paused, her attention caught by something down the road. "Bless me, is that Mr. Darcy? My eyesight is not what it used to be."

Elizabeth whirled around in the direction her aunt looked, her heart pounding unexpectedly.

A light chaise came down the lane towards them, driven by Mr. Darcy. Georgiana sat beside him, her arm linked with his. They conversed together and did not see Elizabeth or her aunt until Georgiana looked up and pointed at them with an excited outburst.

Darcy stopped the chaise at once. Georgiana jumped down and came shyly towards Elizabeth, who clasped her hand with warmth.

"Well, this is a lovely surprise. I am happy to see you, Miss Darcy."

"And I to see you." Georgiana's eyes glowed with pleasure. Darcy jumped down from the chaise and walked towards them. Elizabeth turned to greet him. She felt as shy as Georgiana as she dropped a curtsey.

"Where are you going?" he asked.

"Nowhere in particular. My aunt and I wished to take advantage of this lovely weather, although I fear she is growing tired."

"I confess I am, Lizzy. I am a sore disappointment to my niece, Miss Darcy. She is an excellent walker, but it fatigues me."

"You are not a disappointment," Elizabeth chided gently. "I knew the walk was tiring you. I was about to suggest we turn back."

"I insist on offering Mrs. Gardiner my chaise," said Darcy at once. "I am happy to drive her anywhere she wishes to go."

"Oh, I could not take your time. I am certainly strong enough to return to Lambton."

"Aunt, you know you are fatigued. I should not have come this way. I did not expect we would walk so far."

"You are not responsible for that, Lizzy. If I was tired, it was my duty to speak up, not yours to anticipate it."

As they spoke, Georgiana went to her brother. He stooped to allow her whisper into his ear. He nodded, and she stood back, blushing furiously. Darcy cleared his throat, and the two ladies looked at him.

"My sister has something she wishes to ask you," he said. He gently nudged her forward.

"I was wondering, Miss Bennet, if you and your aunt would like to accompany us back to Pemberley for tea and refreshments? My brother will be happy to put one of his carriages at your disposal to take you home afterward."

Elizabeth and Mrs. Gardiner looked at one another.

"I do not think Mrs. Waters is expecting us home at a particular time?"

"Not at all."

Elizabeth turned to beam at Georgiana. "Then we will gladly accept."

# CHAPTER 24

*a* t Pemberley, Georgiana led them to a saloon where she called for tea. She took a seat beside Elizabeth and, with her brother's encouragement and Elizabeth's, conversed with her guests. Elizabeth made them all laugh with a lively description of the previous night.

"Your brother, Miss Darcy, dances like an angel. He did not tell you this? How wicked of him. You will never be without a partner as long as he is to hand. I am sure I was the envy of every young lady in the room, as well as every not so young lady."

Georgiana smiled. "I did not think my brother cared to dance. He has only danced with me occasionally to practice my steps, but his friend, Mr. Bingley, has complained many times he will walk about a ballroom in what he calls a — what he calls a — I am sorry, Fitzwilliam. I mean no disrespect, and I only repeat his words — in a stupid manner."

Elizabeth and Aunt Gardiner burst out laughing. Georgiana's smile grew in confidence when her brother rolled his eyes but smiled to show he was not at all offended.

"I shall speak sternly to Bingley. He talks too much. I am

surprised he has the leisure to notice what I do when he is too busy making himself charming to all the room."

"He said there had been evenings where you did not dance a single dance," Georgiana went on a little more boldly. "He says there were many balls when more than one lady was in want of a partner, but you would not ask them."

"Bingley says far too many things," said Darcy.

"I should like to meet this Mr. Bingley," said Elizabeth. She gave Darcy an arch smile. "I am sure he could tell us tales of you that would shock us all."

"You would like Mr. Bingley, Miss Bennet," said Georgiana. "He is so warm and cheerful, is he not, Fitzwilliam? Always in good humor and sees the best in everyone."

"He sounds exactly like my sister, Jane. She is just such a person. And if he is anything like my dear sister, I can see why he is such a valued companion."

"He is rather less valued when he tells my sister tales of my doings at balls," said Darcy. His voice was dry, but there was affection in his eyes as he spoke of his friend.

"Or your lack of doings, Mr. Darcy. Those poor ladies."

"I am sure they survived the ordeal."

"Perhaps, but we shall never know. I read enough novels to know what happens to ladies who are slighted. At best, they will flee to nunneries on the continent. Now, shall we discuss our excursion? Captain Waters will return soon, and then we shall be free to go. I cannot tell you how much I look forward to it, Miss Darcy."

Georgiana was interrupted from answering when the door opened, and a footman came in, carrying a tea tray. Mrs. Younge followed, and although she smiled, Elizabeth thought she detected the usual hardness in her eyes at the sight of her and her aunt sitting close to the Darcy siblings.

"Forgive me for interrupting, but I was not aware we had

visitors," she said with a tight smile. "Miss Darcy, you should have told me so I could be here with you to greet them."

"My sister is doing well enough for herself, Mrs. Younge," said Darcy. "But take a seat and join us."

"We were just discussing our excursion to the peaks, Mrs. Younge," said Elizabeth.

"I shall take my paints and papers and draw the scenery. Do you draw, Miss Bennet?"

"Unless you count making messy squiggles on the page and insisting they are trees, I am afraid I do not draw," said Elizabeth. "None of the girls in my family have a talent for it. I once tried to draw a picture of my father, and he congratulated me on my excellent rendition of a monster. He reminded me he has two eyebrows, not one, that his eyes are on one level, not two, and his face is more angular and less shaped like a lumpen potato. After that, I refrained from inflicting any more of my art on my family and friends."

"None of you draw?" Mrs. Younge's eyebrows shot up. "That is most unusual. Your governess must have been remiss." She laughed to disguise her remark as a joke, but Elizabeth did not miss the intended insult.

"We did not have a governess, Mrs. Younge," she said in a cheerful voice. "We were such bluestockings that we educated ourselves." She smiled at Georgiana, who giggled.

"No governess? And this was a genteel home?"

"As genteel as any home can be with five daughters running about. But our education was not lacking. My father has a well-stocked library, and our parents always encouraged us to read. I have an inquiring mind, and it was no hardship for me to devour all the knowledge I could find. I do not feel I lack in that department."

"You do not," said Georgiana with spirit.

Mrs. Younge looked at Georgiana sharply but said nothing. Darcy smiled at Elizabeth.

"Well, you have done excellent work in educating yourself. Your father must be very proud. I have always admired ladies who improve their minds with extensive reading. As far as accomplishments go, it impresses me most."

Elizabeth smiled and thanked him, and to cover her embarrassment at his praise, she turned the subject back to their trip.

"Which peak do you recommend we visit? I want to see the most impressive one. Which is that, Miss Darcy?"

"Kinder Scout?" Georgiana ventured with a glance at her brother. "It is the highest."

Mrs. Younge scoffed. "Oh, come, Miss Darcy. You know it is overrated. You had best see Wibben Hill. It has the advantage of being closer, and we can be there and back within a few hours."

"I agree with my sister that Kinder Scout is the most impressive and the one which will delight Miss Bennet the most. She will also love Mam Tor. It is not as high, but its views over Derbyshire are stunning. But what do you mean by "we", Mrs. Younge? I did not think you planned to join us? I had thought to allow you the day off that you may attend to any concerns of your own. You have been most diligent in being at my sister's side these past few months, so I am sure you would appreciate some time to yourself."

Elizabeth happened to look at Mrs. Younge's face as Darcy spoke, and she saw a flash of anger that she quickly covered with a honeyed smile.

"It is my pleasure, not my duty, to be with your sister, Mr. Darcy. Miss Darcy could not be dearer to me if she were family. Time away from her is a punishment rather than a reward. I would much prefer to join you."

"I am afraid I must insist, Mrs. Younge," said Darcy. "You will tire yourself out if you do nothing but tend to Georgiana. You must take time for yourself. Come now, we shall say no more about it. The matter is settled."

Mrs. Younge looked as if she wished to speak again, but she sank back into her chair and fell into a sullen silence. Eventually, she excused herself and left the room.

Elizabeth noticed the tension in the saloon lift as soon as she left. Georgiana appeared far more relaxed, and with her brother's encouragement, she joined in the conversation with greater ease.

# CHAPTER 25

*A*fter talking a while longer, Elizabeth requested a stroll through the pretty rose garden she could see through the French windows. Aunt Gardiner declined, and Mr. Darcy offered to stay with her.

The girls went outside, and Georgiana showed her some of her favorite rose bushes. The air in the garden was soft and fragrant. Summer was all around them, with bees droning lazily among the flowers. A soft breeze refreshed their faces, bringing scents of woodland and grass. Elizabeth breathed it in with delight.

"I do not believe I have ever seen such lovely gardens. They are a credit to you. Especially these roses." She stopped at a bush and leaned closer to examine it. She reached out a hand to touch the silken petals. "I am no gardener, but I recognize this one in particular. My oldest sister Jane is the gardener in our family, and she mentioned this one is especially hard to cultivate. You must be proud of such an accomplishment."

Georgiana's cheeks were rosy with pleasure at Elizabeth's words.

"I am afraid I am prone to pride. Mrs. Younge tells me it is a flaw because there is always someone better than me and always room to improve."

Elizabeth had been stooped over the rose to catch its fragrance, and she turned to give Georgiana an incredulous look.

"I mean no disrespect to Mrs. Younge, but that is utter nonsense," she said firmly.

Georgiana started at her words, and she softened them at once.

"Forgive me, Miss Darcy. I am prone to speak out of turn. One of my flaws," she added with a grin. "I am sorry. I understand Mrs. Younge is your companion, but I cannot agree with her there. Of course, there will always be those who are better than us, and of course, there will always be room for improvement. It is the nature of human beings that we are always growing and changing. But that does not mean we cannot both take pride in our achievements and still acknowledge we can improve. I do not see the conflict."

She took Georgiana's arm, and the girls walked down the path towards the shrubbery. Georgiana was silent for a while, and Elizabeth allowed her to mull over her words while she admired the cultivated bushes.

"It is true, is it not, Miss Bennet? Mrs. Younge is always so insistent I should not take pride in mastering a difficult song or paint a picture that pleases me." She chewed her lip. "She says it in a way that makes me feel vain and foolish."

"She should not do such a thing," said Elizabeth gently. "You have every right to be proud of yourself. I have not known you long, but anyone can see how much work you put into what you do." She paused as she assessed her young friend's face. "Miss Darcy, forgive me if I speak out of turn

160

but are you happy Mrs. Younge will not join us to the peaks? There was something in your manner that suggested relief."

Georgiana looked up in alarm. "Oh, dear. Was it obvious to Mrs. Younge?"

Elizabeth laughed and patted her hand with affection. "I doubt it. She was too busy glaring at your brother to pay attention. But I am right, am I not?"

"You are right," admitted Georgiana. "It is selfish of me, but Mrs. Younge can be a little overbearing with me sometimes. She often says I am like the daughter she never had, and while it is sweet of her, it can mean she likes to keep me all to herself. I do not like to complain. I should be grateful..."

Elizabeth gently took her arm and drew it through her own. "Do not tell yourself how you should feel and especially do not allow another person to do so. I understand you perfectly. Her affection can be smothering and can prevent you from having the freedom to do what you wish without feeling obligated to her."

"That is just it," said Georgiana. Her eyes filled with relief. "I did not know how to put it into words, but that is just what I feel. Even my brother, who loves me very much, does not place such demands on me. His love encourages me."

"And that is how it should be. I do not wish to be yet another person who tells you what to do, but I will offer this advice; consult your feelings. Do not force them down. They will whisper the truth if you listen."

The girls walked on in silence. Georgiana's head was down, and Elizabeth wondered what she was thinking. The level of control Mrs. Younge exerted over her charge unsettled her, and she hoped she could help Georgiana speak up for herself. She gestured towards a bench, and they sat down. Georgiana tilted her face to the sun and sighed.

EMILY RUSSELL

"It is beautiful here. I miss Pemberley when I am away. This time of year is always sweetest."

A bird darted from a tree nearby, and a rabbit hopped out onto the sweet grass. A light breeze ruffled the bushes. Elizabeth took it all in with a smile.

"I cannot blame you. I have never seen a more delightful place than Pemberley. But surely you can stay here with your brother for the summer? There is no need for you to hurry away so soon after arriving."

Georgiana looked down at her lap. She swung her legs lightly back and forth, prompting Elizabeth to smile at the picture of youth she made.

"I am to go away to Ramsgate in a few weeks," she said. "The benefits of the seaside and all that. It has been arranged already. But I shall be loath to leave here."

"As I said before, consult your feelings. Arrangements can always be unmade, and if the trip is to benefit you, you need not worry about disappointing anyone by changing your mind."

Georgiana did not respond. Once again, she was lost in her thoughts. After a while, she spoke, and as her words showed the subject changed, Elizabeth could not imagine what conclusion she had come to.

"Do you like Lord Byron, Miss Bennet? I confess I am an admirer even though he is so very wicked."

"I saw him once when I stayed in London with my aunt," said Elizabeth. "We were in the park, and he happened to walk by."

"No!" Georgiana's eyes were wide. "What did you do? Did you speak with him? Oh, I could not, even though I would wish it very much."

"He tilted his hat to me and bowed. I should have stopped to speak with him if my aunt had not hurried me past." Eliza-

162

beth laughed at the memory. "I daresay she was right. The man is a scoundrel if ever I saw one. If my mother knew I had read about his exploits in the paper, she would never recover. But it was exciting. I do not believe him handsome, but there is something alluring about him."

"I cannot believe you saw Lord Byron! I should love to see him. I would tremble, but to see the man who wrote *She Walks in Beauty*..."

The two girls were still engaged in an animated discussion when Darcy strolled towards them, Aunt Gardiner on his arm. He smiled at the sight of his little sister, her face flushed with excitement, waving her hands about with more animation than he could ever recall seeing from her. Elizabeth smiled and nodded her head, encouraging her to express herself, and they were almost upon them before they realized they were there.

"What are you ladies talking about?" he asked as he handed Aunt Gardiner to the bench.

"Lord Byron," said Elizabeth. "Do you remember how you hurried me away from him, Aunt? That day in the park?"

"I should not have done anything else. The man has a dreadful reputation."

"I know Lord Byron," said Darcy.

Georgiana's eyes widened, and her hands flew to her mouth. "Fitzwilliam, you do not! Why have you never told me this?" Her words bubbled out over one another in her excitement. He could hardly believe the change in her countenance.

"I did not think of it. We are not what I would call friends, but we are known to one another. We will acknowledge one another when we pass one another. And

Mrs. Gardiner is right." He smiled. "His reputation is terrible."

"But does he live up to it? If we were to converse with him, would we be sorely disappointed? Can the man live up to the legend?"

Darcy grunted. "If anything, I should say he is worse. The rumors do not do him justice. That business with Lady Caroline Lamb..." His voice trailed off as he recalled his audience. "There now, you have almost led me to say things I should not. I am sure you would find him intriguing as young ladies are wont to do with scoundrels. But you are both far too sensible to be taken in by him for long. The man tries hard to be controversial. I find it difficult not to consider him affected. His constant musings on society grow tiresome after a while."

Georgiana squealed and almost danced in her seat. "You have conversed with him. You are more than acquainted. Oh, Fitzwilliam..."

Darcy smiled at Elizabeth. "I did not realize my sister was such an enthusiast. I shall have to take even more care of her when she is next in London if she is not to be abducted."

"Abducted..."

"There, you see, Mr. Darcy? You have just succeeded in making him more interesting." Elizabeth gave him an arch look and turned back to his sister. "I may not have met Lord Byron, but I understand his type. As your brother has said, he tries far too hard to be controversial. Such people are only interesting in the short term, Miss Darcy. I can answer for it as I have a cousin who is of a similar bent — you will soon wish you were anywhere else. Enjoy his writing by all means but do not build him up to be a romantic figure."

"He certainly is not that," agreed Darcy.

"As I am sure William Lamb can attest," Elizabeth said with a grin.

Darcy looked shocked by her words, but he recovered and seemed to try not to smile.

"Now we have had our discussion about dissipated poets with bad tempers, shall we repair to the house? The evening grows a little cooler."

As they walked back, Darcy touched Elizabeth's sleeve to hold her back to him. Aunt Gardiner and Georgiana strolled on together, chatting quietly. Even during that afternoon, Georgiana had lost much of her shyness. Her enjoyment of the ladies' company had caused her to forget much of her usual reserve, and she spoke without worrying about how her words might be received.

Elizabeth waited with Darcy. He watched his sister with a smile.

"I want to thank you, Miss Bennet. I know I said as much last night, but it hits me with new force when I see your effect on my sister. She is quite an altered creature."

"I do not know she is altered. Her qualities were always there, but her shyness prevented her from expressing them. She has only wanted a little encouragement to come out of her shell."

"And you have managed it. I am grateful. I am a poor substitute for a parent, but while Georgie can find friends like you, I do not need to fear for her."

"Your flattery is too much," said Elizabeth with a laugh.

"I disagree. I think it is well earned."

Elizabeth smiled, but it was hard to subdue the fluttering in her stomach at his words. She had received lots of compliments from men, but something about his felt sincere. He was not a man given to idle praise, and his good opinion seemed more worth the earning.

He offered her his arm, and they followed the ladies to the house.

"I am now looking forward to our outing more than ever. If an afternoon has done as much for my sister, I am interested to see what a whole day can do."

He smiled down at her. Elizabeth returned it, but inwardly she sighed. Of course. He valued her in as much as she benefitted his sister. She must not allow herself to be run away by girlish daydreams and fancy he meant more than that.

# CHAPTER 26

$\mathcal{T}$wo days later, Elizabeth was in Lambton, having walked with her aunt to meet old friends. She did not wish to intrude on their reunion, so after staying for fifteen minutes, she told her aunt she would walk back to Trillings. Aunt Gardiner agreed, and after taking her leave, Elizabeth set off on foot through the market square back home. She was passing the parsonage when a barouche turned the corner and rumbled past. Elizabeth stood out of the way and looked to see if she recognized the occupant. Her heart lifted when she realized Captain Waters. He did a double-take and appeared flustered for a moment before calling for the driver to stop.

He jumped down and greeted her with a smile.

"Well, this is a fine welcome home. The very face I am most pleased to see. I missed you, Miss Bennet. No conversation can compare to yours."

Elizabeth laughed. "I am always happy to be useful. But why do you come this way? I thought it would be easier to come by Pemberley?"

"It would have been, but a fellow advised us there was a problem with the road which prevented easy passage. It was easier to come directly through the town rather than waste time to discover if it was true. But come, you must drive home with me. I hired this fellow, and we shall take advantage of the conveyance."

Captain Waters gestured to the driver. The man hopped down from his seat to lower the hood, and Captain Waters handed Elizabeth into the carriage. He took the seat across from her and smiled at her.

"Ah, Miss Bennet. We have known each other a short space of time, and already you feel like a dear friend. But what have you been up to while I was away? Did you get into more tussles with over-zealous landowners?"

"Just the opposite, as a matter of fact."

Captain Waters' eyebrows shot up. "Ah. Indeed. Just the opposite, you say? Does that mean you had a pleasant encounter with a landowner, or does it mean this time it was you threatening one with a gun?"

Elizabeth giggled. "Well, I was hardly threatened. No, Aunt and I met Mr. Darcy and his sister on our walk, and they invited us to Pemberley. We had a pleasant day."

"I am glad to hear it. I hope Darcy has improved on closer acquaintance and is not as severe as we believed?"

"I do not believe he is." Elizabeth's voice was thoughtful, and Captain Waters cried with feigned outrage.

"Well, this will not do at all. I leave the county for a few days, and you already found a fellow of far more consequence to make love to you. My poor mother will be heartbroken. Her dreams are crushed!"

Elizabeth laughed and colored. "Oh, you talk such nonsense. I do not know why I agreed to enter this carriage. I should expect more sense from the birds in the trees."

Captain Waters' eyes danced. "But they will not make you laugh as I do. Ah, forgive me, Miss Bennet. I am merely happy to be home and in high spirits. I do not mean to tease."

"I should hope you don't." Elizabeth tried to look severe. "If you do not, I shall be forced to tell your mama about all the dreadful things you did in Manchester."

Captain Waters gave her a startled look, but when Elizabeth grinned, he laughed. "My poor mother. How we would horrify her. Ah, here we are, almost at the turn by dear old Trillings. I never tire of this sight. I am later than expected, but it will just increase Mama's excitement when she sees me. Ha! There she is, rushing down the steps. She must have been on the lookout."

E lizabeth blushed as Captain Waters handed her out of the barouche. Mrs. Waters' smile deepened when she saw them together, and after she had embraced and kissed her son, she gave them an arch look.

"Well, look at the two of you arriving together. One would think you were a married couple coming to visit your mama-in-law. What a cozy picture you make."

Captain Waters rolled his eyes over his mother's head and grinned. Elizabeth had to stifle a laugh, her initial surge of irritation gone in a moment in the enjoyment of having someone to share the trial with. If they were to marry - and it was still a big *if* - was this what their marriage would be like? The two of them allies, exchanging secret jokes? She had to admit, it was not an unappealing image.

Mrs. Waters shooed them into the house as if they were chickens. Once Captain Waters had washed and changed his clothes, he returned to the parlor where the ladies sat.

"You are still here, Miss Bennet. That is good. I had feared you had gone rambling again."

"Not today." Elizabeth stretched her feet towards the fire with a yawn. "The sky is overcast, and there is a chill. Besides, I have walked so much since I arrived in Derbyshire, a day before the fire will do me good."

"Oh, I am sure that is her reason," said Mrs. Waters. She raised an eyebrow with another of those arch looks. "Yes, Miss Bennet merely wishes to stay home today of all days. She is tired. It can be nothing else. I quite understand you."

"Precisely, Mrs. Waters. It can be nothing else," said Elizabeth with a firmness that would not have been ignored by anyone but a determined mama with the sound of wedding bells already in her ears. She glanced over her shoulder at the window. "It is a shame it is so overcast. I hope it improves again. I want to experience Derbyshire at its best, and there is nothing more enchanting than hills and peaks under a blue sky and bright sun."

Captain Waters gave her a quizzical stare.

"Our outing," she prompted. "Surely you did not forget?" As his face cleared, she laughed. "How forgetful of you. We settled on two days after you returned home. We planned it already."

Captain Waters yawned and stretched. "I admit, I had not forgotten the outing, but I had forgotten the day. You say it is in two days?"

"I hope it is not a problem?" said Elizabeth.

Captain Waters waved her concerns away. "I had planned to see a fellow about a new gun. But I can easily change it. I will not give up our trip for the world. Now, what arrangements have you made? I am sure you must have some. You were not idle while I was away, especially if you were in the company of the Darcys."

Elizabeth told him of their plans to visit Kinder Scout and how they would travel. Captain Waters nodded but seemed preoccupied.

"So you wish to be in a carriage with Miss Darcy. And Mr. Darcy will no doubt wish to drive you." He lapsed into silence. Mrs. Waters joined in the conversation, but Captain Waters hardly responded.

Elizabeth could not account for his odd humor. Was it possible he wished to drive her himself and was jealous that she would be with the Darcys instead?

She could never tell what he thought of her. He certainly liked her a great deal and enjoyed her conversation. When he looked at her, there was admiration in his eyes that told him he liked what he saw, but she could never make him out beyond that. His manner was so playful that it was hard to know when he spoke in jest and when in earnest. However he felt about her, it was clear something about the outing unsettled him.

"Miss Darcy's companion will not be joining us, so there will be room for you in Mr. Darcy's carriage. You will not need to bring out your own," she offered.

Captain Waters made a face. "I have no objection to Darcy's carriage, but I prefer to drive myself. I am my own master."

"And yet you hired a carriage to take you home today," Elizabeth teased.

Captain Waters returned her grin. "Well, that was different. I confess I would prefer to drive myself. Perhaps I shall ride along beside you." He fell silent once again as if considering something. "Hmm, I shall think on it more."

He leaned forward and clapped his hands together. "But enough talking about carriages and horses and whatnot. We have plenty of time to consider everything. Now, what about

171

a game of cards, Mama? Come, you know you like a game, and Miss Bennet is right. The day is far too overcast to make the outdoors pleasant. Here we are nice and cozy with a fire. We shall play for fish. I will fetch the table. Where is Father? He should join us."

# CHAPTER 27

The clouds had disappeared during the night, and the sun had returned by the following day, giving Elizabeth hope that the day of their outing would be a repeat of the beautiful weather they had enjoyed since she arrived in Derbyshire. Captain Waters had gone to town to make new arrangements to view the gun, and Elizabeth hoped he had recovered from his odd humor.

Was he really jealous of her traveling with the Darcys? She had already explained she wished to ride with Georgiana, but it was possible he hadn't given too much thought to the matter until it was just about to happen and then realized the arrangement was not to his liking.

Well, surely when he understood Mr. Darcy only cared for Elizabeth in so far as she was useful to his sister, he would recover from his pique if that was what bothered him. But if he did not, she would keep her distance. She was not about to have their outing ruined by Captain Waters' sulks.

The day was too hot to walk far, but Elizabeth still wished to be active. When she saw Mrs. Waters take a basket and some shears, she offered to gather roses in her stead.

173

"What a dear girl you are, Miss Bennet. Thank you, that is most generous. I confess this heat can be too much for me, but I wished to make dinner perfect for Henry on his first full day home." She handed her the implements. "He particularly likes the yellow ones," she added with a sly smile.

It took Elizabeth some effort not to burst out laughing. Yellow roses, the traditional symbol of jealousy. Was this a sign that her musings about his odd humor were correct? Was there jealousy in the air?

Bees droned in the bushes as she knelt in the grass. It was a perfect lazy summer's day. From the lane opposite the house, she caught the scent of gorse. Birds flitted in and out of bushes. She had plenty of time to gather roses before dinner.

She lay the basket to one side, threw the shears inside, and lay on her back in the grass with her eyes closed. She could almost hear her mama's voice shrieking at her about her complexion, but her mother was far away, and Elizabeth was free to relish the sun without interruption.

Or almost without interruption.

"Well, this is a pleasant sight."

Elizabeth had been dozing when a deep voice filtered through her dreams. She sat up and looked around, still feeling drowsy.

Captain Waters crouched down beside her, a buttercup swirling between his fingers. He grinned at her.

"Forgive me, Miss Bennet. I did not mean to startle you. But no young man could resist the sight of a young woman lying in the grass on a summer's day. You put me in mind of a painting."

Elizabeth laughed and shook the grass from her hair.

"I am afraid you caught me shirking my duties. I promised your mother I would gather roses for dinner to

174

make myself useful, and here you find me doing the precise opposite. I do not know how I shall live down the shame."

Captain Waters smiled and held out his hand. Rising from the grass, he pulled her to her feet.

"Well, we shall manage together. Come, give me the shears. Which roses does my mother wish you to gather?"

"The yellow ones." Elizabeth's lips curved into a smile. "Your favorites."

"The symbol of jealousy." As he took the basket, his smile was sardonic. He turned away towards the roses. Elizabeth could have sworn she heard him mutter under his breath, "How curiously appropriate."

She tied her bonnet under her chin and went to join him. They worked together in companionable silence, Captain Waters cutting the thicker stems and Elizabeth rearranging them and pointing out the more desirable ones.

"Was your gun man satisfied with your change of plan?" she asked.

Captain Waters grunted as he wrestled with a stubborn stem. In his shirt-sleeves, his hat thrown to one side and his fair hair tousled, he was a man who would set many a lady's heart racing. She was still undecided how he affected hers.

"He was a little difficult. He did not take too kindly to the change," he admitted. "But what was to be done? I had promised you first."

"I am sure he was just piqued," said Elizabeth. "There is no reason you cannot go the second day if he is in town. Once you buy the gun, it will not matter which particular day you saw it. I take it he is not someone in town for a limited time?"

Captain Waters stood back in triumph, holding the stubborn rose aloft. With a flourish, he placed it in the basket.

"No, he is here for some time. The gun will be delivered

to him on the day we set out, but it will still be there afterward. Some people just like to be difficult, and there is no accounting for it."

"True enough." She hesitated. "Have you given more thought to how you might travel with us?" She watched him, curious to see if her question would bring on a repeat of his odd humor.

"Oh, as to that." He paused and wiped the sweat from his brow. "Phew, what a day. I do not believe I was so hot in the West Indies. As to your question, I will take my carriage after all. I met the Miss Carters as I returned here. Miss Helen told me all about your dinner with her the other night. I am glad you spent time with her. She is a dear girl for all my mother's prejudices. As we spoke of the weather, I mentioned our excursion. Miss Helen was wild with envy when I told her we would tour the peaks. She has never been, although she has visited Derbyshire many times. I cannot fathom it! Well, I could not turn down her and Rebecca with such an appeal before me. I hope you do not mind, Miss Bennet, but our journey has grown by two more. I hope you are not against the plan?"

Elizabeth was surprised. "Not at all. I like Miss Helen very much. I am astonished they have not seen the peaks. I take it you will convey them in your carriage?"

"Precisely. A carriage is better for a whole day's exploration than a horse, but there was little point in me driving one out alone. Now, I shall convey the two ladies." He hesitated. "Do you — that is, you do not think the Darcys will object to their joining us? I know Mr. Darcy can be particular about the company he keeps, and well, with the Miss Carters backgrounds..."

"As to that, I cannot say." She tilted her head to consider.

"I do not believe Mr. Darcy had any objection to Miss Helen's presence at the dinner the other night at the Altons. He did not speak with her, but I suspect more so because he did not have the opportunity than out of any prejudice. And Miss Darcy is such a sweet girl I do not believe she will object. No, I am satisfied. Mr. Darcy is far more just than I gave him credit for being. He will not mind their presence."

Captain Waters' eyebrows raised, and he grinned. "Mr. Darcy is just, eh? Well, this is more evidence of your change of tune. I was right. You have lost your heart to another man."

"Oh, for shame," said Elizabeth with a feigned scowl. She pulled the basket from his grasp, pretending to be annoyed, although her face flushed at the suggestion. "If you continue to speak such nonsense, I shall return to the house at once."

She gave him a look of mock offense and hurried across the lawn to hide her warm face. Whether Captain Waters looked after her with amusement or jealousy, she could not say.

D arcy called briefly that evening to discuss arrangements for the following day. Elizabeth had expected him to send a note, so her spirits were flustered when she came downstairs to find him in the parlor, his hat in his hand. He rose at once when she entered. Captain Waters was with him.

"Mr. Darcy," she exclaimed. "I did not expect to see you, sir. I hope our plans are not to change?"

"Not at all." Once again, he appeared stiff and formal.

"I was just telling Mr. Darcy of our new companions," Captain Waters explained.

"Ah." Elizabeth turned to Darcy. "I trust you do not object, sir?"

Darcy frowned a little. "Of course not. I am not acquainted with the ladies, but I know nothing that would make me object to their company. I am sure my sister will be happy to meet them."

"And what arrangements have been made for tomorrow?"

Darcy outlined his plan he should call for them at ten o'clock. Captain Waters would travel to the parsonage to collect the Miss Carters, and they would all continue on their journey together.

Elizabeth nodded, although she was slightly bemused. It was five miles to Pemberley. How odd that Mr. Darcy should make a ten-mile round trip to arrange something that might have been managed in a few lines on a note. She and Captain Waters walked with him to the door as he left. He paused in the vestibule.

"Until tomorrow then, Miss Bennet." He hesitated. "Captain Waters."

Elizabeth murmured a goodbye. Darcy placed his hat on his head and turned to say something else. Captain Waters stood by her side, and something about the picture seemed to strike him. Elizabeth had an uneasy suspicion Mrs. Waters' careless words might have started a rumor that had reached his ears. But she might have imagined it because a moment later, he nodded to them without speaking and walked down the path to where his horse waited.

"What a strange fellow," Captain Waters muttered. "Coming all this way just for that. I wonder why he came here?"

Elizabeth felt his gaze on her but could not bring herself to meet it. She shrugged and bid Captain Waters goodnight before climbing the stairs to her room.

From the window, she saw Darcy on his horse as he rode down the lane. He turned back to look at the house, and for a moment, it seemed their eyes met. Elizabeth drew back with a sharp breath, her heart pounding. After a moment, she leaned forward. He continued on his way, and she followed his path until she could see him no more.

# CHAPTER 28

"*W*ell, this is splendid," Elizabeth sighed. She removed her bonnet and waved it slowly to send a gentle breeze over her face. The party had traveled for several hours and exclaimed over the peaks until even Elizabeth had her fill of them. They now rested on a gentle hilltop Darcy recommended, and all the young people lounged in the grass. "I could not ask for more beautiful weather."

"I have never climbed so high," said Georgiana. "How daring you are, Elizabeth. I should never have done so if you were not beside me."

Elizabeth smiled. During their walk, they had agreed to call one another by their first names. "I do not know if I would have done so without you beside me either. It is always easy to be brave when a friend is by your side."

"You are both brave enough," said Captain Waters. He lounged on one elbow. Despite how they traveled, once free of the carriages, the party had divided themselves into two different groups. Captain Waters took charge of Elizabeth and Georgiana while Darcy escorted the Miss Carters. Elizabeth was not all that surprised. One sight of Rebecca Carter's lovely face would draw in any man. "If I had the two of you on my ship, the war would have ended within a month."

"You are so fortunate to travel," said Georgiana. "I should like to visit places I read about, but I do not know if I would have the courage. Elizabeth also wishes to travel. We spoke of it at length on our journey here."

"Well, perhaps you will fall in love with a man who will take you to explore the world?" suggested Captain Waters with a grin. "Find a man who owns a ship, and he will take you anywhere. Isn't that right, Miss Bennet?"

"Georgiana should marry the man she loves, and if he is open to traveling, that will serve," said Elizabeth. His question felt a little too pointed. She did not wish to indulge it, especially as Darcy and the Miss Carters came to join them. Miss Carter had wanted to sketch the view, and Darcy accompanied her. Elizabeth was curiously unsettled by the sight of them together. She forced herself to keep her mind from it by turning her attention to Captain Waters.

Darcy sat down across from Elizabeth, and Miss Carter knelt beside him. Elizabeth tried to appear unconcerned by the sight.

"Why do you speak of my sister marrying? She is a little young yet."

"We were joking, sir. Your sister expresses a desire to travel, and Captain Waters suggested she marry a man who would convey her."

"Miss Bennet would love life on a ship," said Captain Waters. He leaned back on one elbow and smiled at her. "She has the sort of adventurous spirit that would make her a delight as a companion."

"I am not sure about that. You forget I like walking. I am sure I should go out of my mind with boredom if I had nothing else to do but walk up and down on a deck."

"Perhaps, Miss Bennet, you do not yet know your mind? Perhaps you would make a perfect naval wife," suggested Miss Carter. Elizabeth gave her a sharp look, but the one she returned was innocent. "Perhaps Captain Waters should take you on a ship so you could see how you like it."

"Oh, I am sure I would like the novelty well enough for a short time. But for months on end? I think not. Besides, Captain Waters speaks in jest. He will not take anyone out to sea. He has come to settle here and will not take a ship again unless called back into service. Have you told the Miss Carters of your plans for a house, sir?"

Captain Waters obliged them with his ideas, but he did not seem happy to share them. Elizabeth listened and added some opinions of her own, which he took seriously.

As they spoke, Elizabeth thought she noticed Darcy regarding her thoughtfully. She met his eyes and gave a small smile which he did not return. She looked away in annoyance. What on earth ailed him? Why did he come today to be silent and grave?

"Such a house will require a mistress, sir," said Helen when Captain Waters finished his description. "You shall need to wed. A home such as the one you described should be filled with children." There was a knowing smile on her lips.

"Yes, you are right, Miss Helen. And I hope I shall not have to search too far," said Captain Waters. He smiled at Elizabeth. "What do you think, Miss Bennet? Should I find a wife close to home?"

"Oh, do not seek to make me your matchmaker," said Elizabeth with a laugh to cover her confusion. "It is far too hot for such matters. Find your own wife."

"Perhaps I have found her or will very soon."

"Perhaps." Maybe it was the heat that began to grow

oppressive, but Elizabeth suddenly felt irritated. She was tired of knowing looks and suggestive remarks, and now it seemed Captain Waters had joined in on it, although she understood he only did it to tease her.

Miss Carter stood up. Elizabeth saw how the eyes of both men moved towards her at once. She looked down at Darcy, and with the sun behind her, she looked like an angel. What man could resist her, even with her unfortunate origins?

"Mr. Darcy, you offered to show me the view from the very top. Will you take me there now? I have rested enough and this sitting around bores me."

"Gladly." Darcy rose at once. He took her arm and walked away without a backward glance.

Captain Waters' eyes followed them, then he glanced at Elizabeth. He could not speak his thoughts with Georgiana by her side, but Elizabeth thought she understood what he wished to communicate to her. *It seems Miss Rebecca Carter has made a conquest.*

Elizabeth was tempted to agree. She heartily wished Captain Waters had not invited the Miss Carters but then scolded herself for the ungenerous thought. Helen at least was pleasant company, and it would not be fair to deprive her of an enjoyable day out.

"Would you like to walk, Georgiana? There are still some places I would like to view, and it will be time to leave soon."

She took Georgiana's arm, and they walked on. They saw no sign of Darcy or Miss Carter, but Elizabeth reminded herself she did not care where they were or what they did together. It was none of her concern.

"Are you enjoying your day?" she asked her friend.

Georgiana gave her a radiant smile. "Oh, yes. I am so happy to be here. And the Miss Carters are pleasant, are they not? Miss Rebecca Carter is the most beautiful lady I have ever seen. Just standing by her side makes me feel like a tall oaf."

Elizabeth's laugh was strained. "I am sure she makes every woman feel like that. It seems unfair that so much beauty has been given to one lady."

"Captain Waters is amusing, is he not? I enjoyed his stories about his ship. He has lived such an exciting life! And he seems to like you very much. He is so attentive to you."

"He has been attentive to both of us," said Elizabeth evasively. It was true Captain Waters had paid her more attention that day than at any other time. It was as if he was determined to attach himself to her side, and it irked her. She did not wish for more rumors to spread. Even Georgiana and Miss Carter, reserved as they were, had now joined in the speculations about their possible union. It was as bad as being at Longbourn. "Come, look at that view. I can see Derby in the distance. Is it not splendid?"

"Do you like Captain Waters?" asked Georgiana. Her face was so eager, Elizabeth could not find it in her to feel annoyed. She smiled at her.

"I confess, I like him, but I am not sure whether it is a simple enjoyment of his company. I rather suspect it is. He is a pleasant enough fellow, but I can only imagine him as a good friend, not as a husband."

"I see."

"You disapprove?"

"Not at all." Georgiana looked shocked at the suggestion. "He is a fine fellow, but you understand your mind, and if you do not agree he is the man for you, you are the best judge. I am sure he would be disappointed. How could he not be? But you must be free to be with the man who is right for you."

Elizabeth smiled and hugged the girl. "You do not know

how much I appreciate hearing you say that. I have endured more smirks and suggestions than I can tolerate. You are a true friend, Georgiana."

Georgiana was pleased and flattered. For a moment, Elizabeth considered asking her for her thoughts on Darcy and Miss Carter but decided against it. No, she would not put her young friend in the uncomfortable situation of being pushed for information. If Darcy was drawn to Miss Carter, she would find out in her own good time.

# CHAPTER 29

$\mathcal{M}$rs. Younge looked up in surprise when the door to her chamber opened after only a brief knock.

"Miss Darcy," she cried, rising from her seat. "You are home. Did you enjoy yourself?" She came towards her and placed her hands on her shoulders to better look at her. "Oh, you have freckles." She bit her lip. "Well, no matter. I am sure it is nothing Gowland's cannot cure. I shall send for some right away, so your pretty looks are not spoiled."

Georgiana gently pulled herself from her grasp. Mrs. Younge's expression of concern increased.

"Whatever is the matter, child? You have never looked so serious. Did something happen? Did Miss Bennet say something to upset you? Come, you must tell me. It is not like you to march into someone's rooms in this manner."

Georgiana was nervous, but she forced herself to meet Mrs. Younge's eyes without flinching.

"Mrs. Younge, I have come to a decision. I mulled over for some time, and I hope my decision will not upset you."

"Oh?" Mrs. Younge sat back down and patted the seat beside her. "Sit down, dearest. You do not appear well."

"I fell perfectly well, thank you. I have rarely felt better." Georgiana took a deep breath and launched into the speech she had rehearsed over and over again on her way to Mrs. Younge's room. "I decided I do not wish to travel to Ramsgate with you just yet. I wish to extend my stay at Pemberley. If the weather is agreeable at the end of the summer, perhaps we might spend a few days before I return to London, but for now, I do not care to travel there. I am sure it will cause no inconvenience. At this time of the year, the inn will have no problem finding other guests for our rooms, so they will not be out of pocket."

Mrs. Younge stared at her as if she could not believe her ears. Her mouth opened and closed a few times, and she shook her head. She stared at Georgiana as if she did not recognize her.

"Miss Darcy, I must confess, I am disappointed," she said finally. "It is not like you to dismiss your commitments. I said as such to you when we first met Miss Bennet, and you promised me repeatedly with the most heartfelt assurances you would not go back on your word. And yet you have. I confess I do not know what to think. Is this Miss Bennet's influence? Does she pressure you to change your plans that she might use your friendship for her gain?"

"It is nothing of the sort." Georgiana's eyes watered, but she continued bravely. "Miss Bennet has been a true friend, and I am fond of her. As the visit to Ramsgate was for my benefit, I do not understand how I disappoint anyone else when I change my plans. The visit was supposed to be for my health, and if my health can flourish just as well here, it can be of no concern to anyone else if I do not go. I understand you were excited to see Ramsgate, but as I have said, we can go again later, or if the weather does not agree, there is always next year." She paused as a thought occurred to her, and her eyes lit up. "Mrs. Younge, would you like to visit Ramsgate? I am sure my brother would not mind if you traveled in my stead. You can stay in my rooms and have a lovely time. Come, you deserve it. You hardly left my side since you came to us."

Mrs. Younge shook her head. Her eyes were filled with sorrow.

"No, Miss Darcy, I should not like that. And while I agree the trip was for your benefit, that is not what concerns me about your change of heart. I confess I fear what it says about your character. Someone who is so easily influenced and persuaded away from their commitments is a person not to be relied on. I am sorry for speaking so, and I do not wish to hurt you, but as your companion and I hope your friend, I must tell you the truth even though it pains me to say it. I consider myself the guardian of your moral wellbeing just as much as your reputation."

Georgiana was stricken. "But may I not change my mind about a matter that concerns me? If others depend on me, I might agree with you, but as it is, this trip was for me, and only I am affected if I decide not to go. You were coming as my companion, and with all due respect, our stay in Ramsgate was not for you."

Mrs. Younge's hand flew to her mouth. She pressed her fingers to her lips and shook her head. "I am sorry. Forgive me. It is hard to hear you speak in such a way. To treat me as just a companion when I have been there for you all this time. It is harsh and cruel, and I know you do not mean it."

Georgiana softened at the sight of her tears. "I do not mean to hurt you, but I must speak for myself. It will cause no hardship to anyone if I do not go. If the inn cannot cover the cost of my room, my brother will do so. No one will be at a loss. I am sorry, Mrs. Younge, but I am determined to stay here."

Her breath was shallow as she struggled to take a deep breath. Her hands clenched together behind her back, willing herself to stand firm in the face of the other woman's unhappiness. Mrs. Younge slowly moved her hands away and gave her an assessing look. She sighed and shook her head.

"I am sure you see it that way. But if you are determined, I cannot move you. I will write to the inn and inform them you have gone back on your word to stay with them."

Georgiana felt a twist in her chest, but she refused to be moved.

"I am not the first person to cancel a booking, and I will not be the last. I made no vow to them. I changed my plans which is my right. Nothing more."

Mrs. Younge smiled. "Well, I will write to them. I beg you will excuse me so I might write the letter in peace. I will find you later."

Relieved the exchange was over, Georgiana left the room quickly. Once she closed the door, she pressed her back to it and released a breath.

She had done it! She had stood firm in the face of Mrs. Younge's displeasure and spoken up for herself. Elizabeth would be so pleased. She would go at once to tell her the good news.

Just as soon as her legs stopped shaking.

In agitation, Mrs. Younge paced the floor and chewed the skin beside her thumbnail. Of all times for the girl to grow a spine. It was all that Miss Bennet's fault. That pert madam put ideas in Georgiana's head and caused

189

her to become difficult and demanding. If she had stayed well enough away, Georgiana would never have dreamt of refusing her.

Now the plan had changed. Mrs. Younge paced to the window and looked with unseeing eyes over Pemberley Woods. She would have to find another way to bring them together. But what if the risk was too great? Could he be trusted to be discreet? He had an inflated sense of himself at times, which would make it difficult for him to lie low, but she did not see what else could be done.

She went to her desk and pulled out the hot-pressed paper, a gift she had persuaded Georgiana to buy her in London. Taking her pen, she began a letter.

*"My Dear George,*

*I am afraid there has been a change of plan. Our dear Miss Darcy has chosen this of all times to refuse me just when it is most inconvenient. She refuses to go to Ramsgate. She has made a new friend here, an impudent madam called Elizabeth Bennet. Georgiana is in her thrall, and I am afraid has given her the unpleasant habit of speaking up for herself.*

*Come here at once. Be as discreet as you can. Take rooms at the inn on Derby Road where no one will recognize you. Mr. Darcy cannot see you, or we might as well give up. I will find ways to bring her to you, and you must devise a way to woo her while convincing her to keep your presence here a secret from her brother. Do you think you can manage?*

*You must also convince her to keep your presence a secret from Elizabeth Bennet. She is sharp as a tack, and I am afraid might see through you. I do not doubt you could charm her, but it will waste precious time. An advantage to you coming here is it is much closer to Scotland, so at least that is in our favor.*

*Write at once and let me know when you will come. I will spend my time finding ways for you and Georgiana to meet, and I hope her old affection for you will do the trick.*

*I miss you very much. I look forward to seeing you again. It will be a relief to know you are here,*

*Yours,*

*Alice Younge.*

# CHAPTER 30

*E*lizabeth looked up and shielded her eyes from the sun. She smiled when she saw Georgiana run down the garden path towards her, her eyes sparkling.

"Oh, Elizabeth, I have done it. I cannot believe I had done it," she cried.

Elizabeth laughed and took her hands in hers. "You cannot believe you have done what? Whatever it is, I am impressed already."

"I told Mrs. Younge I would not travel to Ramsgate. I wish to stay in Pemberley for the summer."

"Ah." Elizabeth raised an eyebrow. "How did she take it? I cannot imagine she smiled and gave you her blessing."

Georgiana's face clouded. "Not exactly. She said she was disappointed in me and said it meant I could not be trusted to keep my word. I felt awful. I did not think it could be seen in that light."

"And you are right. It cannot. Why that is a ridiculous way to consider it. Plans change all the time, and it is not the end of the world. My uncle originally planned to accompany us to the Lakes, and he was obliged to stay in

London. Does that mean he is not capable of keeping commitments? I do not know where your Mrs. Younge gets such odd notions, but they are not yours to carry. Do not waste another thought on it. Now, shall we plan another outing?"

Georgiana sat beside her, and they chatted together, devising new schemes for exploring. As they spoke, Elizabeth looked up when she heard someone coming down the path to join them.

"Mr. Darcy," she said in surprise. "I did not know you were here."

"I accompanied my sister," he said briskly. She started a little at his abrupt tone.

"I see," she said, matching it with one of her own. After a pause, she could not resist adding, "Did you like our excursion? I am sure Miss Carter enjoyed all you showed her."

"The day was tolerable."

He said nothing and took a seat on the bench across from them. Elizabeth felt irritated. If he joined them just to be dull and miserable, she would not pay him any attention. She turned back to Georgiana and continued talking with her.

"Ah, Miss Bennet. There you are." Captain Waters' cheerful voice called across to them. He came down the garden and stood behind Elizabeth as he greeted the Darcys.

"Did you wish to find me for a particular purpose, Captain Waters?" asked Elizabeth.

"None at all but the pleasure of your company." He sat down beside her and began chatting with the girls with animation.

Darcy sat in silence until he stood up.

"I am afraid I must go." At Georgiana's crestfallen face, he added, "You need not leave with me. I can send the carriage for you later if you would prefer to stay."

"No need for that. We will make sure Miss Darcy returns home safely." Captain Waters smiled.

Darcy looked as if he would like to refuse. He hesitated and then gave a sharp nod. He bowed and left.

Captain Waters exchanged a glance with Elizabeth and shook his head.

"Odd fellow. Gets more peculiar all the time," he muttered so only she would hear. In a loud voice, he said, "Well, I have interrupted you long enough. I will leave you to talk together and will return to bring Miss Darcy home later."

He swept them a bow and left the same way Darcy did.


D arcy was not ready to return home yet. The idea of the empty house with no distractions from his thoughts of Elizabeth gave him no comfort. After driving his chaise around the lane and taking some pleasure from the pure country air, he decided to travel into Lambton to pass the time.

It seemed all in hand. Captain Waters' attitude towards Elizabeth spoke of an attachment and had a familiarity that could not be mistaken. Darcy was sure they had an understanding. Everything about them spoke of it. He could not travel into town without hearing people anticipate when the announcement might be made.

It tortured him, but what could he do? If Elizabeth preferred another man, he would not stand in her way. But something struck him as not quite right about Captain Waters. At first, his honest nature suggested it was his jealousy that made him believe he detected something untrustworthy about him. How could he like the man who courted the woman Darcy had begun to care for?

But it was not that. For Elizabeth's sake, he wished to

believe the man she might marry was worthy of her even if it were not him. And there was something secretive in Captain Waters' demeanor. He was sure the man was hiding something, but what it might be, Darcy could not say. He only desperately hoped it would not lead to Elizabeth being hurt.

He turned down the lane towards the parsonage and stopped. A sight was before him that made him pause. Without attracting attention, he turned the chaise around and went the other way.

Once out of view of the house, he stopped and chewed his lip. He would have to consider what to do. Elizabeth would not take kindly to what she would consider his interference, but he would not sit by and do nothing. He would need to find a way to put her on her guard.

# CHAPTER 31

*E*lizabeth had been pleased to receive Georgiana's note inviting her to spend the day with her at Pemberley. Their carriage arrived for her, and as she traveled down the lane towards the park, she recalled Darcy's odd temper the previous day. She only hoped he would not behave in the strange manner he had done before. If he did, she would spend all her time talking to Georgiana and ignore him as much as she could.

She had been sitting in the garden with Georgiana for an hour before she first saw him. He came down the path towards them. Elizabeth could have sworn there was something less decided in his manner than usual. She gave him a quick smile as he reached them.

"I hope you are well, Mr. Darcy?"

"Quite well."

Earl was with him, and he greeted Elizabeth with his usual ecstatic joy. She bent to stroke the dog's ears, and when she looked up, Darcy was watching her.

"This picture reminds me of when we first met. You were playing with Earl, and I did not know what to think of you."

"Oh, you knew what to think of me all right. You thought me a poacher," said Elizabeth with a smile. "You told me I should not know what a poacher looks like."

"Well, you should not. It is not the business of young ladies to know how poachers look."

Elizabeth rolled her eyes, but she was glad Darcy's manner had thawed a little.

He declined to take a seat with them and paced back and forth. Elizabeth found it distracting. She tried to engage Georgiana in conversation again but with difficulty. She glanced at Darcy out of the corner of her eye. He appeared to watch her, but he often looked at her, and there was nothing unusual in that. She was about to turn back to her friend but decided she would not let him get away with thinking she had not noticed him. She turned back and raised an eyebrow.

"Won't you join us, Mr. Darcy? I am sure you will wear a path into the earth if you continue on this way."

Darcy started and colored. "Forgive me. I was lost in my thoughts." He paused. "Georgiana, I almost forgot. Will you go to Mrs. Reynolds to discuss the menu with her? She is eager for your opinion." He smiled when his sister looked confused. "You are mistress of the house, after all," he reminded her gently. "And your opinion is of great importance."

Georgiana blushed but did not decline. She excused herself and ran lightly across the lawn.

"My sister is still a little reluctant to put herself forward," Darcy said in answer to Elizabeth's unspoken question. "Your influence has done her good, but she still does not exert her role in the house. I am sorry if I interrupted your conversation."

"I am sure she will return soon," said Elizabeth. She smoothed down her skirts. Darcy continued to watch her. He appeared to be trying to work something out. "What is it, Mr. Darcy?" She smiled to keep the annoyance from her tone. "You look at me as if I am a puzzle you cannot make out. Do I perplex you, sir?"

"You know, you do not." He smiled. "You have great enjoyment in expressing opinions that are not your own."

"For shame. You will teach people not to believe a word I say. How ungallant of you."

"Will you walk with me, Miss Bennet?"

Elizabeth was surprised but not unwilling. She took his offered arm, and they strolled down the path towards the shrubbery.

"Forgive me for my silence just now," said Darcy. "You will have wondered at it."

"Yes, just a little."

"You mentioned gallantry, and that has been my difficulty. I have a problem before me, and I cannot tell which is the gallant approach and which is not."

Elizabeth tensed. "Yes?" she asked sharply. "Is there a problem with my friendship with Georgiana, sir?"

Darcy was astonished. "Of course not. None at all. I have told you how much I delight in it."

"What is it, then?"

He hesitated and stopped to examine the leaves on a bush. "Holly," he said. "We will gather it at Christmas and decorate the house with it."

"That sounds delightful, but you did not bring me here to talk about holly," said Elizabeth pertly.

Darcy walked on. "It is a delicate subject, and I am hardly skilled at conversation at the best of times. I hope you will forgive me if my words come out clumsily."

Elizabeth nodded. He stopped and turned to face her. They were out of sight of the house by now. He still held her arm in his. Elizabeth looked at the distance they had come, and a sneaking suspicion came over her. He had sent Georgiana away. He had invited her to walk with him and took her out of sight of the house. He was embarrassed and spoke of gallantry and delicate subjects. Was it possible he...? No, it could not be. She would not allow herself to believe it.

But her heart continued to pound, and she could hardly bring herself to meet his eyes.

"Miss Bennet." Darcy took a deep breath.

"Yes, Mr. Darcy?" Elizabeth murmured.

"May I ask the extent of your acquaintance with Captain Waters?"

Elizabeth blinked. Whatever she had been expecting from him, it was not this.

"May I ask why?"

He frowned. "I am aware it is an odd question. But I must ask. Your aunt and his mother are friends but do you know the man well? How familiar are you with his character?"

Elizabeth could have laughed at her foolishness. To think she had dared believe he would declare an attachment to her. It was how Kitty or Lydia would think, and here she was, falling into the same vain trap.

"You know I have not known him long. Only since coming here. But we have spent several weeks in one another's company. I should say I am well acquainted with him. Very well, I am sure."

Darcy looked over her head into the distance. He swallowed. "And how trustworthy is he?"

"I should say he is very trustworthy. Mr. Darcy, may I know where these questions tend? I cannot make you out."

Darcy paused. "Have you ever had reason to suspect Captain Waters is not all he says he is?"

"I beg your pardon?"

"Do you have reason to suspect he is hiding something?"

Elizabeth pulled her arm from Darcy's and took a step back. "Why on earth would you accuse him of hiding something? What is he hiding?"

"I hardly know." Darcy looked at a loss, far different from his occasional haughty self. "It is difficult for me to say for sure. But I merely wished to put you on your guard."

"Put me on my guard for what?" Elizabeth's irritation was growing. "Captain Waters has been nothing but pleasant and welcoming to my aunt and me since we arrived in Derbyshire. He has been all ease and friendliness. I see no reason to arouse suspicions. He is a fine man, and I am proud to be his friend."

An idea struck her. A memory of Captain Waters teasing Georgiana about marrying a sailing man so she may travel. Darcy had come along at just that moment and had not seemed pleased. Of course. That was his concern. "I believe I know the nature of your worry," she said. "And it is ill-founded. I will not name names as this conversation has been indelicate enough as it is, but I can assure you there is no need for your concern."

"You know my worry?" Darcy's eyebrows came together in a frown though whether it was anger or concern, Elizabeth could not say.

"I do. You suspect him of trifling with a lady, do you not? That is what you mean by his untrustworthiness? Well, I can assure you there is nothing of the sort going on. Believe me, I am in a position to know."

Far from reassuring him, Darcy reacted as if she had slapped him. He stared at her, and a closed, guarded expression came over his face.

"The day is rather warm," he said. "I shall escort you back

to the house." He offered her his arm, but Elizabeth was too annoyed to take it.

"I am not too warm. I shall stay out a while longer."

"As you wish." Darcy bowed to her and walked away.

Elizabeth shook her head. Did he consider Captain Waters so dishonest he would court Darcy's fifteen-year-old sister right under his nose? She was sure if Captain Waters had any designs of the sort, he would declare them openly. Besides, she suspected he made his interest in Elizabeth herself quite clear. Miss Darcy was in no danger of being whisked away to become the new Mrs. Waters.

"Miss Bennet."

Elizabeth turned around. Darcy had stopped. His expression was still guarded, but his next words took her by surprise.

"I believe we are safe from whoever was harassing my tenants. If you wish to walk in the woods again, they are at your disposal." He gave a curt bow then walked away.

Georgiana eventually came out to join her. She spoke about her menu choices and was anxious that Elizabeth should approve them, but Elizabeth could hardly take it in. She smiled and nodded but still felt too annoyed at Darcy's words. It was disrespectful for Darcy to accuse Captain Waters of such designs. And even if he suspected him, why should he come to her? Why did he not speak to his sister or, indeed, Captain Waters directly? For him to involve her struck her as cowardice. Did he wish her to go to Captain Waters and put him on his guard because he did not dare himself? She did not like such underhanded behavior, which struck her as going against everything she believed Mr. Darcy to be. He had always seemed so direct and honorable. Even too direct at times. When she considered it, she wondered if that was the real cause of her irritation; her disappointment that Darcy was not the straightforward, noble man she took him to be.

She declined Georgiana's invitation to stay for dinner, citing her aunt as an excuse. When Georgiana stood on the steps to see her off, Darcy was nowhere to be seen.

# CHAPTER 32

Elizabeth did not see Mr. Darcy over the next two weeks. He did not accompany his sister to Trillings, and when she visited Pemberley, he was not in sight. Georgiana told her he had matters to attend on his estate, but even she seemed distracted of late. Her visits to Trillings had tapered off slightly. Elizabeth was worried Darcy had put the idea in her head she was not safe around Captain Waters. Sometimes, Elizabeth noticed she stared off into the distance with color in her cheek, and frequently, Elizabeth had to repeat a question while Georgiana stared at her blankly and blinked.

"Georgiana, you are quite in another world," she told her one morning as they walked around the garden. "Whatever is the matter? Has something upset you? Is all well?" She tried to keep her voice light to hide her worry.

"Forgive me, Elizabeth. I am being rude, am I not? I find it hard to concentrate." She chewed her lip.

"Sometimes, speaking with another can help with a problem," said Elizabeth gently. "I hope you know you can speak with me if anything concerns you?"

Georgiana looked back towards the house. The family was inside and in no danger of intruding on them. Captain Waters had gone to Derby, so they would not need to worry about him joining them and overhearing their conversation.

"I must ask you, Elizabeth - I hardly know how to say it, and I beg you not to think me foolish."

"I could never think you foolish."

"You are very kind." She played with a loose curl hanging over her shoulder, and although her expression was worried, there was something in her eyes Elizabeth could not put her finger on.

"Elizabeth, may I ask if you have ever been in love?"

Elizabeth recoiled slightly at the question. It was not at all what she had been expecting. Her mind at once went to Mr. Darcy, and she forced it away firmly. She would not ask herself why his face should come to mind at the mention of being in love. It was only because of their last conversation about his sister and nothing more.

"I — I cannot say. I do not know," she said uneasily. "May I ask why you wish to know?"

"I hope I am not indelicate..."

"Not at all. I am merely surprised." She smiled. "Has someone taken your eye?" Her mind flew again to her last conversation with Darcy, and she felt uneasy. Had he been right after all? No, he could not be. It was one thing for Georgiana to fancy herself in love with Captain Waters. It was quite another for him to court her when he was more than ten years her senior, and she was only just fifteen. She tried to hide the anxiety from her face as she waited for Georgiana's response.

"Yes, he has," she said slowly. "But it is difficult to understand how I feel. I think of him all the time. I look forward to seeing him again. I feel a constant fluttering, and I do not know if it is fear or excitement."

Elizabeth nodded, once again pushing thoughts of Darcy from her mind. "Am I acquainted with the gentleman?" She willed her young friend to say no.

"No, you have not met him. I knew him once before and had not seen him in some time, but now he has returned..." Her eyes widened, and she took a deep breath. "He is all I can think about."

Elizabeth took a seat on a bench and patted the spot beside her. Georgiana sat down and stared off into the distance chewing her lip.

"Have you seen much of him?" she asked.

Georgiana blushed and gave her a self-conscious smile. "I confess I have. You will think me very sly, but I have seen him several times this week."

"And your brother..?"

Georgiana's face clouded over. "Ah. There is the difficulty. It is the place where I feel most shame. I have not told Fitzwilliam of my meetings. I cannot. George begged me not to until the time is right."

Elizabeth frowned. Something about this made her uneasy. She would have to tread carefully. While Georgiana possessed none of the pig-headed stubbornness of her younger sisters, she understood young girls had a perverse habit of cleaving strongly to any young man they were warned against. She was not sure if Georgiana were such a young lady, but the risk was a concern.

"I admit, that gives me some unease," she said carefully. "Why should he ask you to keep his presence and his interest in you a secret from your brother? Why not court you openly?"

"I do not understand the particulars," said Georgiana. "He

has known my family all his life. He and my brother used to be close, but they fell out over a matter. I am still not clear on the details, but he tells me it was a misunderstanding. My brother is proud — I love him, but it is true, as I am sure you have noticed. George returned out of a desire to renew his friendship with my brother, but he wishes to go about it correctly. He did not expect to see me again. It has been several years, and I suppose I am grown up now..." She broke away and blushed.

"And has he made any attempt to speak to your brother?"

"He wrote a letter, but it was returned unopened. He even showed it to me, and it was so handsomely written and spoke of his true heart and good character. I was disappointed my brother would not read it. George begged me not to intervene. He said this is between him and Fitzwilliam, and he will do what he can to mend bridges in his way. And now he says he has an added incentive." She blushed even deeper.

"Very noble of him, I'm sure," said Elizabeth. She still did not feel easy about the affair, but she had to admit, she could imagine Darcy being the sort of man whose pride would prevent him from wishing to renew an old friendship. He was not a man who would admit his faults readily. But it might not be so simple. "Have you no inkling what caused this separation? Forgive me for speaking so frankly, dear Georgiana, and I hope you take it in the spirit it is intended. You know I only have your best interests at heart. But is it possible whatever they fought over was so dreadful, your brother has good reason not to see him again?"

Georgiana swung her legs lightly. Her hands were folded in her lap, making her seem much younger than her fifteen years.

"I confess, the same idea did occur to me. But George insists it was just a misunderstanding. They both said things they did not mean, and George said he is anxious to make amends for his side of it even if Fitzwilliam never forgives him. But of course, now he has met me, it is even more important my brother forgives him."

"Has he proposed to you?" Elizabeth looked at her directly.

"In a manner. He has told me he loves me and wishes to take care of me. He said he could not say the words directly until he knew where matters stand with Fitzwilliam, but he has made his intentions as clear as he can. He said he is willing to do anything for us to be together."

"And do you wish to marry him?"

"I think so." Georgiana twisted her hands and tugged at the edges of her shawl. "Maybe? I do not know. Perhaps I do. He is not an acquaintance of a week. I have known him for many years. He loves me so much, and I think I feel the same. He was so good to me when I was a child. He would devote hours to my amusement, and nothing was too much trouble for him. And now, here he is, wishing to make amends for a falling out. I believe that does him credit."

"I am sure it does," said Elizabeth slowly. She looked around the garden. Summer was at its height. The trees were full and green. Had she really been in Derbyshire so long? "I cannot tell you what to do, of course, but I will say the subterfuge makes me uneasy. But perhaps it is as you say. Perhaps it is best if he wishes to make amends to Mr. Darcy in his way. And the fact that he will not make a positive declaration until he knows where matters stand speaks of his good sense. Just be careful, dearest. You are a sensible girl and will take your time to understand what you are about."

Georgiana smiled and seemed almost ready to worship her for this advice.

"I will be careful. But I confess, it is hard to be sensible. Every time I am away from him, I long to be with him again."

Elizabeth smiled, but her uneasiness increased. She only hoped her young friend would realize the importance of telling her brother before her reputation was compromised.

"Do not look so uneasy, Elizabeth," said Georgiana. She smiled at the worry in her friend's eyes. "I never see him unaccompanied. I am in no danger."

"Of course not. But if it goes on much longer and the matter is still unsettled between him and Mr. Darcy, I would urge you to speak with your brother. It is always best when these things are out in the open."

# CHAPTER 33

*E*lizabeth was out of spirits for the remainder of the day. Georgiana left soon after their conversation, eager to meet her mysterious suitor. Her relief at having unburdened herself to Elizabeth was great, but it left Elizabeth uneasy. She decided it was a good thing Darcy avoided her as she was not sure how she would behave around him, knowing she was keeping such a secret.

But she would have faith in Georgiana's good sense. Georgiana loved her brother. She would not willingly do anything to cause him pain. And she assured Elizabeth if the matter dragged on, she would speak to him herself. Perhaps if Darcy understood his sister's happiness depended on him putting aside his pride and making amends with his old friend, he would accept the offered olive branch, and they would make peace.

But Elizabeth was still unsatisfied with the situation. Something did not sit well with her. There must have been more she could have done. Why did she not persuade Georgiana to decline her meeting with her gentleman until she had spoken with Darcy first? Elizabeth did not believe she had done right by her young friend there. She regretted her decision almost as soon as Georgiana was out of sight. She had been about to run after her to persuade her not to see him again until the matter was settled with her brother, but she resisted the temptation. She would see Georgiana tomorrow. She would urge her to talk to Darcy then.

Captain Waters was still away. He left early that morning to visit Derby and had not returned. Elizabeth felt too restless to stay in the house. After sitting in the garden trying to lose herself in a book, she decided she needed a long walk.

And she knew just where she would go. Pemberley Woods was at her disposal once again. On a summer evening, it would appear even more beautiful than it had the first morning she saw it. If she did not encounter Mr. Darcy with a gun again, she would have a pleasant walk.

There was no sign of another person. The trees swayed gently in the evening breeze. Birds called to one another, and the undergrowth rustled with the presence of timid woodland creatures. Elizabeth's boots crunched pleasantly through the springy loam, and she took deep breaths to relish the pure air. She tilted her head back to admire the blue sky through the tops of trees. Was there anything more delightful than this? She would feel like a queen if she had all this at her disposal. No wonder Georgiana had been so keen to remain in Pemberley, and no wonder Darcy rushed back home as soon as an opportunity presented itself. She did not blame them. If she had a chance to spend her life here, she would take it in a moment.

Despite the late hour, the heat of the day remained. She had run along the path clutching her bonnet in her hand to enjoy the exercise, and she was soon out of breath and sweating. A sound caught her ear, and she wiped the sweat from her forehead as she paused to listen. It was the welcome noise of a stream. She picked her way through the undergrowth, trying to avoid catching her clothes in the snags when she reached it.

The stream was quite wide. It foamed and bubbled over the stones, and its clear water was inviting. It was perfect for her purposes. She pulled the pins from her hair and shook it out so it fell over her shoulders. The heat of the day was in danger of giving her a headache with it bound so tight.

Elizabeth kicked off her half-boots and picked her way to the water. She held up her skirts and allowed it to run over her ankles. It was deliciously cool. She bent down and splashed her face and arms, then drank from her cupped hands. She looked all around her and sighed with pleasure. Here she was, all alone in nature, not another soul around. She was free from pins and shoes that pinched and could enjoy her surroundings as she was meant to. It was perfect.

A large, flat rock sat in the middle of the stream. The water surged all around it, but the top was high enough out of the water to provide a dry seat. She picked her way carefully through the water, wobbling now and then as her foot caught a stone. She clambered up onto the rock and allowed her legs to dangle in the water, kicking them back and forth to let it splash up her legs.

Covered up as she was most of the time, it was a giddy sensation. If her mother saw her now, her shrieks would send the birds flying from the trees in alarm. She smiled at the thought. Her mother was far away. No one knew she was here. She could be as free as she liked. Nature did not have rules about how she should behave or dress.

She leaned back on her elbows, still kicking her legs in the water as she looked up at the azure sky. Birds circled lazily overhead. The breeze tempered the heat and made it just right, blowing through her loose hair and cooling her neck. She allowed her mind to wander as she gazed up at the blue sky and the vibrant trees.

"I heard we had nymphs in these woods, but I never expected to encounter one."

The voice cut through her daydreams. Elizabeth bolted upright with a cry and looked around wildly at the same time, hastily rearranging her skirts back over her legs.

To her horror, Darcy stood at the water's edge. He wore no jacket and looked much as he had the first time she had seen him apart from the lack of a gun over his shoulder. His sleeves were rolled up, and he looked a million miles away from the formal man he so often appeared to be.

And he had seen her like this. Elizabeth felt the heat rise up her neck as she scrambled for some semblance of dignity.

"Mr. Darcy," she said. "I did not know you were there."

"Evidently."

Suddenly, her lazy mood vanished, chased away with anger.

"What are you about, sneaking up on me like that?"

His brow furrowed.

"I did not sneak up on you." His heated tone declared him highly offended. "I spoke to alert you to my presence as soon as I saw you."

Elizabeth climbed down from the rock. He held out a hand to help her across. She was about to refuse but grudgingly took it. With her luck, she would decline his offer in a fit of pride, only to stumble on a rock and fall at his feet in the water. She felt foolish enough without wishing to add more to it.

"Thank you," she said coldly. She glared up at him. He

returned her look with one she could not decipher. "You need not mock me," she said.

"Mock you?" Darcy's eyebrows flew up. "When did I mock you?"

"Your remarks about nymphs. I trust you did not mean it in any other light."

"I do not know where you got such an idea. Are you suggesting nymphs are repulsive beings, and one would only wish to call a lady such to insult her? If that is the case, I should like to see your childhood books, Miss Bennet. Mine portrayed them quite differently."

Once again, he seemed more at ease with himself out here in the woods in casual clothes. Apart from their last encounter, he had grown easier and more relaxed in her presence, but it was nothing to how he appeared now.

He sighed. "I own I am astonished you could take my remark in any other light than the one I intended, but to be clear, I meant it as a compliment. You made a fetching picture, lying there in the center of the stream. If I were an artist, I would have begged leave to paint you."

Elizabeth could not think of a response to that. She continued to glare at him, still unwilling to let go of her embarrassment.

"Where are my boots?"

"Your boots?" Darcy blinked.

"My boots. You do not think I walked here barefoot, do you?"

"May I say it would not have surprised me if you had?"

Elizabeth pushed past him and found her boots where she had left them with her stockings. Behind her, she heard Darcy give a low laugh. She sat on a tree stump and looked up at him. He raised an eyebrow and turned away politely to allow her to dress in privacy.

"I wondered if you had taken advantage of my woods," he said as she pulled on her stockings and boots. "I have walked them many times myself over the past few days, but I did not meet you."

"I only came today. I have been attending other matters."

"No doubt." His voice was suddenly cooler.

He turned around when she was ready. She knelt on the loamy woodland floor, pushing aside leaves and twigs.

"Have you missed something?"

"My hairpins. I thought I had put them in my pocket, but I have either lost them in the stream or laid them with my boots, and now I cannot find them. They are not here." She sighed. "Perhaps I left them on the rock."

Before she could say anything else, Darcy walked back down to the stream. He strode over the rocks until he reached the one where she'd been resting.

"There are no pins here," he called over the sound of the rushing water. "I am afraid they are gone, Miss Bennet."

Elizabeth clicked her tongue and continued to search around her pins. She looked back to see Darcy still standing on the rock, looking up among the trees as she had been doing when he found her.

"You know, I can understand the attraction of lying here. There is a feeling of peace in being surrounded by nature with all cares of the human world behind us."

He looked so handsome in his shirt sleeves, his hair tousled, Elizabeth had to look away.

"When you are quite finished, Oberon," she said tartly. Darcy looked at her in amusement and leaped back to her side with the same easy strides as before.

"Interesting you call me that. I had thought of you as a Titania when I saw you."

Elizabeth rolled her eyes. "Nonsense."

"Not nonsense. I speak as I find. Now, can I escort you anywhere?"

"I can find my way home."

Darcy gave her a searching look, then nodded. He gave her a brief bow and stood back to allow her to find her way through the undergrowth again.

# CHAPTER 34

*T*he undergrowth was thicker than Elizabeth recalled. Surely it had been much easier to walk when she first made her way through here? Had there been so many trees? She did not remember that fellow lying on its side as if it had been struck by a storm.

She looked around and chewed her lip. Perhaps it was that direction? She started to walk, but the growth was even thicker and snagged her frock. She grabbed her hem to release it from the brambles, biting back an unladylike curse of frustration. How on earth was she to get out of here?

She looked back at the way she had come. There was only one thing she could do. She could only hope he had not left, but somehow she doubted it. She had a feeling he was still there waiting for her until he was satisfied she was safe. She started to trudge through the undergrowth towards the stream. Her frock snagged again, and as she struggled to free it, she stumbled forward into a pair of strong arms. She cried out and recoiled at once. Darcy's hands went to her waist to steady her before he released her.

"I assumed you knew where you were going, but when I

heard you thrashing about, I thought I should investigate," he said.

Elizabeth struggled to regain her breath. Darcy raised his hand to her face. She stared at him, too astonished to move. What on earth was he doing? He touched her hair, and she could not breathe. The blood pounded in her ears and only subsided when she felt a gentle pull on her hair, and he held up a twig.

"Thank you," she murmured. Feeling slightly dazed, she took it from him as if he'd offered her a flower. When she realized what she had done, she quickly threw it to one side and tried to look as if that was what she'd intended all along. She swallowed.

"Which way do I go?"

Darcy looked over her head around the woods.

"Hmm. It has been a long time since I have been in this part of the woods. Not since I was a boy. Let us return to the stream, and we will find our bearings from there."

Elizabeth nodded. She pulled at her frock and stumbled again as it came loose. Darcy caught her hand to prevent her from falling, and without realizing what she was doing, she curled her fingers around his. Hand in hand, they helped one another through the tangle of thickets and briars, one reaching for the other when they stumbled.

Finally, they found their way back to the stream. Darcy strode down to the water and looked about him. He still held Elizabeth's hand in his, and she wondered if he noticed or if she should mention it. She decided against it. After all, the ground was still uneven. It was better they continue to hold on to one another in case one of them should need it. That was the only reason. If she told herself that emphatically enough, she might even believe it herself.

"I came upon you — upon the stream from this angle." He

pointed with his free hand. Elizabeth turned to face the stream from the direction he came.

"I did something similar. Why did you come upon the stream, by the way? There is no path to it. I just crashed through the bushes when I heard the sound."

"I imagine I did something similar. The evening was still hot, and when I heard the stream, I wished to cool off."

Elizabeth shivered. The sun had sunk lower in the sky, and twilight had fallen. Midges swarmed about them in the late summer evening. Twilight was long at that time of the year, but it would not last forever, and her aunt would worry.

"It is not so warm now."

Darcy nodded. "And you have been splashing in the water. Part of your frock is wet. That cannot help."

Elizabeth scowled, and he shook his head. "I am not making fun of you. Come, let us go this way. I am sure this will take us to a path."

Still hand in hand, they made their way through the thickets. Elizabeth was growing tired, but she would not admit to it. But oddly enough, she did not wish the adventure to end. Walking hand in hand through the woods with Mr. Darcy — there were worse ways to spend an evening.

"I am surprised you came out alone," said Darcy. "Although I am not sure why I should be. I know you enjoy your own company."

For a moment, Elizabeth thought he referred to Georgiana, and she tensed. Did he suspect her whereabouts? She had almost forgotten about Georgiana's meeting with her suitor. She did not care to be reminded of it when she was in Darcy's presence.

"I would have thought Captain Waters would come with you. He does not enjoy walking?"

"Captain Waters is away at present, in Derby. He will not return until tonight."

"I am sure that is a hardship."

Elizabeth released a frustrated huff. "I do not understand why you have taken such a dislike to him. Your suspicions are unfounded. He has been nothing but kind to you. But let us not speak of him. It will only irritate us both."

Darcy said nothing. She looked up at him. His jaw was set as he helped her over a branch that blocked their path.

Surely he did not still suspect Captain Waters of trifling with his sister? It was a ludicrous idea. However, Elizabeth knew he was not far wrong. Georgiana had a secret suitor, but his suspicions did not come from her behavior. Only Captain Waters caused him concern.

But that was often the way. Men were frequently disposed to see suspicion in other men while their female relatives' behavior passed them by unnoticed.

"My sister had the pleasure of seeing you today?" he suggested.

"She did." Elizabeth blushed. "We spent a pleasant after-noon in the garden."

"I was worried you two had a falling out."

She looked up in surprise. "A falling out? Georgiana and I? Of course not. Why should you think such a thing?"

"My sister has been quiet lately. She keeps to herself more and seems distracted. I was concerned something had happened between you, especially after my words a few weeks ago. I am delighted to hear it has not come between you."

"Why should it? That conversation was between us. I did not speak of it to Georgiana." She was about to say she, too, had been afraid their conversation had come between her friendship with Georgiana but caught herself at the last moment. To do so would be to bring the conversation around to dangerous territory.

*Oh, Georgiana, what are you about? You must speak with your brother. You cannot keep this from him. It will hurt him, and it forces me to lie to him. Why did I not persuade you to return home?*

"I am glad. But I am still concerned about her behavior. This morning, I invited her to walk with me tonight, and she made an excuse of being tired and wishing to retire early. I feel I am out of my depth at parenting a young girl her age."

Elizabeth kept her face turned to the undergrowth so he would avoid seeing the color there. This was not right.

Georgiana had invited Elizabeth to tea the following evening at Pemberley. She would talk to her then and tell her she must speak with her brother. If this George was honorable, he would not wish her to deceive Darcy.

"She is at a trying age," said Elizabeth carefully. "I am sure if she wishes to speak with you, she will do so in her own time."

Darcy nodded. He stopped walking for a moment and looked as if he was about to say something else. Elizabeth's heart raced, dreading his next words, words that could oblige her to either betray her friend or tell an outright lie to a man she — well, she would not think about that now.

Whatever he was about to say, Darcy had changed his mind. "Perhaps you are right," was all he said.

They walked on, and Elizabeth felt a rush of shame. No, this could not go on. As soon as she arrived at Pemberley the next day, she would speak to her friend alone and impress her with the vital importance of talking to Darcy.

She was still picturing the conversation she would have when Darcy used his free hand to bring her to a stop.

"What is the — "

"Shh!"

Elizabeth looked at him in bewilderment. He was tense, his whole body prepared for — what she could not say. His grip on her hand tightened, and he appeared to be straining to hear something. She listened as well.

At first, she heard nothing but the rustling of trees and the breathing of the man by her side. Nothing to cause alarm.

But then she heard it. A thrashing sound through the overgrowth. Then another sound. She could have sworn it sounded like chickens but smothered somehow.

Instinctively she moved closer to Darcy. Just as instinctively, he wrapped his arm around her and drew her close to his side and a little behind him. The pair peered through the gloom. The twilight had deepened, and the night was almost upon them, making it difficult to see.

"Wait here, Miss Bennet," Darcy whispered in her ear.

She looked up at him in alarm.

"What are you about?"

"I believe we may be about to meet our thief. I was wrong about him having finished with us."

"But you know there's a chance he might be armed. What do you propose to do?" Elizabeth gripped his arm to prevent him from charging off as if she could have stopped him.

"It is dark. If I can come upon him without him seeing me — "

"Out of the question," Elizabeth snapped back in a fierce whisper. "You would just as easily get yourself shot. This is foolhardy!"

"If he is armed, I shall do nothing. But I may see his face. The moon is coming out. I might see him without him seeing me."

"And you might just as well get shot." She glared up at him, and he met her glare with a look as stubborn as her own. "Fine. If you mean to do this, I am going with you."

"What? Elizabeth, do not be ridiculous."

"No more than you are being."

"It is out of the question — "

This time it was Elizabeth who held up her hand. The sounds came closer. A voice carried over the night air. They could not make out individual words, but it sounded like...

"Is he singing?"

"Yes. Thievery makes him cheerful."

The sound passed them by. There was far less thrashing coming from the person's direction than had come from theirs.

"He seems to have fared better than us and found a better path," said Darcy. "All right, Miss Bennet. Stay by my side. We shall follow him from a distance."

Elizabeth nodded, satisfied with the plan. But then she felt him press her even tighter to his side. He bent his head so his face was only inches from hers. She could hardly breathe as she looked up at him.

"But if I tell you to run, you will do as I say and run. Is that understood?"

Too shocked by his closeness, Elizabeth simply nodded. He did not move away. The moon passed above them, lighting his face, and she could see the glint in his eyes as he looked at her. His eyes dropped to her lips, then, with a sigh, he moved back.

"Let us go then."

Elizabeth felt a wave of disappointment wash over her, but she could do nothing else but nod. "Let us go."

# CHAPTER 35

*T*he path was close to where they had stood. If they hadn't been distracted by the sound of the thief, they should have soon reached it. They paused to catch the faint clucking of poultry, and Darcy nodded. They followed at a distance, keeping well back.

"There he is," Darcy whispered.

Elizabeth looked to where he gestured with their entwined hands. In the moonlight, she could make out a man perhaps a few years older than Darcy. He had taken a seat on a rock and opened a sack before him. The sound of protesting chickens came to them louder than ever, and Darcy's jaw set.

"I wonder which of my poor tenants have lost the fruit of their hard work this evening? All because this man decided he had the right to take what others have worked for without exerting himself. I despise people like this."

"Do not let it overwhelm you," Elizabeth said. "Remember, you are no help to your tenants if you get yourself injured."

"I will not allow it to overwhelm me." His face still

looked angry. He leaned out to get a better look. The thief had forced the chickens back inside, and their squawking had calmed to an occasional cluck. He took out a pipe and lit it.

"I do not believe he has a weapon," said Darcy. "I am going to confront him while he is here."

"What?" Elizabeth stared at him in alarm and tightened her grip on his hand. "Do not be foolish. Just because you cannot see a weapon, it does not mean he doesn't have one. You could get yourself killed. Remember what he did to your tenant."

"That is what I remember."

"You need not confront him. We can see him quite clearly from here. We can describe him to the magistrate. I am confident a fellow like this is already known to him."

Darcy continued to watch the man. Elizabeth could not tell what he was thinking by his expression.

"Mr. Darcy, I beg you not to do this," she whispered.

He looked down at her, and something about the expression on her face made his eyes soften. Almost absently, he ran his thumb along her knuckles in a comforting gesture.

"As you wish." He glanced back at the man and shook his head. "I will have this fellow brought to justice. I will not have him terrorize my tenants."

"He will," said Elizabeth. She was almost dizzy with relief. "Come, shall we leave him be and find our way out?"

"I should like to follow him and discover where he goes. Not all the way, but if I can see his direction, it might give me information for the magistrate. But I understand if you do not wish it."

Elizabeth glanced at the man. They had followed him a little distance without attracting his notice. Surely they could do it a little longer. She nodded.

"Let's hope he hurries up with this pipe. If he tarries every time he comes to a tree stump, we shall be here all night."

Darcy gave a low laugh.

The man eventually finished smoking and walked on. Darcy and Elizabeth followed at a distance, keeping close to the trees that they might slip between them if he turned around. The moonlight that allowed them to follow with ease would also prove their undoing if he turned quickly.

"Do you know what direction this is?" whispered Elizabeth.

"This path leads directly to the mountains. There are some small hamlets there, and the people mainly keep to themselves."

"Good places for a thief to hide out, then."

The man walked on, and Elizabeth and Darcy grew more confident. He believed himself all alone and did not suspect for a moment he might be followed.

A sound came ahead. As soon as Darcy heard it, he pulled Elizabeth with him behind a tree. He kept an arm around her while he peered out. Elizabeth recognized the dawning horror on his face.

"What is it?"

"Keiths."

"He is coming towards him?"

Darcy nodded grimly.

"You must wait here, Miss Bennet."

"What are you going to do?"

"I cannot allow Keiths confront this fellow alone. He has seen him. Wait here."

Elizabeth nodded and reluctantly stood back.

"What are you doing — HEY!"

She leaned forward to see Keiths running towards the thief. To her horror, the thief dropped the chickens and drew

225

out a pistol. He aimed it at Keiths, who skidded to a halt. Darcy still advanced on the man who was too focused on Keiths to notice him.

"Go back the way you came, or I'll shoot," said the man. Keiths put his hands up and backed away.

At that moment, Darcy grabbed him from behind. As he swung him around, his gun fired. Keith tumbled to the ground, and Elizabeth cried out in horror. Darcy grabbed his arm and pulled him around, trying to wrestle the weapon from his grasp. The man kicked backward, and Darcy stumbled, almost releasing him before catching him again.

Elizabeth could not bear it. Keiths on the ground and Darcy struggling with an armed man. Promise or not, she would not stand there while he fought alone. She moved among the trees and ran swiftly through them. She found a tree branch that was coming loose. It might serve as a weapon. She grasped it and twisted it, struggling to snap it free. She glanced towards the fight and cried out as the thief swung his gun on Darcy and fired. Darcy ducked and lunged at him. Almost sobbing with urgency, she gave the branch one last twist, and it came loose. She picked it up and rushed out onto the path, throwing herself in front of the thief.

Unknown to Elizabeth, she made a startling sight. With her hair loose and filled with leaves and twigs, her pale blue frock bleached white by the moonlight, torn about the hems and covered with stains from the wood, and the moon lighting up her face, she looked more ethereal than human. The sight of her startled the thief so much he let out a high-pitched scream and scrambled backward to get away from her.

Darcy lunged for the gun. The thief was startled back to attention and tried to aim it at her, but he was too slow. Darcy brought his hand down on his arm and forced him to drop it, then pushed him back against a tree. Elizabeth ran forward and picked up the gun. She ran towards Keiths. She was weak with relief when he struggled to sit up, rubbing his head.

"Are you hurt?" she asked anxiously. She knelt beside him and examined him for wounds. Apart from one on his head, there were no other injuries.

"He didn't shoot me," he replied. "I jumped out of the way, and like a fool, I bumped my head."

Elizabeth helped him to his feet. He shook his head, still slightly woozy. The focus in his eyes grew sharper. "I am alright now. Not the first time I've banged my head and probably won't be the last."

"If you two are done getting reacquainted," said Darcy through gritted teeth. "Perhaps you'd like to assist me?"

Keiths ran towards him and grabbed the man's other arm. Knowing he was defeated, he had lapsed into a sullen silence. Darcy was much larger than him, and Keiths, though slight, had a wiry strength. Between the two of them, the man knew there was no chance of getting away.

As they pulled him along the paths towards Pemberley, Darcy turned to Elizabeth.

"I thought I told you to stay where you were."

"You did. And I might have done if I hadn't thought Keiths shot and you about to be the same."

"What did you think you would do?"

"Distract him and grab the gun while you captured him," she said pertly.

Darcy shook his head and then laughed. "Well, I cannot argue you succeeded in your aim."

"Thought she was a bloody ghost," murmured the thief.

He refused to look at Elizabeth, and they were the only

words he would utter before the magistrate came to Pemberley to take him away.

D arcy insisted on accompanying Elizabeth back to Trillings.

He looked up at the house as he handed her out of the carriage. All the windows were dark.

"They are not waiting for you?"

Elizabeth shook her head. "I often return by a side door and go to my room. They will believe I am back from my walk and in bed already. They do not keep late hours in this house."

Darcy nodded. He looked at her, his eyes bright in the light of the carriage lamp.

"I must confess, I am glad you were with me tonight," he said.

Elizabeth smiled. "I am glad I was with you. The thief, perhaps, is not."

Darcy gave a low laugh, but she thought there was a hint of sadness in his eyes.

"I hope I shall see you again soon. Goodnight, Miss Bennet. And God bless you."

Elizabeth looked back at him. It was as if her willpower to leave him had deserted her. She did not want to go. She sighed.

"Goodnight, Mr. Darcy."

# CHAPTER 36

None of the family was aware of Elizabeth's adventure or her late return. Her maid noticed odd marks and tears on her frock, but apart from a raised eyebrow, she said nothing. She had grown accustomed to Elizabeth's rambles by now.

After the previous night, Elizabeth had expected to sleep late. Instead, she felt a strange energy coursing through her body, and it prevented her from resting. She could not stay still. She wished to be up and moving. She hoped that she would see Darcy again when she visited Pemberley later. Apart from wanting to know what had happened to the thief, she longed to be with him again.

Elizabeth's night had also been interrupted by her worry for Georgiana. More than once, she wanted to kick herself for not persuading her young friend away from this suitor of hers. The sooner she could speak with Georgiana, the easier her mind would be. She could hardly believe she had waved a friend off to a situation that could end in ruin without at least attempting to convince her away from it. Georgiana had confided in her as a trusted friend, and Elizabeth had the uneasy feeling she had not done well by her. She wished to rectify it as soon as she could.

"Lizzy." Her aunt greeted Elizabeth with pleasure when she came down for breakfast. "Did you sleep well, my dear? I must say, the air here agrees with you. You have quite a bloom about you, even more than usual. Your eyes are bright. Does she not look well, Abigail?"

"She does indeed. And I am sure if a certain other person were here, he would agree with me." Mrs. Waters gave her a coy look over her teacup.

Elizabeth almost declined to answer when the woman's words sunk in. "If he were here? Has Captain Waters not returned then?"

"Oh, you knew I referred to him? How odd when I mentioned no names…"

Elizabeth remained impassive while the woman continued to tease her. Finally, Mrs. Waters relented.

"Henry is still not home," she explained. "I am disappointed. I expected he would return yesterday. But he warned me he might stay longer in Derby. Such is the way of young men, I suppose. But do not fret, Miss Bennet. I am sure he will return soon."

"That is a great comfort, Mrs. Waters," said Elizabeth dryly.

She helped herself to toast and hot chocolate as the ladies chatted. Her mind drifted back to the night before. The memory of holding hands with Darcy made her smile, and even the terror that came afterward had a sweetness to it because they'd shared it together. She wondered what he was doing right now and if he thought of her. Her visit to Pemberley could not come soon enough.

"You are in a world of your own, Lizzy," said Aunt Gardiner. "Has something pleasant occurred? You have the appearance of someone who is dwelling on a happy memory."

"Perhaps she has a sweet secret," said Mrs. Waters. She smiled eagerly. "I know that look. I have seen it in many a lady's eyes."

Elizabeth put down her cup. Her feelings were still too close to the surface, and any potential resolution of them too uncertain for her to endure teasing with good humor.

"You are mistaken," she said as firmly as she could. "I was merely looking out at the weather and enjoying the beauty of the day. That is all."

She pushed back from the table. "If you will excuse me, I would like some air. It is too nice to be indoors."

She walked out into the garden, leaving the older ladies to stare after her in confusion.

"She is in love, Marianne. I can guarantee it. She cannot fool me." Mrs. Waters sighed in contentment. "She is miserable because my son has not yet proposed, and his staying away is causing her uncertainty. But when he returns, he will make all right. We will celebrate a wedding before the season changes; you mark my words."

Aunt Gardiner could not agree. There was a light and an uneasiness about Elizabeth, but she had never seen a marked preference for Captain Waters that might suggest he was the cause. Her niece enjoyed his company as they both had lively high spirits, but she had detected nothing beyond that.

No, something or someone else troubled her niece. She hoped whatever it was would not cause Elizabeth unhappiness. It would be too dreadful if, by bringing her here, she had led her favorite niece to misery.

·  ·  ·

The day could not pass fast enough. Elizabeth walked in the lanes and even returned to Pemberley Woods, hoping to see a sign of Darcy.

But of course, he was not there. He would have much to do today with visiting the magistrate and reporting on the previous evening's events. He would not have time for walking in the woods. She would manage her impatience and see him that evening as expected.

She laughed at herself when she realized what she was doing. Moping around after a man like a calf. This was not like her. If her father saw her now, his teasing would never end. If she weren't careful, she would find herself writing bad poetry and composing dreadful songs about her heartache. She would turn her face to the wall and declare she would never love again. She shook her head, amused at her silliness, and turned back to Trillings.

As she walked along the lane, she heard a carriage coming behind her. She turned to step back out of the way, but it drew to a stop. To her astonishment, Mr. Darcy jumped out. He ran to her, his face pale and tight with worry.

"What is it?" she asked in alarm. "Surely the thief did not escape?"

"No, it is not that. Miss Bennet, I need your help and also your discretion. Can you do that?"

Elizabeth nodded. Her heart was in her mouth as she waited for Darcy to continue. She had never seen him look so distraught, and a possibility immediately flew to her mind.

"It is not Georgiana, is it?"

"Yes, yes, it is Georgiana. How did you know? No, it does not matter now. Miss Bennet, do you know where my sister is?"

"I have not seen her. Do you mean to say she is not at Pemberley?"

"Not only is she not at Pemberley, but she did not come home last night after she visited you. Where did she go? Come, you are close friends. She must have told you something."

Elizabeth felt the color drain from her face. She knew she must appear as pale as Darcy.

*Oh Georgiana, what on earth have you done? Foolish, foolish girl! And what have I done? I let you go!*

"You know something, Miss Bennet. Come, I know you do. For god's sake, tell me."

Elizabeth took a deep breath. "I am afraid your sister has been meeting with a suitor."

"What?"

"She only told me yesterday. She went to meet him after seeing me."

Darcy shook his head. He turned from Elizabeth and walked up and down, everything about him proclaiming his agitation.

"My sister — I cannot believe it. She would not — she is too good to do such a thing. And you — " He whirled around to face Elizabeth, his eyes dark with fury. "Why did you keep this from me? You were with me for hours last night, and you did not think to tell me?"

"For god's sake, keep your voice down," snapped Elizabeth. She glanced at the carriage driver, but he did not seem to hear. "I did not tell you because it is not my place to tell you. I cautioned your sister and told her she should speak with you because it was better if it was all out in the open."

"But why would she not tell me? Why would she keep it from me? Did she say who the fellow is?" He paused, and she

233

saw the dawning suspicion grow in his eyes. He strode towards her. "Tell me who he is, Miss Bennet."

"It is an old friend I believe you are no longer on speaking terms with," said Elizabeth. "His name is — "

"George Wickham." Darcy's jaw tightened. "I should have known — who else could it be if she felt the need to keep it a secret?"

"Georgiana said he sought to make amends with you. He sent you a note, but you returned it unread."

"I received no note. Another of Wickham's lies, no doubt. I wonder his tongue is not forked. Did she say where she would meet him?"

"She did not. Just that she would not be unaccompanied."

"Mrs. Younge." Darcy almost spat the words. "She is missing too. What is she about? She should have known better than to expose Georgiana to such a man."

"Where is Wickham likely to stay?"

"There is a tavern called the White Stag. It is the sort of place he would stay as I am familiar with his gambling habits. He will not have much money. If he has my sister there — "

"You can think of what you'll do to him on the journey," said Elizabeth. "Come, we must go."

"We? I cannot allow you to come with me."

"Oh, do not start this again. You were happy enough for my company last night, were you not? Even despite your warnings. We can argue about this and then go, or we can go now. But Georgiana is my friend, and I will be there to help her either way."

Elizabeth turned on her heel and climbed into the carriage herself. Darcy had no choice but to follow her. He gave the orders for the inn then turned to the window to stare out. They traveled in silence towards Lambton.

# CHAPTER 37

*E*lizabeth watched the scenery roll by their window without taking it in. Her anxiety for Georgiana and her guilt at not offering her better advice was overpowering. She could not bear sitting at home waiting for news. She needed to see her friend and know she was safe.

At the White Stag, Darcy jumped out of the carriage. This time, he was firm. Elizabeth would not come with him.

"If she is there, I will send her out to you. She will be glad you are here. But I will not risk your reputation in such a place. Trust me, Miss Bennet. If Wickham is here, I will deal with this matter faster on my own."

Elizabeth reluctantly agreed. She sat back against the seat so she could not be seen and kept her eyes on the entrance to the inn, desperate to see Georgiana emerge. She knew Georgiana would never willingly stay the night with this Wickham. Something must have prevented her from returning home. Elizabeth's stomach churned as she imagined what that might be. She bent her head and sent up a small prayer, pleading that Georgiana was unharmed.

Few minutes had passed before Darcy climbed back into the carriage. Elizabeth stared at him in dismay.

"Where is she?"

"Not there. No sign of either of them. I asked at the stables, and a lad told me Wickham and two ladies left last night. The description of one fits Mrs. Younge, and the other was veiled, so he did not see her face." Darcy thumped his fist against the side of the carriage. "I will kill Wickham when I find him," he snapped. "And what is Georgiana about? Why would she have left with him? I do not understand."

"Do you have any idea where they might have gone?"

Darcy shook his head. "London seems like the obvious choice. I shall have to inform the magistrate and have the roads searched. Wickham has few friends - he isolates everyone he has. He will not have many willing to protect him. Forgive me, Miss Bennet, but I must return you home so I may continue the search."

Elizabeth offered to walk, but he insisted on taking her to Trillings.

D arcy's face was white when she climbed out of the carriage.

"If I can do anything, please let me know," she said.

"I am sure you will. All I can ask now is for your discretion. My sister's reputation might already be impaired, but I would not like it spoken of until there is no help for it. It cannot stay hidden for long."

Elizabeth nodded.

She walked slowly to the house. Her stomach roiled with guilt. Poor Georgiana. What on earth could she be thinking? Had she left willingly? Elizabeth could not believe that. It was so unlike her. Why did Elizabeth not persuade her to return to Pemberley yesterday instead of waving her off as she went to meet this man? Georgiana had confided in her, trusting her judgment, and Elizabeth let her down. She had been no friend to Georgiana Darcy.

As Elizabeth walked past the table where Mrs. Waters kept letters and calling cards, she half-glanced at them as she always did to see if it contained a letter from Jane or any of the rest of her family at Longbourn.

She glanced away, then did a double-take. Her name! She grabbed the envelope. It had not been there this morning. It must have arrived when she was out. And she recognized that handwriting.

She ran out to the garden to read it undisturbed. Her hands shook so much she had trouble opening it. A slip of paper fell out, and she grabbed it, almost tearing it in her haste to read it.

*"My dear Elizabeth,*

*I do not know what to say. I cannot think straight, and I am at a loss for what to do.*

*I write this in haste to tell you I am leaving for Gretna Green, and I hardly need to tell you who I am traveling with. I will leave this note with a servant, so you will know what has become of me.*

*You will wonder why I do not tell my brother, but the truth is, I am too ashamed. I will leave it to you to do what is best."*

Georgiana.

Elizabeth gasped. Oh, Georgiana!

She fled down the steps and out the gate. Darcy had only left her moments before, and she saw the carriage rumbling down the lane. She gathered her skirts and ran after him, crying his name for him to stop. He must have heard her as the carriage halted so abruptly it lurched to one side. It had not come to a complete stop before Darcy jumped out of the carriage and ran towards her.

"Miss Bennet, what is the matter?"

Elizabeth was too out of breath and agitated to speak. She pushed the note in his hand, and he walked away from her to read it. His frown was fierce.

"What has he done?" he snapped. "Gretna Green with my sister? How dare he!"

"How long will it take to reach there?"

"If I leave now, I can be there by nightfall tomorrow."

"You might overtake them. Wickham will not travel with four horses."

"But he has had a greater start."

"And it only grows larger while we stand here talking."

Their eyes met.

"I shall leave at once."

"I am — "

"Coming with me. Yes, I do not doubt it. But I cannot allow it this time. I am sorry, Miss Bennet, but you cannot spend two days on the road with an unmarried man. If anyone discovered it, your reputation would be ruined."

Elizabeth clicked her tongue and walked away in frustration. She turned back to him.

"Mr. Darcy, your sister confided in me yesterday, and I am afraid I did not advise her as well as I might have done. I should have persuaded her not to go, but I did not. It is my fault Georgiana is in this situation, and I will not be satisfied if I do not help recover her."

Darcy's eyes flashed at her words, and she braced herself for his anger at her failure. She deserved whatever he might say to her. Instead, he looked away. His jaw tightened, and with a struggle, he relented.

"I cannot allow you to take the blame. I knew something

was not right, but I did not pursue it. And I did not look in on Georgie as I usually do. I thought she was tired and needed her sleep when she refused to walk with me. I was in a hurry to go to the woods because — well, that does not matter. But it is no more your fault than mine, Miss Bennet. Your conscience is clear, and you may feel no guilt in remaining here."

Elizabeth shook her head. "No, that will not do. You say it is as much your fault as mine, yet you can do something about it while I must remain idle." She looked at him helplessly, willing him to understand. "I will not sit here and wonder what is happening to Georgiana. I love her too. It is cruel of you to expect me to wait here."

Darcy shook his head and opened his mouth to argue, but Elizabeth interrupted.

"No one will know who we are, so how can my reputation be destroyed? I daresay no one we encounter will know who you are either. We will not be visiting your landowning friends along the journey." She fixed him with a steady look. "Mr. Darcy, I am traveling to Gretna Green. If you do not allow me a place in your carriage, I understand, and I accept that. I will take the public coach instead. It will take longer, but I may still be there the morning after you, and I daresay the sorts of places the public coach will stop at will allow me a greater chance of finding Wickham if he frequents the places you say."

Darcy looked away. He appeared to struggle with himself as he looked down the dusty lane along the road they would travel. He glanced up at the sun. It had risen higher in the sky since he had first discovered Georgiana was missing. He muttered something under his breath and shook his head.

"Make your excuses to your aunt and then join me at once. We need to be there as soon as possible."

Elizabeth was surprised but pleased. She ran back to the house before Darcy could offer her the carriage.

She heard the low murmur of her aunt and Mrs. Waters in the parlor. She raised her hand to open the door but paused. What would she tell her? That she was going on a wild chase to Gretna Green with Mr. Darcy? No, her aunt would rightfully forbid it and demand an explanation that would only cause harm to Georgiana. It would take too much time.

Elizabeth ran up to her room and quickly threw clothes into a small trunk. Her father had given her money before she left Hertfordshire. She was thankful Lambton did not offer her many opportunities to spend it. There should be more than enough for a few nights on the road.

The thought made her freeze. What was she about? Was she really about to risk her good name to travel alone with a man? And to Gretna Green, of all places. Darcy was right. If they were discovered, she would be ruined.

Georgiana's face came before her again, looking up at her with eyes filled with trust as she confessed her secret. Elizabeth shook her head and resumed her packing. No one would discover them. For all anyone knew, they were brother and sister, traveling together. They would not encounter anyone they knew who might spread rumors about her. If all went well, once they caught Mrs. Younge and this Wickham, that deceitful pair certainly would not be in a position to say anything.

Elizabeth pulled her trunk downstairs as quietly as she could and returned to the little table where letters and cards were kept. She took a pen and paper and wrote her aunt a brief note. She sealed it and left it where she would see it and then ran down the lane to where Darcy paced in agitation.

"What did you tell her?" he asked after they had climbed into the carriage.

"I left a note. I told her I was going to Georgiana. Not exactly a lie, and she will not fear for me. I told her I would spend a few days with her. She will find it odd I left a note without telling her, but I am sure she will put it down to not wanting to endure any more of Mrs. Waters' teasing."

"Teasing?" Darcy raised an eyebrow.

Elizabeth didn't respond. She leaned against the seat and looked out the window as they left Lambton behind. Mr. Darcy decided not to pursue the subject. He, too, looked out the window, drumming his fingers lightly on his knee.

"I wonder what this Wickham said to make Georgiana leave with him? The tone of her note suggested she did not do so willingly."

Darcy nodded. "I am not sure, but I can guess. My sister is sweet and eager to please. Wickham can charm when he wishes, and he would find it easy to beguile her. If she said anything that would compromise her, he might use it against her to make her leave with him. That is the most likely explanation I can imagine."

"What sort of man is he? Georgiana seemed to believe him misunderstood, but I can tell by your countenance that is not the case."

Darcy gave a bitter laugh. "Oh, I have no doubt he portrayed himself as misunderstood. It is what he does best. My father was taken in by him, and he was a clever man. George Wickham is the son of my father's steward, Miss Bennet. My father was fond of him and raised him like a brother to me. Indeed, he felt like a brother. We played together as boys. When Georgiana was born, he doted on her almost as much as I did. They were fond of one another — another way he might have imposed on her."

"So, what went wrong? Why should he turn against you?"

"As I said, my dear father was taken in by him. He promised his father, a good man, he would provide for Wickham's future when he died. He decided to bestow a church living on him when it became available that would have seen him settled for life." Darcy shook his head. "But by this time, Wickham and I were young men. It was increasingly clear Wickham was not cut out for the church. My father paid for his university education, but he preferred to drink, gamble, and pursue women. No one's spiritual welfare could have been entrusted to him.

When my father died, Wickham approached me about the living. I knew he was not suited for that life, but I would not have gone against my father's wishes. So I was relieved when Wickham told me he did not wish to take it. He decided to study the law. I gave him money in exchange for the living, and he accepted it. Word reached me now and then that he'd squandered it. I received letters from him begging me for assistance with discharging this debt and that. The sums he demanded were outrageous.

At first, I sent him some small amounts to assist him, but as is the nature with that sort of man, the more he received, the more he demanded and the angrier he felt when denied. He asked for more and more, and when his language became abusive when refused, I ended all communication with him. I had not heard from him and did not expect to hear from him again until this happened. No doubt he wishes to avail himself both of my sister's fortune of thirty thousand pounds, as well as avenge himself on me. Men like him will always see themselves as deprived of their due when they are refused."

Elizabeth had remained silent while Darcy told his story.

She shook her head. "I sometimes feel myself very naive when I learn of such wickedness."

Despite the strain on his face, Darcy smiled. "It is not naivety. People incapable of treachery and dishonor find it difficult to recognize it in others. Their minds do not work in such a manner. Men like Wickham are the opposite. They are dishonest, so they believe everyone else is as well. Just like our friend last night. Thieves believe everyone steals."

"It is shocking he came and imposed on Georgiana. I wonder how he came by the plan? How did he contact her and meet her?" Elizabeth's voice trailed off as she realized the answer. "Mrs. Younge," she said. "I always thought her odd. Her attitude towards Georgiana was so intense and controlling. Georgiana felt the same. Mrs. Younge was set on getting her to Ramsgate. It is strange, is it not that she should be so eager to get her away from you, and when Georgiana refused, Wickham is suddenly seized with a desire to offer you an olive branch?"

"You think Mrs. Younge arranged this?"

"I think it is likely."

Darcy lay his head back against the seat, suddenly looking exhausted. "And I hired her. I brought her into my sister's life. I exposed her to someone like this."

"You were not to know. You cannot take responsibility for the world, Mr. Darcy. The lady presented you with references, yes? She played the part of a good companion to Georgiana?"

"Oh, she had references. False, no doubt. As to being a good companion to Georgiana, it seems you picked up on my sister's discomfort when I did not. There were things about her I did not like, but as Georgiana seemed to have no complaint as far as I could see, I chose not to interfere."

"You had much on your mind. And besides, it is not

unusual that a young girl should find it easier to confide in another lady than an older brother."

Darcy nodded, but he was not convinced. He lapsed into silence as the carriage rumbled through towns and villages, taking them further north.

Elizabeth tried to imagine Georgiana traveling the same way. Had she been afraid? Did she wish to stop and come back? What had Wickham and Mrs. Younge done to convince her to take such a step?

# CHAPTER 38

$\mathcal{D}$arcy and Elizabeth broke their journey in Lancaster. The sky was almost dark as they entered the courtyard of an inn. It was not as fine a place as either of them would usually choose, but it was the sort of place Wickham might stay. It also meant there was less chance of meeting anyone who might recognize Darcy. Darcy made arrangements for rooms and came back to hand Elizabeth out.

After she had refreshed herself in her room, she went downstairs to find Darcy. He sat at a table near the window, and he rose at once when she came towards him.

"The food is not the finest fare, but I am so hungry I will eat anything they put before me," he said as they took their seats.

"I cannot disagree with you. They can bring me rodents, and I will be content."

"I am afraid they served their last rodent some hours ago. Will bread and stew satisfy you?"

"It will serve."

The innkeeper carried their plates to the table. From its

taste and texture, the stew had been made very early that week and left to sit uncovered. The bread might have been made any time within the past month. But Elizabeth and Darcy did not care. They ate their fill as if it was the finest they had ever seen.

"I shall have to send my cook up here for the recipe," said Darcy as they finished.

"Old stew and stale bread. Who knew it could be so delicious?" Elizabeth agreed.

Darcy smiled, but it faded.

"I had hoped we might catch them," he said. "I told myself they might throw a wheel and had to stop. A horse might lose a shoe. But nothing. They might be in Scotland already."

"There is no pointing thinking that way. We cannot fly ahead of them. We might pass them tomorrow. Do not lose hope, Mr. Darcy."

Darcy pushed some of his remaining stew around with a chunk of bread.

"No, you are right. There is no point in borrowing trouble, as my mother used to say."

"She sounds like she was a wise woman."

"She was. You would have liked one another."

"Why so?" Elizabeth could not help feeling flattered.

"Because you are alike in many ways. She was lively and adventurous like you. She loved to walk in the woods. I think you would have been great friends."

Elizabeth could not be insensible to such a compliment, and it was with difficulty she did not smile too much.

"What is your mother like?" he asked. "Is she anything like you?"

Elizabeth burst out laughing. "No. No, I would not say that. I am more like my father. My mother is like Mrs. Waters. Excitable, talkative, and — "

"Eager to marry off her children?"

Darcy looked horrified when he realized what he had said.

"Forgive me. I did not mean to disrespect your mother or Mrs. Waters. I only meant — "

"I know what you meant. And as a matter of fact, yes, they have that in common. But it is normal, is it not? I am sure your mother would have been concerned for your marriage prospects if she were here?"

Darcy smiled. "She told me before she died she was sorry she would not see me wed. Despite my family's attitude, I know she wished me to find a woman I could love and admire. Someone who was my equal in all things, who would be a true partner to me."

"You were lucky even if you lost her when you were young," said Elizabeth softly. "It sounds like she valued your happiness above all else."

"She did. She was unique in that way. For all he was a good man, my father wished me to marry someone who would bring fortune and connections to the family, and my aunt and uncle hold the same view. I did myself for a long time..." His voice trailed off, and he looked at his empty bowl. He pushed it away and cleared his throat. Elizabeth stared at him, an agony of sensation running through her.

Was he thinking of Rebecca? Or someone else?

Darcy rose from the table.

"We shall have to leave early in the morning. We should retire now."

Elizabeth was startled by the abrupt change, but she nodded.

They walked up the stairs to their rooms.

"Goodnight, Miss Bennet."

"Goodnight, Mr. Darcy."

As she put her hand on the door, he stopped her.

"It is a shame your family is so far away. I have an idea I would enjoy your father's company."

Elizabeth smiled.

"Goodnight," she said again. She shut the door. He stood staring at it for some moments before going to his room.

T hey stopped in Carlisle to change horses for the last time. Elizabeth was relieved the journey was almost at an end. They had left first thing that morning and would be in Gretna Green in a few hours. As they waited, Darcy spoke to the grooms. He returned to Elizabeth, his face grim.

"They saw no one of their descriptions. Only a gentleman and a lady stopped by on their way, but from the description they gave, it was not them." He rubbed his jaw. "I am hopeful we made it ahead of them. If we make it there first, we can get to Georgiana before she is married. If you will excuse me, I will speak with the innkeeper."

Elizabeth nodded. She had been walking around the courtyard to stretch her legs while Darcy tended to the payment for the new horses. The evening was still warm, but there was a slight cool breeze, and she wrapped her arms around herself to keep warm. In their haste to pursue Georgiana, she had not thought to bring a coat or a shawl.

When Darcy returned, he noticed her shiver and immediately removed his jacket. Elizabeth tried to refuse, but he would not hear of it.

"After all, it is only fitting that a husband should offer his wife his jacket when she is cold," he said dryly.

Elizabeth gaped at him. "Excuse me? Are we in a play now, sir?"

Before Darcy responded, the innkeeper came out with parcels of bread and cheese wrapped up for their journey.

"Something for you and your wife," he said humbly. He also handed them two cups of water. Elizabeth drank it gratefully, but she still eyed Darcy with surprise.

"What is all that about?" she asked when the man left. "Forgive me. I do not speak to wound, but if we are married, I have entirely forgotten it. When did such a joyous event take place? How long have we been married? Are we blessed with children?"

Darcy handed her back into the carriage. The new horses had been hitched, and they would leave soon.

"We have been married two years. We are the parents of a little boy who people say looks like me, but he has your eyes. He is the apple of our eye, and I hope many more will follow. The wedding was a delightful ceremony. Everyone said you were radiant."

He took the seat across from her and tapped the roof with his cane. The carriage pulled away. Elizabeth continued to give him a quizzical look. Darcy shrugged. "He referred to you as my wife. I am not accustomed to explaining my affairs to strangers, so I did not correct him. I should have told him you were my sister, but it did not occur to me to think of you as..." He hesitated. "Well, we do need to do all we can to preserve your reputation," he finished.

There was an odd tension about him, and Elizabeth found she could not bring herself to wonder what it might mean. She laughed to lighten the mood.

"That is true," she said playfully. "Well, my dear husband, I hope you will be open to discussing our little boy's education once we return. I know you prefer the London masters, but I would not wish him far away from me just yet. I am sure the village school will serve just as well."

Darcy raised an eyebrow, then he smiled.

"Thank you, Miss Bennet."

"Whatever for?"

"For making me smile. I thought nothing could do so when I realized my sister was missing. Your presence brings me great comfort."

Elizabeth returned the smile. "Your presence seems to bring me great adventure. I have had more excitement since I met you than in my whole life together. From being held at gunpoint —"

"I did not hold you at gunpoint."

"To being lost in woods, to capturing thieves and now a wild race to Gretna Green to save your sister. My life will be dreadfully boring after all this is over."

"I rather hope it is. I hope this journey has a happy but boring end where we travel home with Georgiana safely by our side."

The sky grew darker. They spoke quietly as the remaining miles raced by. Elizabeth told him of her sisters, and he told her of his parents and growing up in Pemberley. The ordeals they had been through removed all barriers and restraints, and they spoke openly, confiding their hopes and fears and wishes for the future. Elizabeth found it strange that such a terrible journey would create such warmth around them both.

At one point, the carriage stopped so the driver could consult with Darcy about their road ahead. Darcy climbed back into the carriage, and almost without thinking, he took the seat beside Elizabeth. If he realized his mistake, he said nothing, and Elizabeth was not about to persuade him to move. The sky was dark now, and as the carriage rocked gently from side to side, Elizabeth felt her eyes grow heavy.

. . .

A hand gently shook her awake. "Miss Bennet. Elizabeth. We are here."

Elizabeth blinked awake and looked around in bewilderment. Where on earth was she? She felt something warm against her cheek and sat up to see what it was.

She was suddenly wide awake. The warmth beside her was Mr. Darcy. Of course. They were on their way to Gretna Green.

And she had slept on his shoulder. How mortifying. What must he think of her? He would believe she had done it deliberately.

She looked around and then tidied her hair, trying to look as if she did not notice how she had slept.

"What time is it?"

"Almost eleven o'clock." Darcy's jaw was shadowed with stubble, and his eyes were slightly red. After two days of traveling, she could not imagine how tired he must be. But despite his appearance, his body was alert. "We shall go to the blacksmith's shop and find out if they are married. If not, and I pray they are not, we shall try to discover if they have lodgings. Gretna Green is not large."

Elizabeth hesitated. "And if they are married?" she asked gently.

Darcy rubbed his jaw. She found herself seized with a compelling desire to touch his face and smooth away the tired lines. He did not deserve to carry so much on his shoulders.

"I will worry about that if it happens. For now, I simply hope they are not wed."

Elizabeth allowed him to hand her out of the carriage. The night had grown cooler, and she was grateful for the jacket she still wore, but she was worried about him. In his shirt sleeves and waistcoat, he must feel the cold. But if he did, he gave no sign of it.

They walked to the blacksmiths. No candles were lighting the windows at such a late hour. Elizabeth walked around while Darcy banged on the door. A disgruntled face peered out a window.

"Don't you fine folk sleep?" he demanded.

Darcy walked around to see him as Elizabeth joined him.

"Ah. In a hurry to wed, are you?" the man's grin was sly. "Well, I suppose I can do a quick ceremony if you are eager to spend the night without sin. It will cost you extra, though. I was already in bed and need to be awake early in the morning."

"We are not here to marry," said Darcy. He glanced down at Elizabeth. She stood beside him, her hair tousled, his very male jacket wrapped around her. "We are already married," he added hastily. He put an arm around her and held her close. Elizabeth was astonished but not averse to the subterfuge. She gave the blacksmith a smile she hoped was both confident and wifely.

"Almost two years now. We have a little boy already. He is the image of his father," she said.

The man looked a little perplexed.

"Well, if you do not wish to be wed, what do you want? I cannot mend your horse's shoe. The forge is not hot enough."

"You are the blacksmith then?"

"Aye."

"I wish to ask you about a couple who have passed through. They will have been joined by a lady in her thirties and probably arrived in Gretna Green earlier today. Did you see them?"

The blacksmith's face took on a closed look.

"Why do you ask? I don't want any trouble. If they ran away without permission, you can take it up with them."

"But were they here? We want no trouble. The couple are friends of ours, and we are anxious to attend their ceremony."

The blacksmith did not seem convinced.

"No, we have had no one of that description. A few couples but none of them brought witnesses with them, so they do not answer your description."

"You are sure?" Darcy's voice was urgent. "The bride is young with blonde, curling hair."

The blacksmith pulled a face. "No. We have had no lady like that. We had a man with fair hair and a few ladies with dark hair but no blonde lady."

Darcy narrowed his eyes. "You are sure? If you have information about the people we seek, I can pay you handsomely."

The blacksmith laughed. "And I would allow you pay me handsomely, friend, but I would take your money under false pretenses. I cannot tell you anything because I did not see these people."

Darcy's fingers tightened on Elizabeth's shoulder, and she felt him exhale. They had not been married yet, not by the blacksmith at any rate. There was still a chance they might take Georgiana home. He started to respond but fell silent. Elizabeth could hear the catch in his throat and spoke for him.

"Thank you, sir. We are most relieved to hear that. We would not miss the wedding for the world, so we hope we have beaten them here and can surprise them." She smiled at him. The man returned it with a skeptical look. Elizabeth gently nudged Darcy. He fished in his pocket and drew out some coins.

"We will be much obliged to you if you keep our surprise

if you meet with such a party. My wife and I were disappointed when our little boy appeared ill, and we thought we could not attend. They will be thrilled to see us."

The blacksmith huffed and muttered something that sounded like "Not bloody likely," but he accepted the coins Darcy tossed to him.

"May I ask what time you start your ceremonies?"

The blacksmith shrugged. "I rise at five, and I will see anyone who passes through. The marriage only takes a few minutes over the anvil."

"Thank you," said Elizabeth. "You have been most helpful." She reached for Darcy, and he took her hand. They started to walk away when the blacksmith laughed.

"Aye, you are married, then. I confess I did not believe you at first, but anyone can see it."

Elizabeth was glad the darkness hid her blushes. Darcy raised a hand in salute and escorted her back to the carriage.

"What do we do now?" she whispered.

Darcy looked towards the tiny village. "I would prefer to find Georgiana right now, but I cannot believe she is here. Wickham would have been sure to marry her the moment they arrived. I suggest we take a room for the night and then return first thing in the morning."

"A room?" Elizabeth raised her eyebrows, and she was amused to see Darcy color slightly.

"All right, Mrs. Darcy, have it your way. Separate rooms."

# CHAPTER 39

*E*lizabeth waited in the carriage while Darcy went into the inn. He was gone some time, and Elizabeth was afraid there was nowhere for them to stay when he returned. He opened the carriage door and leaned in to see Elizabeth.

"I have asked around, and they have seen no one who matches Georgiana's description, or indeed Wickham's or Mrs. Younge's."

Elizabeth was relieved. "Do you believe they are telling you the truth?"

"I suspect so. As I said, Wickham would not risk waiting a full night to marry if he were here. He would drag the blacksmith from his bed and order him to perform the ceremony at once. No, I am satisfied they are not here."

"Thank god," Elizabeth breathed. She leaned back against the seat and closed her eyes. God, she was tired! She opened them again to look at Darcy. He was watching her with a curious expression on his face. She self-consciously put a hand to her hair. "And rooms? Do they have a place for us to stay?"

"They have room, yes," said Darcy in a careful tone.

"Oh, thank god," said Elizabeth in relief. "I imagined sleeping across the carriage seats."

Darcy nodded, but he paused. For the first time, Elizabeth noticed a look of intense discomfort over his face.

"What is it?" she asked.

"There is only one room."

Elizabeth's mouth fell open. "Oh," was all she could say.

"But of course, I will sleep in the carriage," Darcy added hastily. "It will be no hardship. I am sure I shall not sleep much, anyway."

Elizabeth stared at the floor while her mind raced. Darcy looked dead on his feet. She was sure he had not slept a wink since discovering Georgiana was missing. He had probably not slept much the night before either with attending to the magistrate. He was likely to collapse if he did not get some repose.

Could she do that? Spend a night alone with Darcy? She would be ruined if they were found out.

But who would discover them? They knew no one here. If her family found out about it, they would not need to know details of sleeping arrangements. They were hardly likely to let the information become public knowledge, anyway. She glanced at Darcy. He looked down towards the village, and his demeanor was just as embarrassed as she felt. He raised a hand to stifle a yawn. He was exhausted.

"I am sure — that is — perhaps we might see the room?"

Darcy nodded.

A girl led them up the stairs and pushed a door open. In the flickering candlelight, Elizabeth could see the room was plainly furnished. There was a large bed in the center she could hardly look at. On the opposite side, there was a couch.

A table, chair, and washstand were the only other furnishings.

Elizabeth glanced at Darcy and nodded towards the couch. He looked at it and raised an eyebrow. He shook his head.

"No," he mouthed silently.

Elizabeth leaned towards him. "You are about to collapse, sir," she whispered as the girl occupied herself with hastily covering a stain on the bed cover. "You will be no help to Georgiana if you do. You cannot face Wickham in such a condition." She took a deep breath and averted her eyes. "No one will know of this. I mean — it will not come back on us in any way. I am sure neither of us will want news of it to spread…" She hoped the dim light hid her blushes. She had never felt so mortified in all her life.

Darcy stared at her for a long moment. She could not bring herself to meet his eyes and see his expression, and she did not know if she was thankful for that or not. She was unsure she wanted to know what he thought of her bold suggestion. He yawned again and almost stumbled as he tried to keep it in. He gripped the door frame and sighed. He gave Elizabeth one last look, then nodded.

"We will take it," he said.

After arranging for food to be brought to their room, Elizabeth sat on the bed. Darcy moved to the couch, and they both tried to seem busy while unable to look at one another. A deep embarrassment replaced the closeness they had developed on the carriage journey.

When their food arrived, they ate it at the table and spoke of their hope that Georgiana remained unmarried.

"I would like to be at the blacksmith's just before five," said Darcy. "I will not risk missing them if they should arrive."

"Is there a chance they married elsewhere? Anyone can marry them here, can they not?"

Darcy nodded. "I do not believe they have married here at any rate. Wickham is unlikely to ask some poor cottager to marry them. He will want his own peace of mind that the matter is done properly."

"I will go with you to the blacksmith's tomorrow," said Elizabeth. "If they have not arrived by eight, I will go to the village and ask around while you remain there."

Darcy agreed to the plan.

Finally, there was nothing else for them to do but sleep. Darcy tried to sound casual as he suggested checking the common room for any new arrivals. Elizabeth took the hint, and as soon as he left, she stripped to her petticoat and pulled the pins from her hair. She jumped into bed and pulled the covers to her chin. After a few minutes, he knocked. She told him to enter, hoping her voice sounded sleepy enough to prevent further conversation.

Darcy moved to the couch, and she heard him remove his boots. She held her breath but could hear nothing else but the couch creaking as he lay on it. She took a peek and saw him lying fully dressed on the couch.

"Goodnight, Miss Bennet," he murmured.

Elizabeth swallowed. "Goodnight, Mr. Darcy."

The next morning, Elizabeth stirred and murmured to herself in irritation. Her usually soft bed felt harder than usual, and the sheets far coarser. She opened her eyes and sat up in confusion to see the dim room. An early sun shone through curtains threadbare with age. The windows had been opened to allow fresh air to circulate the stale room. She looked around quickly and saw Mr.

Darcy sitting at the table where they had their meal the night before. He was looking out the window, lost in thought but turned at the sound of her stirring.

"Good morning, Miss Bennet."

Elizabeth tried to reply, but the words would not come. Instead, she gave a smile then self-consciously touched her hair to feel its disarray while trying not to seem like she was doing it. As she did so, the sheets fell around her waist, and she hastily grabbed them. Darcy swallowed and averted his eyes.

"What time is it?" she asked.

"A little after half four. I would like to be at the blacksmith's and wait for them before five. I do not wish to leave anything to chance, but you can join me later if you wish to sleep a little longer. It has been a long journey, and we are not finished yet."

Elizabeth shook her head. She could not endure lounging in bed while Darcy waited alone and Georgiana — well, who knew what Georgiana was experiencing.

Poor girl. What was she doing right now? Was she in despair she was about to be married and possibly against her will? No one deserved to marry under such circumstances. Well, perhaps this Wickham might deserve it, and certainly Mrs. Younge. Elizabeth would not weep if they found themselves in the situation they pushed on Georgiana. But a sweet, gentle girl of just fifteen who probably dreamed of being loved by a good, kind man deserved far better than that.

"I thought to walk around when I first woke up hoping to see them, but I would not risk it," said Darcy. "If Wickham is here after all and should see me without me seeing him, he would escape, and my poor sister is lost to me. I have been sitting here instead, hoping one of them might pass by, but I saw nothing apart from a few villagers starting their day. A sudden worry has seized me, Miss Bennet. What if they traveled to another town? Wickham might have discovered Georgiana sent you a note. He might have changed his plan to any other town on the border. They might not come here at all."

He looked so distraught, Elizabeth wrapped the sheet around herself and went to him.

"We must not borrow trouble," she said. "Let us only think what is in front of us right now. Take it one step at a time. Let us go to the blacksmith and wait for them. If they do not come, we can think about our next step from there."

Her hand rested on the table. To her surprise, Darcy took it. He raised it to his lips, and she froze, her eyes wide. He caught himself at the last moment and instead squeezed her hand gently and released it.

"Thank you, Miss Bennet. You have been a great comfort. I am glad you are with me." He looked away to avoid meeting her eyes. "I only pray I have not damaged your reputation by doing so."

Elizabeth felt a slight chill, and she covered it over with a laugh. If he compromised her, he might have to marry her, and he made it plain he had no wish to do that. "Yes, I rather hope it has not been."

Darcy looked at her then turned away towards the window. "I am sure it would cost you a great deal if it did."

His tone was aloof, and after the warmth of his other sentiments, it felt even colder than it might otherwise have done. She could not account for these odd moods of his at times. She was about to ask him what he meant by it but bit her tongue. It would keep for later. They had more important things to worry about.

She moved away from him.

"I will dress now."

Darcy nodded, and without a word, he strode from the room. Elizabeth looked after him as the door closed and shook her head in irritation. For all she liked him, and her feelings for him had grown, his sudden changes in mood for no reason were something she would never find tolerable. She could think of no reasonable explanation for them.

She tried to make herself look as presentable as possible after two days on the road. The one mirror in the room was chipped and faded, but she attempted to pin her hair, then washed her arms and face at the water jug.

There. That was as well as she could expect to look.

# CHAPTER 40

*D*arcy was in the common room when she came downstairs. He sat at a table near the window. His legs were crossed, and he jiggled his foot up and down as his eyes scanned the road outside. He drummed his fingers on the table. He was so focused on the road he did not realize Elizabeth was there until she cleared her throat. He scrambled to his feet with a mumbled apology. He nodded towards the sleepy innkeeper who sat at another table, yawning loudly.

"Do you wish to break your fast before we leave?" he asked.

She shook her head. "I am too nervous to eat. If all goes well, we can eat with Georgiana later."

Darcy nodded. "My sentiments exactly. Shall we?"

They walked to the blacksmith's shop in silence. Darcy looked about them for any sign of Georgiana or her companions, but any couples there to be wed were not about yet.

"Would anyone really come here to be married so early?" asked Elizabeth.

"If they believe they are being chased, as many couples

who come here are, they will want to be wed as soon as they cross the border. No matter what time it is."

They had arrived at the blacksmith's.

"Should we go in?" Elizabeth asked. Darcy looked up at the building, considering.

"No, not yet. We should wait somewhere nearby where we can see if they arrive and intercede."

Elizabeth nodded. The area at the front of the blacksmith's was exposed, and if they wanted to catch Wickham, they would need to be in a position where they would see him before he would see them.

A small copse of trees stood nearby. It would allow them a clear view of the road and to approach the blacksmith's without being seen. Darcy nodded to it, and they hurried towards it. Elizabeth seated herself on a rock and smoothed her skirts to calm herself as Darcy paced. His eyes were fixed on the road, and he muttered to himself. The sun rose higher in the sky. The first villagers appeared to start their day. Darcy grew more agitated.

"It must be near seven. What if they are not coming here? What if they married at Springfield while we wait here like idiots?"

"It was always unlikely they would come this early. No public coaches will arrive yet, and if they spent the night somewhere, they might still be several miles away."

Darcy continued to pace, and his behavior made Elizabeth even more nervous. She closed her eyes and murmured a brief prayer that within a few hours, they would have Georgiana with them, safe, unharmed, and unwed. She wanted to embrace her young friend and know she had escaped her ordeal unscathed. And she wanted to see Wickham and Mrs. Younge brought to justice.

She was startled from her prayers by Darcy making a harsh sound.

"Elizabeth! It is them. He has her."

Elizabeth jumped from her seat. On the road leading to the village, she spotted a small cart drawn by a pony. It was driven by a man who could only be a farmer by his clothing.

A tall, handsome man sat next to him. Even from that distance, Elizabeth saw his red eyes and stubbled jaw. He looked exhausted and irritated.

Two ladies sat in the back of the cart. Elizabeth recognized Mrs. Younge's rigid back. Her hair stuck out from under her hat like a bird's nest. However they had passed the night, it had not been in comfort.

As the cart moved, the person across from Mrs. Younge came into view. Elizabeth's hand flew to her mouth. Georgiana! Her friend looked just as exhausted as her companions, but she seemed otherwise unharmed.

And if they just arrived now, it could only mean they were not married.

Darcy drew in a sharp breath. "Let us go," he said. He took Elizabeth's hand and hurried towards the blacksmith's.

Wickham jumped down from the cart. He strode into the anvil room without bothering to attend to the ladies. Georgiana and Mrs. Younge climbed down with the farmer's help and followed him inside. Georgiana trailed behind, her head down as if she were attending a funeral.

"Blacksmith," Wickham roared. "Anvil priest. Whatever cursed name you go by. Come marry us at once, and there will be a reward for you."

"Wickham," snapped Darcy. The man spun around, and his face fell as Darcy lunged towards him and pushed him back against the wall. Mrs. Younge screamed, and Elizabeth reached for Georgiana. Georgiana looked shocked as Elizabeth pulled her into her arms.

"Thank god we have you," she whispered. As Georgiana's shock subsided, she wrapped her arms around Elizabeth and clung to her, burying her face in her shoulder.

"Elizabeth, you came. I hoped you would when you read my note, but I was afraid to believe it. I did not know what to do."

Wickham struggled against Darcy's grasp and tried to swing a punch at him, but Darcy ducked, and while the other man was off-balance, he knocked him to the floor. Mrs. Younge screamed again and tried to run, but Elizabeth released Georgiana in time to stick her foot out and send her barrelling to the floor.

The blacksmith strolled in, his head too buried in a mug of ale to notice what was going on. He smacked his lips with satisfaction and peered into the end with one eye closed to see how much was left. He sighed in disappointment before releasing a hearty belch.

"Who comes here to be wed? Names and birthplaces, please..."

His voice trailed off as he witnessed the sight in front of him; the bride sobbing, the witness trying to crawl away while Elizabeth grabbed her, and the groom groaning on the floor while Darcy stood over him. He slowly lowered the mug and cleared his throat.

"Well. I see you have some disagreements to smooth over. I will — I will allow you to —" He hiccuped then gestured vaguely towards his house with his mug. "Yes, well —" He sidled towards the door, then bolted.

"What are you going to do, Darcy?" asked Wickham. He staggered back against a pillar and examined his bloodied hands as they came away from his face. "She is already compromised. She has spent two nights with me already. Allow us wed, or she is ruined forever."

"That is a lie," said Georgiana. Her voice trembled, but she spoke bravely. "I did not spend the night with you. I shared a room with Mrs. Younge, and you slept elsewhere."

"Who will believe that?" said Wickham with a sneer. "Wherever you lodged, you are still ruined when people know you came with me to be wed." Darcy loomed over him, and he sunk into silence.

Mrs. Younge had decided she had nowhere to run without Wickham and had sensibly stopped trying to escape. She leaned against the anvil and buried her face in her hands.

Elizabeth turned to Georgiana.

"How did he convince you to leave with him? I know you did not care about him enough to take such a step."

"She cared enough about me to do lots of things —" Wickham began but broke off as Darcy grabbed him by the front of his shirt.

"You will not speak of my sister ever again."

"You overestimate your charms, sir," cried Georgiana at the same time. "Do not listen to him, Elizabeth. He is a liar." She flushed and ducked her head. "I sent him notes through Mrs. Younge. At first, I planned to help him be reconciled with my brother, but after some time, I imagined I had feelings for him myself. I know it was wrong of me to send him notes, but Mrs. Younge was so persuasive that I felt I was as cruel as she said I was to deny one who had grown up with us.

But they changed the notes. I only sent brief information about meeting him in Lambton, but they used my handwriting to change them to something far more compromising. They threatened to use them to destroy me if I did not elope with

Wickham at once. They told me by visiting him, I led him to believe I would marry him, and it would dishonor myself and my brother if these notes came to light. I did not know what else to do. They both spoke so fast and so often I could not think straight. Wickham promised me all would turn out well. He would be reconciled with my brother after the marriage, and we would be as we were before. I saw no way out."

Elizabeth embraced her again until she regained her composure. "Where are these notes?" she asked.

Before Georgiana could answer, Wickham lunged to his feet and tried to run, but Darcy was too fast for him. He caught him and pinned him down.

"Your actions answer the question," he said. Wickham tried to struggle, but Darcy was stronger, and he soon pulled a packet from inside his coat. He handed it to Elizabeth, still holding Wickham down.

Elizabeth opened the packet, and she perused them with Georgiana.

*"I will meet you near the clock, sir, and Mrs. Younge will accompany me. We shall be there by four,*

*All my love, Georgiana.*

*I open this letter again to tell you I cannot wait to be with you. I long for you. Do not be late."*

"My note was simply the first line and signed Georgiana. Everything else was added afterward, but so convincingly I could not deny them if they were shown to anyone," said Georgiana. "George told me he did it out of desperate love for me. He said my brother stood between us so he could not bear it, and he only did this so we would be forced to take the step we both wanted. He claimed he would not have done it if he did not love me so much."

"A twisted sort of love," said Elizabeth. She threw

Wickham a disgusted look. "The sort of false love seen in a man who will bring nothing but misery to a woman."

"She does love me, though," said Wickham, his words a little strangled from the weight of Darcy on him. "I barely needed to convince her to come away with me. She was relieved I'd forced her hand, were you not, my little love?"

"You would well to be silent, sir," said Darcy. His voice was like ice. "We are in a forge, do not forget. There are many ways for an accident to befall a man."

Whatever Wickham saw in Darcy's eyes made him fall silent. For all his blustering, he was a coward.

"I never loved him," said Georgiana. "I had an affection for him, and he was so charming, I imagined it was love. But I also felt uneasy with him. That is how love should be."

Elizabeth looked through the rest of the pages. They were in the same vein.

"They were correct about one thing. These notes are rather incriminating. They have copied your handwriting flawlessly. Which one of you did that?"

"I did," said Mrs. Younge sullenly.

"No doubt you learned to copy her hand from all the times you followed her about, afraid to leave her out of your sight. Was that your plan for Ramsgate? That Wickham should join you there? And you wrote and asked him to come here when Georgiana changed her mind."

Mrs. Younge threw Elizabeth a look of pure poison and turned away as if Elizabeth was beneath her notice.

"She is Wickham's cousin," said Georgiana. Mrs. Younge looked at her sharply, and Georgiana returned it with a steady one of her own. "What? Did you think I would not hear your conversations when you thought I was asleep? I heard you call him Cousin Georgie. You have debts like he does, and you planned to have a share of my fortune if you arranged our marriage."

Darcy still held Wickham, but he looked at Mrs. Younge in disgust.

"All references were false, I take it? Well, do not look too pleased with your deception. You will find it most difficult to deceive anyone else after this."

"It explains her strange sense of ownership towards Georgiana. She was her passage to an easy life." Elizabeth shook her head. "Well, the matter of these letters is easily remedied." She walked towards the forge. Wickham and Mrs. Younge watched in defeat as she held the letters over the coals. She was about to throw them on but paused.

"Georgiana, why don't you do the honors? They are your letters, after all."

Georgiana smiled and swiftly joined Elizabeth. She took the letters and threw them in, then watched triumphantly as they curled and turned to black.

"There. Gone forever," she said with satisfaction.

# CHAPTER 41

$\mathcal{M}$r. Darcy found the blacksmith huddled in his house. He ordered him to send for the local magistrate. The magistrate, a small man called Mr. Cameron, arrived before long, and Mrs. Younge and Wickham were taken away.

Elizabeth and Mr. Darcy brought Georgiana back to their inn, and as soon as she lay down on the bed, she fell fast asleep.

"Thank god she is unharmed," said Mr. Darcy. He clutched the bedpost, his fingers white. "I could not have endured it if she were forced to live her life with that cad. I could not have borne the life of misery she would have led."

"You do not need to worry about that now. She is safe with us. The farmer who brought them here confirmed she was never alone with Wickham. That is one thing she was forceful about, and thank goodness for it. And she was raised with Wickham, almost like brother and sister. She has that in her favor if the matter should come to light." Elizabeth looked at the girl with affection. "She is growing stronger all the time. Soon, she will not be the sort of young lady easily manipulated by unscrupulous people. She grows wiser and will make a fine match with a man who is worthy of her."

Darcy smiled while she spoke, and he nodded. "It was a fortunate day for us when you came to Derbyshire, Miss Bennet."

"I feel just as fortunate. It has been an interesting summer, and I have gained new people who I feel have changed my life forever."

Darcy looked away from her and swallowed. Elizabeth realized how her words must have sounded and looked away in mortification. She would not have him think her indelicate.

She stood up. "I think I shall walk around and explore the village. It looks an interesting place, and who knows if I shall ever have a chance to leave England again."

She turned to leave, and as she reached the door, Darcy spoke.

"If you do not object to my company, I will join you, Miss Bennet. I feel the need for movement. That couch made rather an uncomfortable bed, and I am feeling the effects of it now."

They walked down the stairs and out into the courtyard together.

"When shall we return to Derbyshire?" Elizabeth asked. Darcy did not respond. She looked up at him to repeat her question. He stared straight ahead, his body rigid. Elizabeth turned to see what had caught his attention, and the sight made her freeze.

A couple walked into the courtyard. Their arms were wrapped around one another, and the man bent his head to kiss the lady. From their open affection and the gold

EMILY RUSSELL

wedding band glinting on the lady's finger, it was clear they were newly married. An unremarkable sight considering where they were, but it was not that which caught Elizabeth and Darcy's attention.

Elizabeth took a step towards them. Darcy reached for her but stopped himself. He allowed his hand to fall to his side as he watched her helplessly.

"Captain Waters," she called.

Captain Waters looked up, still smiling. The color drained from his face when he saw Elizabeth and Darcy. His bride, Rebecca, looked equally shocked. She froze, then looked from left to right as if she did not know where to hide her face.

"Miss Bennet. Mr. Darcy. What are you doing here? You did not come here to —""

"No, we did not. We are here on another matter. Miss Darcy is with us."

Elizabeth looked at the plain band glinting on Rebecca's finger. Rebecca noticed her glance and rather foolishly tried to hide it.

"So I take it this is the reason for your late return from Derby?" she asked.

Captain Waters drew himself up and wrapped an arm around Rebecca, pulling her close.

"Yes, it is. You know my mother. She would not have agreed to the match otherwise."

Rebecca looked pained. "I am sorry for the deception, Miss Bennet. We became engaged in Portsmouth. I thought our situation hopeless when I saw how set his mother was that Henry should marry — marry another. I was prepared to end the engagement."

"But I would not hear of it. I prevailed on Rebecca to

272

elope with me. My mother will not be happy, but now we are married, there is nothing she can do about it."

Elizabeth stared at Captain Waters. She did not know what to say. All this time, she had to endure his mother's meddling, and all along, he had been engaged to another. All the times he flirted with her, no doubt to distract everyone from his true feelings for another. He had used her in an infamous manner. True, she did not have feelings for him, but he did not know that. She could hardly stand to look at him.

"My congratulations," she said tartly. "I will not disturb you on your honeymoon. I hope you will be very happy together."

She dropped a curtsey and hurried past them, her face burning.

Elizabeth left the courtyard and turned towards the tiny village. She started to walk in that direction but then stopped. No, she did not wish to be among people just now. She had too much to think about.

She turned in the other direction towards a pretty meadow where she could be alone to think.

She pulled her bonnet from her head as she wandered in the direction of a small stream, its banks covered in wildflowers.

"Miss Bennet. Elizabeth."

Footsteps ran towards her, and she turned reluctantly, almost expecting to see Captain Waters coming after her to plead his case.

Darcy caught up with her. He looked down at her, at a loss for what to say. He took her hand and held it between both of his. Elizabeth stared at it, then up at him.

"Your pain will ease," he said gently. Elizabeth frowned in confusion as he continued. "He is a scoundrel, and he has used you ill. But he is not worth your tears. He is a disgrace to the name of man, but I know your heart will heal in time."

Elizabeth tilted her head. He looked at her with such concern and tenderness she started to suspect there might have been some confusion.

"Why do you speak of my heart, sir?"

"Because I know what it is to love someone and to know they love another."

It was then Elizabeth's heart was affected. The knowledge that he loved another pierced her like a dagger. He saw the pain in her eyes and took a step towards her. He held their entwined hands against his chest where she could feel the steady beat of his heart. It was faster than usual after his chase to reach her.

"Your excellent sense will soon help you see he does not deserve you. You will laugh and realize you had a lucky escape from him. Poor Miss Carter. I believe she deserves better than a man who will flirt with another woman to hide his true feelings for her. But that is not your fate. You will recover."

"Mr. Darcy, I must speak now as I fear there is some confusion. Are you — do you believe me attached to Captain Waters?"

Darcy hesitated. "You are, are you not?"

"Not in the slightest. I have enjoyed his friendship but nothing more. I have never loved him. My heart is quite unattached."

*From Captain Waters, at least.*

Darcy was silent. He looked at her so earnestly, Elizabeth felt a fluttering in her body.

"Is this true? You have never loved him? You never hoped to marry him?"

"Never. Well, I must admit when I first met him, I was

open to considering the idea. But when I grew to know him better, I realized that although I was fond of him, he would not suit me as a partner." She frowned. "But why should you believe me attached? You spoke to put me on my guard because you believed him interested in Georgiana, did you not?"

"Georgiana? No, never in the slightest. It never crossed my mind." His face cleared. "Is that what you thought I referred to when I sought to warn you? That I thought him interested in Georgiana?" At Elizabeth's nod, he closed his eyes. "No. I believed you had feelings for him. I had suspected him of hiding something for some time. The day before I spoke with you, I saw his phaeton at the parsonage. Although I had my suspicions about him and Miss Carter, I did not know for sure, but I wished to put you on your guard. I was afraid your heart would be broken if he proved himself untrustworthy."

"Oh." Elizabeth was astonished.

"But tell me. If you are not attached to him, why did you run away just now? You fled as if you could not be in their company a moment longer."

"Did you think I did that because my heart was broken?"

"I confess, I did."

Elizabeth laughed. "Forgive me. I can see how it might have looked that way. No, I was merely annoyed he had used me in that manner. Combined with Mrs. Waters' relentless hints at marriage which gave me no peace, and my worry for Georgiana, I needed to be away from them. It was not the effects of a broken heart that made me leave. Rather it was that of an exhausted, irritated spirit."

Darcy stared at her as if afraid to speak. He seemed overcome with a powerful emotion. She was afraid to hope what it might be. His lips moved, and he looked at her earnestly.

275

"Miss Bennet, please allow me to ask one more time, so I am sure. Do you mean what you say when you tell me you do not love Captain Waters? That you have never loved him, and your heart is not attached to him?"

"I am completely clear in what I say." She smiled. "You are good to be so concerned for me, but I am completely unharmed. My heart is not broken. I sincerely wish them well, although I have my doubts about a relationship that began in secrecy and deception. However, if his parents can be reconciled to it, I believe they have as good a chance as any. But you need have no fear for me."

She smiled at him and gently pulled her hand free. He released it, and she started to walk again. He fell into step beside her. She wondered at his manner. He glanced at her often and seemed to be thinking how to express something he very much wished to say. Was this an effect of his over-powering sense of responsibility again, feeling guilty he had not sufficiently warned her? Did he doubt her claims she had not been injured by Captain Waters?

Or was it something else? Something she was afraid to think.

They knew not where they walked until they came to a small hill that overlooked the village. The Scottish country-side rolled out before them, allowing them to see for miles. Darcy stood by her side as she commented on its beauty. He cleared his throat.

"Miss Bennet, I must speak with you." His voice was urgent. He moved around so he faced her. "I have kept my silence until now, believing you attached to another man. But now I know your heart is free, I will regret it for the rest of my life if I keep silent any longer."

Elizabeth was shaken by the fervor in his voice. "What is it, Mr. Darcy?"

He took a deep breath. "You must allow me to tell you how ardently I admire and love you. I do not expect you to return feelings for me right away. But if I may have a chance to win your heart, you would do me the greatest honor any man could have."

Elizabeth stepped towards him. He gazed down at her, and his eyes were bright with emotion. Her legs suddenly felt weak, and her heart pounded.

"You love me?" she said.

"You bewitched me from the first moment I saw you. I was moved to mix more with the neighborhood that I might spend time with you. I have thought of you night and day since we met, and it pained me more than words can express to think you gave your heart to a man who did not deserve you. It is not easy for me to speak this way, Miss Bennet. I have never said these words to another woman. But I say them to you now, asking for nothing more than a hope that I might win your heart."

"Mr. Darcy —" Elizabeth hardly knew what to say. "I am — this is most unexpected."

Darcy's face fell, and she smiled quickly to reassure him. "I am almost afraid that at any moment, I shall wake up and find myself back in my bed at Longbourn and discover that all this has been a wonderful dream." She felt a prickling in her eyes.

Darcy inhaled sharply and took a step towards her. He touched her cheek.

"Does that mean what I think it means?"

"It means my heart is already yours and has been for some time."

The look of heartfelt delight diffused over his face made him more handsome than ever. He took her hand in both of his and stared down at their entwined fingers. He smiled.

"I cannot believe it. I was so sure you were to marry Captain Waters. I believed that was your main motivation in worrying about your reputation. And now you tell me that which I have longed for has been mine all along."

Elizabeth laughed. "I did wonder at your occasional odd moods. Was that it? You were jealous because you thought I loved another man?"

"A flaw I did not know I had until now," he smiled. "I told myself I was unfair to Captain Waters for disliking him, but I believe I can now safely think of him as a splendid fellow after all."

He bent his head and kissed her. Elizabeth never knew she could feel such happiness. Her heart felt fit to burst. He finally released her and pulled her against his chest. They looked at the view together in contented silence, happy merely to be close to one another.

"I suppose then I have another question to ask you," he said after some moments. He stroked her hair, and she snuggled closer to him. "You have already answered my first one, and it seems I have already succeeded in my aim of winning your heart. So I must ask you my next question."

"And what would that be?"

Darcy moved her back slightly so he could look down at her but kept his arms firmly around her.

"Miss Elizabeth Bennet — scourge of my woods, nymph of my forest, and my partner in adventure — will you do me the honor of becoming my wife and being my partner in all things?"

Elizabeth tilted her head as she pretended to consider it, but it was not easy to look composed.

"Well, I suppose I shall have to, won't I?" she said with a sigh of feigned regret. "You have taken me to Gretna Green. Friends have seen us here together. Even after all our caution, my reputation has been well and truly tarnished by now."

"Absolutely destroyed. There is no hope of recovery after this." Darcy smiled. "Never mind. I am willing to redeem you." He kissed her again.

# CHAPTER 42

hen Darcy and Elizabeth returned to the inn some hours later, there was no sign of Captain Waters or the new Mrs. Waters. It was not unexpected. Elizabeth suspected Captain Waters was nervous about speaking with her after his actions and would avoid her as much as possible. He had no way of realizing Elizabeth was too happy to care. But when they returned to the room, they were alarmed to find no sign of Georgiana. Elizabeth looked over the pillows and table, but there was no note to explain her absence. Darcy ran down to the common room and demanded to know if anyone had seen his sister. His face was grim when Elizabeth came to join him.

"Someone saw her speaking with the magistrate and a couple. They spoke together for some time, and she was in some distress when she left with them. They said the man, in particular, was quite heated. If Wickham and Mrs. Younge are free and they came back for her..."

"They wouldn't dare," Elizabeth soothed him. "How were they to know you were not here? Wickham would never risk a confrontation with you. I am sure they are not free.

Perhaps the magistrate wished to ask her a few more questions."

Darcy looked around in agitation. "But why would he bring Wickham and Younge for such a purpose? He does not need their assistance. Come. I will not be easy until we find her."

He gave brisk orders to have their carriage prepared. It was ready in minutes, and they traveled down the coaching road out of the village.

"The innkeeper says Cameron's house is not far from here if we keep to this road," said Darcy. He drummed his hand on his knee, hardly able to keep still. "He said we would recognize it by its red bricks and the church beside it."

Elizabeth slipped her hand inside his, and he wrapped his fingers around it gratefully. Darcy had lowered the window, and they leaned out, eager to catch some sign of the house.

"There it is," said Darcy. "And it is just near a church, as they said." He tapped the roof with his cane to bring the carriage to a stop. He jumped out almost before it ceased moving. Elizabeth followed close behind, scarcely less anxious than himself.

"Why could he wish to speak with Georgiana?" Darcy muttered as they rushed up to the house. "He should have waited for me."

"We do not know the particulars," said Elizabeth. "Let us discover what has happened first."

Darcy raised her hand to his lips then hurried on.

The magistrate's house stood at the end of a long lane. Darcy ran up the path and banged on the door with his fist, shouting the magistrate's name. He raised his hand to bang again when the door opened. A maid gave him an apprehensive look and stood back to enter.

"Mr. Cameron is speaking with someone, sir. He will see you when he is done," she said in a soft lilt.

"I know who he speaks with, and I will see him now," said Darcy. His face was dark with anger, but Elizabeth could see the fear in his eyes. She squeezed his hand and threw the maid an apologetic smile.

"I am sure it is Mr. Darcy Mr. Cameron wished to speak with, and he is here now. We must see him."

Elizabeth's explanation was interrupted by a door opening. Darcy's loud voice had attracted Mr. Cameron's attention, and he poked his head outside.

"Ah. Mr. Darcy. I waited for you, sir, but there was no sign of you returning, and I wished the matter resolved at once. Can you come in, please?"

Darcy had already marched into the room before he finished his sentence. He bristled with anger, ready to confront Wickham at once, but he stopped when the occupants of the room turned to face him.

"What the — what are you doing here?"

Elizabeth hurried after him and stopped in astonishment.

"Captain Waters. Miss Carter. I mean, Mrs. Waters. What are you doing here?"

Captain Waters sat opposite the magistrate's desk while Rebecca and Georgiana sat in more comfortable armchairs. Elizabeth crossed to Georgiana at once and took her hand.

"I am so sorry to worry you, Elizabeth. I wanted to wait for you to return, but we did not know where you had gone, and we waited for some time. Where were you?"

"We — we went for a walk, and we were delayed —" Elizabeth hoped the heat in her face would be attributed to the rush to get there. "What is going on?"

"Yes, what is going on? Why did you need my sister, and why are the Waters here?" Darcy glowered, but some of his tension had faded in his relief to discover Wickham and Mrs. Younge had not taken Georgiana.

The magistrate went to sit at his desk and sighed.

"We have been having trouble with our new guests. Mr. Wickham, in particular, is being quite belligerent. He insists your sister ran away with him willingly, and he says if he is punished, everyone will know your sister eloped with him, and her reputation will be destroyed. I wished to talk to you and Miss Darcy as it puts me in a difficult situation."

"I met Miss Darcy in the common room when she came in search of you and Miss Bennet. We invited her to join us for a meal when Mr. Cameron arrived to speak with her." Captain Waters' eyes met Darcy's. "I told him there was some mistake. Miss Darcy traveled to Gretna Green with you and Miss Bennet to celebrate our wedding. You did not arrive on time, but my wife and I are touched by the gesture."

Darcy nodded warily, and Elizabeth sat on the arm of Georgiana's chair, watching Captain Waters carefully to see where he was going with his story.

Captain Waters swallowed. "Well, we did not see the disturbance this morning, of course, but from what we gather, this Wickham heard of your plans to travel to Gretna Green for our wedding through Miss Darcy's companion, Mrs. Younge. The pair spotted an opportunity and traveled after you. They attempted to coerce Miss Darcy into marriage, but luckily, you and Miss Bennet arrived at the blacksmith's on time to prevent it."

"I see..." Darcy's voice was faint as he tried to take in this sudden change in events.

"Mr. Wickham swears he traveled with Miss Darcy and Mrs. Younge. He said there is a farmer who brought them to the village in his cart, and he can vouch for him. I know of no farmer with his description," said Mr. Cameron. There was a blandly innocent expression on his face. "The village is a small place, and I know all the farmers who travel through. His description rings no bells."

"That is fortunate," said Elizabeth cautiously.

"Most unfortunate for them," said the magistrate. "Mr. Wickham then insisted I visited the blacksmith who could tell me they'd arrived alone. I did as he asked, but he says he saw nothing but Miss Bennet and Mr. Darcy trying to save Miss Darcy, which is rather damning for Mr. Wickham. He swears up and down he knows nothing else."

"Wickham accosted Miss Darcy this morning when he found her walking in the village hoping to meet with us. Is that not right, Miss Darcy?" Captain Waters looked at Georgiana. She glanced between him and her brother and opened her mouth to speak but did not find the words. "Miss Darcy was trying to find myself and my wife to discover if they were on time for our wedding when Wickham and Younge found her and forced her to the blacksmith's. Dreadful fellow." Captain Waters shook his head sorrowfully. He caught Elizabeth's eye. They shared a flicker of a smile, and for a moment, some of their old easiness had returned.

Darcy shook his head. "Well, this is all — I am glad the matter has been cleared up."

"Yes, it has. Most decidedly," said the magistrate. "Wickham also demanded I speak at the inn where I found Miss Darcy and discover she had not been there with you last night because she was traveling with him and this farmer no one else has heard of. I did as he asked, of course."

Darcy and Elizabeth drew in sharp breaths. At Elizabeth's side, she felt Georgiana stiffen.

"Oh yes?" said Darcy carefully.

The magistrate twirled a pen around between his fingers and shrugged. "The innkeeper and the maid insisted there were two occupiers of the room, which of course refers to the two young ladies. The innkeeper said he came down to the common room early this morning to see Mr. Darcy seated at a table. He worried you passed an uncomfortable night there, sir, and he was sorry he had no other room for you. They have no recollection of anything else. It is an extraordinary thing about Gretna Green; people remember just what you ask them to."

"I see," said Darcy. He swallowed. "Well, I must thank you for taking the time to clear matters up, Mr. Cameron. Miss Bennet, my sister, and I are most grateful."

"It is my pleasure. And as I am sure we will have many people who remember seeing Wickham and Mrs. Younge accost Miss Darcy in the street, a conviction should be quite straightforward."

He rose from his chair and came around the desk to shake Darcy's hand.

"Now, I hope you will enjoy the rest of your stay here. It is a beautiful place. I am only sorry you did not arrive in time to see your friends' wedding and had to deal with such a dreadful event."

Darcy thanked him.

They left the house and walked out onto the lane in silence. Once outside the magistrate's room, their earlier awkwardness had returned.

"We should thank you for what you have done for us," said Elizabeth.

"You do not need to thank us," said Rebecca quickly. Her grey eyes looked into Elizabeth's, pleading for some understanding. All at once, Elizabeth forgot her own grievance and felt a rush of compassion for her situation. Poor girl. To have to marry the man she loved under such circumstances, knowing it would bring joy to few people. All because of a situation that was not of her making. She did not deserve that.

"Yes, we do," said Darcy firmly. "Captain Waters, that was some fast thinking. I congratulate you."

Captain Waters shook his head. "It is a small matter. Gretna Green is used to covering up indiscretions. Wickham will find no allies here. We were happy to help Miss Darcy."

His eyes met Elizabeth's. She smiled at him and nodded. She could not forgive him for using her quite so fast, but she was grateful to him and Rebecca for saving Georgiana's reputation. Wickham had only dug himself in deeper, and it would be far harder for him and Mrs. Younge to take in another poor girl once the law had dealt with them.

She moved towards the new Mrs. Waters and offered her hand. Rebecca looked astonished and tentatively reached out with her own.

"I am afraid I was remiss earlier when I heard your news. Allow me to congratulate you properly on your marriage. I hope you have every happiness together."

Rebecca glanced at her new husband. She swallowed, and Elizabeth saw tears in her eyes. Her heart went out to her. To have so little expectation that anyone would be happy about her marriage that the smallest kindness made her cry.

"Thank you, Miss Bennet," she said in a voice that almost cracked with emotion.

"Yes, thank you, Miss Bennet," said Captain Waters. He gave Elizabeth a look that showed his appreciation.

It was a promising start. Even though the Waters' deception had threatened to ruin any possibility of friendship between them, they redeemed themselves, and soon, both couples and Georgiana were firm friends.

# CHAPTER 43

*L*ongbourn
*One Month Later*

Elizabeth and Jane threw themselves into each other's arms as soon as Elizabeth emerged from the carriage.

"Oh, how I have missed you, my dear sister," said Jane. "It has been a long summer without you."

"I have missed you too, my dear Jane." Elizabeth drew back to look at her, then threw her arms around her again and squeezed her tight. "I have so much to tell you," she whispered.

Before she could say anything further, the rest of her family spilled out of the house to greet her, putting any confidences out of the question.

"I hope it is good news, Lizzy," said Jane. She laughed, but her beautiful face was anxious. "There have been no new young men in the neighborhood all this summer, and it has made Mama more nervous than ever. We have heard her express her fears every day that we will be turned out into the hedgerows when Father dies because none of us has succeeded in finding a husband. We have heard nothing but stories about how our cousin Collins will turn us out of the house before Father is cold in his grave. I hope your news will distract her."

Elizabeth had to bite her tongue to prevent herself from laughing. Dear Jane! If only she could tell her.

But if she could not find the time to speak with Jane, she would certainly need to find the time to speak with her father. She needed to find a chance to be alone with him before many hours passed.

After all the merry-making and demand for news Elizabeth had endured, it was difficult to find time alone with Mr. Bennet. She glanced at the clock uneasily. Darcy would be here soon, and she needed to speak with her father before he arrived. She would not allow him to walk into the situation unprepared.

"And what's this I hear about the Waters boy being married this summer?" demanded Mrs. Bennet. She sighed the sigh of one who had been greatly ill-used. "I sent you away to a house with a young man of suitable age, and still you return unmarried. Not only that, another lady took him right from under your nose. Have I taught you nothing? Did you not faint when he was close by and oblige him to catch you in his arms? Did you not listen attentively when he spoke?" Her eyes narrowed. "You did not say anything too intelligent, did you? I have told you and told you, men do not like it."

"Hard for us to know if we would like something we have never experienced," murmured Mr. Bennet. "My dear," he said in a louder voice. "You have not listened to Lizzy. She made it quite plain the couple was already engaged. Long before she arrived. Would you have him break his word to one lady and marry another? Would you want your daughter married to a man like that?"

His wife opened her mouth to speak.

"Don't answer that question," he added dryly.

"I dropped my handkerchief for James Lucas last week," announced Kitty proudly.

"Yes, and he thanked you and blew his nose in it before returning it to you," retorted Lydia. "You must be craftier. Do you recall how I pretended to stumble and landed in George Lark's lap? He went as red as anything..."

"Probably because he couldn't breathe..."

As the youngest Bennet girls bickered, Mrs. Bennet sat back against her chair and fanned herself, although the evenings had cooled. "I do not know. I do not know what is to become of us all. Mr. Bennet will die, and Mr. Collins will descend on us and turn us out on the road before he is cold in his grave. And all because Lizzy does not have the wit to captivate a man. Oh, she has the wit to engage them and entertain them with her pert remarks. But she will not accept that men do not like it in a wife. She will die an old maid, and does she care? Of course not. Too busy gallivanting through woods to meet young men, I suppose. That is just like her..."

Mr. Bennet sighed and rose from his chair. "I am to my library," he said before Mrs. Bennet could get in full flow. He bent and kissed Elizabeth's forehead. "I am glad you are come back, my dear. Apart from Jane, I have not heard two words of sense strung together since you went away. Promise me you will not run away to Derbyshire again."

"Run away to Derbyshire? What a lot of use that will be if

she spent the summer there and could not capture a husband," cried Mrs. Bennet.

Elizabeth waited until her father closed the library door then followed him in.

"I must speak with you," she said.

Mr. Bennet stood at one of his shelves, holding a volume. "What is it, my dear? Cannot bear listening to your mother's laments? Well, spare a thought for me. I have had them the whole summer. As a matter of fact, I have had them these past twenty-three years."

Elizabeth glanced uneasily at the clock. They had agreed Darcy should take rooms in the inn at Meryton and would not visit Longbourn until the evening to give Elizabeth time to prepare her father for their news. But with all the commotion of homecoming, the day had passed quickly. Darcy would arrive within half an hour.

"Mama is wrong," she said. Mr. Bennet closed the book to look at her closely.

"Oh, yes?" He walked to his desk and gestured for her to sit across from him. "Well, that is hardly surprising. I have never known her to be anything else. But what is she wrong about this time?"

Elizabeth took a deep breath. The story poured out of her, all about how she met Mr. Darcy, and he banned her from his lands. How she had befriended Georgiana and thought herself interested in Captain Waters. How Georgiana had been blackmailed into eloping to Scotland '*But you must not tell anyone about that, Father*', and how she and Darcy had pursued them in a carriage. How they had recovered Georgiana in time, and finally;

"Mr. Darcy and I are engaged to be married, Father."

Mr. Bennet's eyes narrowed. He steepled his hands and

leaned forward. He sighed, took off his glasses, cleaned them, and replaced them.

"This is a lot of information to receive all at once," he said finally. "Allow me to understand you. Do you mean to tell me you traveled alone with this man in a carriage for two days?"

Elizabeth flushed. "I know you are disappointed in me, but there was no time for delicacies. I am Georgiana's friend, and if I had advised her better, she would not have been in a position to be blackmailed. It was my fault and only right that I helped recover her. I could not sit at home and wonder what had happened to her. It is not my nature…"

Elizabeth was interrupted by a commotion outside. They both looked towards the door, and their conversation was momentarily forgotten. Mrs. Bennet's high shrieks were accompanied by giggles that could only belong to Kitty and Lydia. And a deep voice Elizabeth would know anywhere…

"That is him now," she said. "He will wish to speak with you."

"Oh, and I wish to speak with him too," said Mr. Bennet grimly. "Well, go ahead. Fetch your young man before your mother or sisters terrify him into insensibility."

Elizabeth's heart sank. She had hoped to make a better beginning than this. It was a poor start, and while the news was still fresh in her father's ears, poor Darcy was to be thrown into the middle. She hurried to the door.

Darcy sat in the parlor. His hat was clutched on his knee, and he eyed the young ladies perched around him, looking as stiff and formal as he so often appeared. Mrs. Bennet stood over him, clutching her hands to her chest, and breathlessly offered him tea, coffee, brandy, or anything, anything at all he might like. Darcy refused all offers and said he only wished to speak to Mr. Bennet. From his tone, Elizabeth guessed he had repeated his request several times.

"Are you new in the neighborhood, sir?" asked Lydia. "I will be happy to show you around." She reached out a hand and let it rest just beside his. "I am at your disposal."

Elizabeth hurried into the room before her family could say anything else to expose themselves. Darcy rose from his chair at once, all stiffness and formality melting away at the sight of her. His face lit up with a warm smile.

"Miss Elizabeth," he said softly. "I am happy to see you again."

"And I to see you, sir," said Elizabeth. It took all her restraint not to go to him and wrap her arms around him.

Mrs. Bennet and the girls looked between them, their mouths open in shock.

"Lizzy, do you know this young man?" Mrs. Bennet asked in an awed tone.

Elizabeth cleared her throat.

"We met in Derbyshire, Mama."

"In Derbyshire..." Mrs. Bennet covered her mouth with her hands. She turned slowly and stared at Darcy as if he were a woodland creature she was afraid of chasing away by making any sudden movements. "And he wishes to speak to your father..." She appeared to be holding her breath, and Elizabeth knew in her mother's eyes at least, they were already as good as married.

"I will take Mr. Darcy to him," she said firmly. She started to reach out a hand towards him just as he did the same. They recollected themselves and dropped their hands, then Elizabeth led Darcy to her father's library. Once alone, Darcy looked down at her. His eyes dropped to her lips, but a sound behind them caught his attention. Kitty, Lydia, and Mary peeked from behind the door to watch them. He sighed then discreetly ran a finger along her bare arm where they could not see.

"I will find you as soon as I have spoken with him."

"He is not happy," whispered Elizabeth. At her glare, her sisters had run back inside, but she knew they listened intently. "I only had a chance to tell him before you came along, and he was not pleased."

Darcy nodded. "I cannot blame him for that." He took Elizabeth's hand and glanced towards the door before dropping a swift kiss on her lips. "Do not worry, my love. All will be well."

Darcy knocked, and her father called for him to enter. His voice was cold and distant. Elizabeth sighed. She could not bear sitting with her mother and sisters while waiting for news of their conversation. She could not have even endured Jane's company. She pulled on a cape and went out to the garden.

The chill and dampness in the air reminded her summer was coming to an end. Autumn would soon be here. She wrapped her cape around her as she walked under the trees. She wished she knew how the conversation was unfolding. Was her father really so unhappy with her? She must find a way to convince her that she married Darcy for love. He would be miserable if he believed she, his favorite child, would marry someone she could not love and respect.

The wait felt like it took forever. Elizabeth blew on her hands to warm them and sat on a stone bench, trying to distract herself from the conversation taking place in the house by looking for any changes since she went away. That new bed of roses had not been there before she left. Perhaps Jane had…

Oh, she could not bear this any longer. She would go mad if she did not know what was happening. She rose from the bench and paused when the sound of deep laughter carried across the garden. She waited where she was, and her heart lifted as she saw Darcy and her father walk across the garden. Darcy said something, and her father burst out laughing.

Well, this was promising. What on earth was Darcy saying that her father found so amusing?

Mr. Bennet looked up and saw her. He raised his hand to invite her to join them. She hurried across the lawn towards them. Darcy gave her a smile.

"Mr. Darcy has been telling me of some of your escapades, my dear. I particularly enjoyed the one where you frightened a thief almost into a state of insensibility. That is a fine story."

Elizabeth looked at Darcy in wonder. Was her father really as reconciled as he appeared?

"I will leave you to converse in private," said Darcy. He bowed and looked towards the house. The faces of Mrs. Bennet, Lydia, and Kitty were all squashed against the window. "Perhaps I will walk about the park..." he said.

"Excellent idea, sir." Mr. Bennet clapped him on the shoulder. Darcy smiled, and with a last look at Elizabeth, he walked away.

Mr. Bennet walked on, and Elizabeth fell into step beside him. She waited for him to speak.

"I will admit, I like your young man," said Mr. Bennet. "He speaks of you with great regard and holds a high opinion of your intelligence and spirit. I know I will not have to fear him trying to break you into an obedient wife with no mind of her own. But I do not know what you think of him, so I am not satisfied yet. He is a wealthy man, and you will have a great many clothes and carriages. All those things your mother believes are the basic necessities of life. But do you love him? Can you esteem him as your partner? Or do you marry him to preserve your reputation?"

Elizabeth took a deep breath. "Father, I do love him. We do not marry because my reputation has been ruined. No one who knows of our flight will spread gossip about it, after all. We told you because we did not wish to keep it from you. When Darcy proposed to me, it was because we had just learned of our feelings for one another. And realizing he cared for me as I did for him was…" Elizabeth tried to speak. She clammed up, then shook her head, still in awe from the wonder of it. "It was the happiest moment of my life."

Mr. Bennet stopped walking. He turned Elizabeth to face him and watched her carefully. Whatever he saw there made him smile though there was a hint of sadness in his eyes.

"Yes, I see that."

They walked on.

"I am still not happy about you traveling alone with him to Scotland."

Elizabeth started to speak, but he stopped her. "I am satisfied Mr. Darcy is not to blame for that. I know myself how headstrong you are, my dear. If he refused you, I am sure you would have strapped yourself to the carriage roof and traveled with him, regardless. And you did it to help a friend. I am just glad it has all worked out as it should." He smiled. "Now, tell me more about you frightening the thief into thinking you were a ghost. I have heard it from Mr. Darcy, but I wish to hear it from you as well."

Mrs. Bennet had never been happier than the day Elizabeth and Darcy married. All mention of Elizabeth's inability to attract a man was forgotten, and Elizabeth became a model to her other daughters for how to catch a wealthy husband. Elizabeth, Darcy, and Mr. Bennet had agreed the rest of the family should not know about their journey to Gretna Green. It would only serve to damage Georgiana's reputation. There was also the very real fear that Elizabeth's ill-advised journey alone with a man would have an unintended effect on Kitty and Lydia.

"I do not have faith that any man they might run away with would marry them unless hunted down and forced to it in exchange for a great deal of money," was how Mr. Bennet described it. Elizabeth could not disagree.

Darcy's closest friend, Mr. Bingley, traveled to Hertfordshire when he heard the news of Darcy's engagement. He was as pleasant and cheerful as Elizabeth had been led to believe. He was entranced by Jane Bennet's lovely face, and when he heard word that a nearby estate called Netherfield Park was available to rent, he went straight away to make an offer that he might spend more time with her. The marriage of Jane and Mr. Bingley came the following spring, six months after the hands of Elizabeth Bennet and Fitzwilliam Darcy were joined in Longbourn church.

After such an outcome leading to the glorious marriages of two daughters, Mrs. Bennet never again complained of Elizabeth's escapades in the woods. In fact, Kitty, Lydia, and Mary complained bitterly of being dragged away from their toilettes and books to take long tramps through the woods and lanes around Meryton in the hopes they too might collide with wealthy, eligible young men.

# CHAPTER 44

*S*ix Years Later

This was the day. After all the planning and preparation, it had finally arrived. Darcy sat alone in his room, his hands clasped between his knees as he contemplated the hours ahead. He would do all he could to push his own sense of loss to one side and make Georgiana proud. She deserved this happiness.

Darcy glanced up at a painting that took pride of place above the fireplace. It was his favorite, and it never failed to soothe him. It had the same effect on him now. He smiled. Elizabeth was seated on a rock in a soft blue gown that left her arms bare in the heat. Darcy stood by her side, one hand protectively on her shoulder. The artist had asked them to look straight at him as was fashionable for elegant couples, but when the two could not resist looking at one another and smiling, he had relented and captured them just like that. Behind them rose the Parthenon, lit up by moonlight. Once

Napoleon had been defeated once, and for all, Elizabeth and Darcy took advantage of their dearest wish to travel together. They had many souvenirs of their time in France, Switzerland, Italy, and Greece, but this painting was Darcy's favorite souvenir of their travels.

This painting and a certain mischievous little boy with his father's dark looks and his mother's sparkling eyes.

He pulled himself together and walked to the mirror to have one last look over himself. He would not let Georgiana down on her special day.

E lizabeth leaned against the door and smiled as she watched her husband smooth his hair down. His hands shook slightly.

"How do I look?" he asked.

"I believe you will serve," she said, admiring his handsome form. He turned to her and smiled to see the yellow silk gown she wore.

"You look beautiful. You haven't changed a bit from the girl who threw herself in my path in the woods that day."

"I did not throw myself in your path." She came towards him and adjusted his cravat. "You have not changed a bit from the man who held me at gunpoint."

He laughed and pulled her into his arms. "We both know I did not hold you at gunpoint."

"Shh. Do not tell the boys that. They will be heartbroken."

"Why will we be heartbroken, Mama?" Their two eldest children, William and Richard, burst into the room and threw themselves on the bed. Elizabeth turned to scold them. It had taken long enough to make them presentable. If they were left to their own devices for a second, they were sure to revert to their usual rapscallion looks.

Darcy strode across the room and pulled them apart. Elizabeth joined him and patted down their hair.

"Where is your sister?" asked Darcy.

The nursemaid knocked on the door and came in, apologies already spilling from her lips for the boys escaping her. Clutching her hand was their youngest child, Georgiana Darcy. She was as pretty and golden-haired as her aunt but had more of her mother's adventurous spirit. She tried to wrestle free to charge towards her brothers.

"The sooner this ceremony is over, the better," said Elizabeth. "Then they can relax and run free. I do not care how untidy they look once we return from the church."

"You are not the only one who cannot wait for it to be over. But at the same time, I dread it," said Darcy. "It will be hard to lose her."

"You will never lose her. She is settling within ten miles of Pemberley. It is hardly a separation at all. We shall see her all the time. And besides, you are giving her away to a good, kind man who adores her and makes her very happy."

"That is true." Darcy sighed. "But I would have been quite happy if this day had been postponed for several more years."

"You would have been happy if it had never come along at all," said Elizabeth with a teasing glint in her eye. "I know you. You believe no man good enough for dear Georgiana. But Anthony Ainsworth is a good man. I have liked him ever since I met him at the Altons. The poor fellow was terrified when he first came here to ask permission to court Georgiana. Do you remember?"

Darcy smiled at the memory. "He almost spilled his coffee when I addressed him. It took time for him to grow easy with us. But then, I recalled my anxiety when I visited your family." He smiled and lowered his voice so only his wife could hear. "At least Anthony had not taken my sister on a wild adventure to Scotland before asking for her hand. I am lucky your father did not kill me."

The nursemaid had the children in hand, so Elizabeth and Darcy walked to Georgiana's room to greet the bride.

Georgiana was as radiant as they expected. Her eyes glowed with joy, and Darcy's filled with tears at the sight of her in her wedding gown.

"Are you happy, Georgie?" he asked.

She crossed the room, threw her arms around him, and then hugged Elizabeth. "Happier than I can say. I feel as if my heart will burst with joy." She sighed and stood back, holding each of their hands. Her eyes grew misty as she smiled at them. "My only unhappiness is in leaving you, my dearest brother and sister. But I own I cannot wait to start a life with my husband. I feel I shall be as blessed in my marriage as you have been. You have set us a fine example."

"I have every faith you will have a splendid marriage," said Elizabeth. "Anthony is the very man for you. Anyone may see the love between you and the very high regard in which you each hold the other."

Georgiana's face lit up at the mention of her beloved.

"He is the very man for me. I have no doubts about that."

The voice of her aunt, Lady Catherine, called to her. Georgiana pulled a face.

"I am summoned," she said with a mischievous smile.

Darcy kissed her and then stood back as she left the room. Elizabeth saw him discreetly wipe a tear from his eye. She leaned up on her toes and kissed him.

"Come now, none of that. This is a happy day. And after their honeymoon tour, it will be as if we have not been parted at all."

"I wonder if Anthony — "

"He will not agree to move to Pemberley," said Elizabeth

firmly. "We have discussed this, remember? His legal profession requires him to be in Derby. But they will stay with us all the time."

Darcy sighed and nodded. "I suppose it must be that way."

"If you are like this over a sister, I cannot imagine how you will be when little Georgiana gets married."

"She shall not marry until she is fifty, and her husband certainly shall live with us," said Darcy firmly. The couple laughed and followed Georgiana from the room. Soon, they would leave for the church, where the groom waited anxiously for his bride.

Afterward, Darcy and Elizabeth walked in the garden while the happy couple celebrated with their family and friends. Among them were the Waters. Mrs. Waters had been horrified when she learned of her son's elopement. For the first few weeks, she could not look at him without bursting into tears. But she eventually came around and was now as happy with Rebecca as a daughter as she would have been with Elizabeth.

There had still been a little uneasiness between the two couples for the first few months of both marriages, but now the Waters, who had built a beautiful home not far from Pemberley, were frequent visitors there with their two small girls. How differently might it have turned out if the wishes and interferences of others had prevailed?

The evening sun began to set, lighting up the gardens of Pemberley and the woods where they first met. Darcy sighed and lifted Elizabeth's hand to his lips to kiss it.

"Everything has turned out just as it should," he said. "Here we are, surrounded by family and friends. Georgiana happily married and us together as we belong."

Elizabeth smiled. Most of the neighborhood had attended the wedding. Darcy's marriage and his fatherhood had encouraged him to mix more with the neighborhood, and now he had many friends among the people of Lambton. She sighed and tilted her head back. It was a beautiful summer night.

"It was a night like this when we walked through the woods together," she said.

Darcy smiled. "I remember. You were lying on a rock, dangling your legs in the water. I had never seen a more bewitching sight."

He turned Elizabeth to him and kissed her. When he finally released her, he glanced towards the house.

"I know it might make us ungracious hosts, but — "

"The bride and groom are too happy and in love to notice anyone else, and all our guests are too busy eating. I am sure we shall not be missed for a while — " said Elizabeth.

They smiled at one another, and hand in hand, they disappeared into the woods where they had first met and which, despite all their travels, would always remain their favorite place in the world.

# ABOUT THE AUTHOR

Emily Russell lives in Ireland. When she isn't writing historical fiction, she loves studying social history, especially that of the eighteenth-century. She also enjoys rambling about the countryside and getting lost, which explains why Elizabeth Bennet is one of her favourite characters.

If you would like to receive updates and news on Emily's new releases, you can sign up for her mailing list here.

ALSO BY EMILY RUSSELL

Made in the USA
Middletown, DE
30 December 2023